Deadly Grief

By the same author

The Heart of the Rose
Rooks Nest
Kindred Spirits
A Time to Love
Generations
Ghosts at Cockrow
Portrait of Maud
Time Will Tell
Familiar Acts
Swifter Wings Than Time
Daughter of Haworth
Family Snapshots
No Time Like the Present
The Villa Violetta
First Finds
Another Summer
Loving and Learning
First Loves
The Family Face
Stephanie and Josephine
Emma Eliza
The Ways of Love
Family Circle
Settling Down

Deadly Grief

B

June Barraclough

ROBERT HALE · LONDON

ISBN 0 7090 7853 6

Robert Hale Limited
Clerkenwell House
Clerkenwell Green
London EC1R 0HT

2 4 6 8 10 9 7 5 3 1

Typeset in 11/12½ Sabon
Derek Doyle & Associates, Shaw Heath.
Printed in Great Britain by
St Edmundsbury Press Ltd, Bury St Edmunds, Suffolk.
Bound by Woolnough Bookbinding Ltd.

Let's make us medicine of our great revenge,
To cure this deadly grief. . . .

Macbeth act 4, scene 3

CHAPTER ONE

It was almost the end of August and Susan Swann was sitting on the grass under the pale glare of the immense Spickhanger sky. She felt cross about all the work there was in prospect for her in September. It didn't seem fair for a teacher to have to spend such a lot of precious holiday time analysing and writing out in detail her 'objectives' for next term. When you finally got round to the actual teaching, more time was expended ticking little boxes to check whether your 'aims' had been fulfilled. It wasn't really the fault of Eastminster School but was one result of the new system of targets and tests and checks. She was a teacher of drama, not a manager of projects, or a bureaucrat. She wanted to enjoy the last ten days of the holidays without the nagging thought of planning.

The plans that interested her most were her own for the next school play. She felt guilty that she had so far done nothing much about that either, apart from rereading it and casting it in her mind. Oh well, she was lucky even to be contemplating a school play. If she left, there would be no more theatrical adventures at Eastminster High. The new head was not keen. So many enjoyable activities had already disappeared from lack of time: the things that had formerly made this particular school quite a pleasant place to work in. Teaching could be an interesting, if exhausting, experience but she hated thinking of it as a chore. There had used to be the Saturday sketching classes, and the choir, and the welcoming of pupils who came from Germany in exchange for the pupils in Year Ten who went abroad . . . and there had been trips to the theatre, and exhibitions of pupils' paintings. Now, even the school library had been allowed to run down, to make room for computers.

As the town had expanded, with new houses for the overspill from the larger towns, and from London, the school had become

bigger and more impersonal, and there were more discipline problems. Adolescents who might actually do some work, never mind
their abilities, were fewer on the ground, and the organization of
the school did not make it easy for them. Meanwhile, more and
more directives arrived from on high.

She just wanted to forget school for a few more days. At the
beginning of the holiday at the end of July she had almost decided
to apply for a post she had seen advertised in a smaller school
across the estuary, starting in January. Someone must be taking
maternity leave. If she got that job she could give in her resigna-
tion at the beginning of next term, allowing her present head
enough time to find someone else. She had hesitated, and now the
autumn term would begin on 8 September. Before that, though,
she would have to go into school two or three times for year meetings and departmental meetings and staff meetings. She had
discovered yesterday that the specification for the job at
Whitecoats had been altered. They'd be lucky to find anybody, for
now it would start as soon as possible, too late for her to apply,
unless she was totally immoral. She was not quite that yet.

At present, she wanted to make the most of the extraordinarily
fine weather. By rights, she should just be returning from Corfu
with her friend Richard, but a bitter argument at the beginning of
the holidays had changed their plans – and any possibility of a
future together.

Some of the other inhabitants of Heron Close were also making
the most of the heat wave, though the older ones said they didn't
like it too hot. Spickhanger was not famous for sun and warmth,
being at the edge of the broad estuary, freezing in winter and
usually cool in summer. It was not often that it enjoyed a few days
of hot sun, which almost made up for the cold, dank or windy
weather usual on the eastern coast of England. This late summer
was a surprise, much warmer than usual, and the others were out
in the sun too, scattered around on his or her special piece of
pebbly beach or grassy bank.

The close was a small development of seven modern houses set
at odd angles to each other, begun when it seemed there would
always be work for the professional classes as managers at an
extension of the local nuclear power station, which you could see
a few miles away where the estuary bent towards the North Sea.
Today, mercifully, the heat haze hid it from view.

Susan sat up and looked around her. Except for Mrs Maitland

and her next-door neighbour, Patrick Dawson, the neighbours were all outside. People said Mr Dawson was unfriendly, but perhaps he was just shy, thought Susan. He was said to have been an alcoholic, but was now 'on the wagon'. He was probably indoors reading. It was certainly true that Eva Maitland disliked going out even on fine days. In this strong sun she might easily burn. You could tell she had once been red-haired from the freckles on her neck and shoulders.

Half an hour ago, on a short walk, Susan had seen the two young Smiths sunbathing, Lisa looking relaxed for once, lying by her husband at the far end of the shore where it met the grassy bank up by the old coastguard's cottage. Earlier, she had heard Anthony Smith shouting at his wife in their garden. He was an awful bully.

Even Susan's landlady, Dorothea Kant, was out in the garden at the front of her house. She had her large sun-hat on, and old-fashioned sunglasses, which she probably did not realize were now once more fashionable, and was sitting in her deckchair with a book. The elderly chap at number one, Mr Cobb, was stopping to pass the time of day with her. He was a sunburned, athletic-looking elderly man who had perhaps once been a Rugby player. He must also once have been handsome and his hair was still black, most unusual for a man of his age, which was, she guessed, in the late fifties. Perhaps he dyed it? Some politicians and TV announcers dyed their hair. You could never tell, but she didn't think he did. Cobb was a widower and had been the last person to come to live at the Close. So far, he had kept himself to himself, though he had had a word or two with Miss Kant, since she was nearer his own age.

They were a typical bunch of mostly retired or semi-retired middle-class people, thought Susan, and she quite liked them all, except for Anthony Smith, who aroused her sense of justice. He was always bossing Lisa about. Poor little Lisa, she did rather ask for it, often looking as though she was about to burst into tears. Lisa was one of the school secretaries over at Susan's school in Eastminster and Susan knew her quite well because she often gave her a lift to school in the morning in her old car. It was six miles by road round the estuary to Eastminster, but being able to live in such a peaceful place as Spickhanger made the daily journey worthwhile. Many of the other members of staff commuted from the county town, much further away. Oh dear, she must stop her thoughts reverting to school. . . .

It looked as though Miss Kant might have fallen asleep. Susan thought about her landlady, whom she admired. The title was ridiculous, conjuring up a vision of a censorious busybody who grumbled about the electricity meter. Miss Kant was a retired college lecturer, not at all interested in meters or spying on her tenant. Why should an ancient stereotype come to mind? Probably, thought Susan, it came from novels, of which she read too many.

Mr and Mrs Whitwham were sitting on a rug on the beach under a large umbrella. Mrs Whitwham was very quiet; her husband made enough noise for them both. He was a retired bank manager and had a bee in his bonnet about vandalism and lawlessness. Susan couldn't blame him; she could have told him quite a bit about his favourite subjects from her recent school experience. He must be seventy, but was full of energy. Probably they would all have to listen to a diatribe from him that evening when the two men at Number 4 gave their party.

Sandy Robson and his friend David Fairbairn liked to give parties, and as they were good cooks and wine-lovers, the parties were excellent. She had seen David further down the beach with his easel earlier this afternoon, looking over to the island, which lay flat and tree-fringed a mile away across the water. Sandy was with him, his camera slung over a shoulder. They sometimes painted or photographed the same subjects – flora and fauna, birds and clouds – but the results, as you might expect, were very different. David Fairbairn used both oil- and water-colour and specialized in landscape and in migrant geese and waders, of which there were many in Spickhanger.

Sandy Robson earned a living selling photographs of formations of swallows, and twee little house martins, to periodicals like *Country Life*. He enjoyed snapping people too, but that was not so lucrative. It was said that David had had several exhibitions in London; he did not appear to go there very often. Both men were in early middle age and savoured their life in the country. They were obviously gay, thought Susan, rather good-looking fellows, different types in spite of their common orientation. David was quiet, somehow not what you might expect of a painter, whilst Sandy was younger, more camp. There she was again, attaching stereotypical descriptions to people when they were individuals. As a teacher, she didn't think of her pupils as 'types', though it was hard not to sometimes.

She turned over on to her stomach and opened her book, a detective story, written by a man under a female pseudonym. The story was rather slow in getting going and she was soon half-asleep. She hoped she was getting a nice tan. She need not worry about skin cancer; she was sallow-skinned, and she did not burn very easily.

Spickhanger was an unusual spot to choose to build seven modern houses, all slightly different in design. Since their construction the price of houses further afield had 'gone through the roof'. A farmer who thought there was more profit in selling land to builders than in growing oil-seed rape had sold the developers of Heron Close the piece of land, and profited thereby. The farmer let the builder discover for himself several long bones under one of the fields, bones that he had been told as a child might have belonged to monks from the period of the Dissolution of the Monasteries. His father had ascertained they were not modern bones.

It had been a one-off project for the builder and he had retired on the proceeds when he discovered that the nuclear power station was to be run down and that well-off professional couples usually preferred to live in 'proper' villages. All the present inhabitants owned 999-year leases and had banded together to pay service charges, which covered painting the exteriors, and having the communal lawns mown and the trees pruned. At present some of the work was being done by an odd-job man and gardener, one Percy Thrush, who lived a mile or two away. He also worked for the small yacht marina round the corner of the point where amateur small-boat sailors, owners of water skis and, occasionally power-boats, kept their craft.

When Susan eventually roused herself, she felt stiff. The beams of the sun were now slanting lower over the estuary behind the island, but it was still warm and pleasant, in spite of the midges. They had not been too bad this year. Susan decided to go in to Number 2 soon to make a cup of lemon tea. She rose and stretched, hoping she wasn't going to become arthritic at thirty-one, and took a little walk around.

The Whitwhams must have returned, for their large parasol was leaning against the front door of Number 7. Anthony Smith was standing over his wife, arms akimbo, obviously telling her to hurry up. Little Lisa was packing her bits and pieces into a beach-bag, about to do as she was told. Miss Kant was still there, reading away in her deckchair. Her subject had been history, and Susan wished she had been taught by her. She was generous in lending books to her lodger, and her enthusiasm for local history had sparked Susan's own interest. Susan confessed to great ignorance about the 'Hundred' to which Spickhanger belonged and was confused about dates. The Bronze Age, the advent of the Romans, Boudicca, St Cedd, the Celtic Christian who had brought the Gospels to these parts, and even the Domesday Book, had been, to begin with, a jumble in her head, but Miss Kant had set her right. She was glad that she'd jumped at the offer of the small flatlet she had seen advertised on the school notice-board. A year in a noisy, shared flat in the big town had cured her of any romantic ideas about flat-sharing. Here, she was far more independent, even if the flatlet was a large studio room with a small kitchenette under the high sloping roof of Number 2. She did not mind being a tenant sharing someone else's house and it had turned out well.

The houses on the close were all different but shared a faintly Dutch-barn air, and the larger ones, like Miss Kant's, had the top floor built to look like a granary. Susan's room led down a little open staircase to the first floor where Miss Kant had a bedroom, large study and bathroom. The stairs descended from there to the ground floor – a long, wide, open-plan sitting-room with a kitchen leading off at the side, planned like a ship's galley, and a small cloakroom.

Once Dorothea Kant had ascertained that Susan was not likely to blast out rock music at all hours, she had been welcomed and given free run of the sitting-room, and even sometimes the kitchen downstairs, in return for sixty pounds a week, which was very cheap indeed. Susan had only once peeped into Miss Kant's study, feeling rather nosy. All the walls were lined with books; they even climbed on each side of the window. She had felt rather small when she invited her landlady up for a cup of coffee in her own quarters, where her own two bookcases of paperback and second-hand fiction, and of text-books and school books, were sited. Miss Kant said she was welcome to borrow any of her books, so long as she put them back in the right place.

'The one thing I can't abide is losing my books – but I can't resist lending them to people who might profit from them. Must be something to do with the urge to educate, mustn't it?' she had said, but not waited for an answer. Susan had been pleased to take her at her word and had borrowed many books on local history as well as poetry, dictionaries and reference books of all kinds. It was better than the public library, for Miss Kant had many interests. Not for the first time Susan had wished that she herself taught a less exhausting subject than drama. History would have been restful, though Miss Kant said all they had to study for exams nowadays were Hitler and Stalin, who poked out like rocks in a sea of ignorance. But still, no capering about 'expressing yourself', or trying to sort out groups of sullen adolescents into 'drama therapy' projects, or sewing for school plays or teaching theatre arts to the sixth form, or the endless collecting of money for trips to the theatre in London, to 'widen their horizons'. Not that there had been many trips recently. Susan had always been out of pocket, mathematics not being her strong point.

She walked back to Number 2, where Miss Kant was still sitting in the garden, and raised a hand in greeting.

'I'll make us both a cup of lemon tea, shall I?' asked Susan.

'That would be lovely.'

Miss Kant went back to her book. Susan went into the downstairs kitchen, which was cool and boasted a pale-lemon sunblind, sliced a matching lemon and boiled a kettle. She looked through the window where she could see some of the houses at the other end in their semicircle round the former duck-pond. Fairbairn's easel was now standing outside the front door of Number 4.

She made some Earl Grey in two pretty cups and took one of them out to Miss Kant, who smiled her thanks. For a moment Susan stood crunching a ginger biscuit, wondering what Richard was doing, and with whom, but by the time Dorothea came in at six o'clock she was up in her studio considering what she should wear to Number 4's party.

A slight breeze had arisen, and the masts were tinkling now in the distance as Lisa Smith trailed home to Number 3 in her husband's wake. Instead of welcoming the breeze, she shivered abruptly. She would like to have slept all afternoon and evening; she slept so badly at night.

Mr Cobb at Number 1, Miss Kant's neighbour on the other side, at the end of the higgledy-piggledy semicircle of houses, saw her and raised his hand in greeting. He was busy watering the yellow rock-roses in his garden at the front. As he had the end house, he had a larger garden at both front and back and a small shrubbery at the side. Not for the first time Cobb speculated as to why Anthony Smith, who was owner of a garden centre and did landscaping jobs, should so neglect his own front garden, leaving it to his wife to weed and plant. He supposed it was a case of not doing for nothing what you got paid for elsewhere.

Cobb creaked to his feet as the Smiths shut their door, and walked round to his back garden, fenced off from the field, which sloped down slightly to the estuary. Not much of a slope. Was it Noël Coward who had said:

'Very flat, Norfolk?' He must ask Miss Kant. South of Norfolk, East Anglia could be very flat too. He wished there were hills in the distance, as there had been in his birthplace in Yorkshire. When his wife died, he had decided to retire and come down south to try to escape his grief.

He had seen this place advertised when only one house was still unsold and he had thought it might suit him. Quiet, only a few neighbours, near enough to London on the newly electrified train from Eastminster if he wanted a day out. His colleagues had thought he was wrong, thought he would go mad alone down there with nothing to remind him of the past. They had said nothing, but he had guessed their thoughts. One day perhaps he might go back home, buy a cottage in the Dales.

For the moment Spickhanger would do. It had no memories for him. He could pretend to start again, forget everything, cultivate his garden, do a bit of studying, might even start a course at the Open University. He was not *really* old – and anyway they always said the older students were the best. Spickhanger was a bit of history and he had become interested in the place, an interest that enabled him for stretches of time to forget himself.

He had always been interested in the past and had discovered that an abandoned end of wall, standing at the side of the lane from Spire, the nearest village to the Spickhanger houses, was built of stones that had once belonged to a Cluniac monastery on this very site. Spickhanger had once been quite famous, larger than Spire. He had also discovered for himself from the builder that, way underneath the houses and lawns, were the mass graves of the monks of that monastery. The builder had not been sure whether they had died in the Black Death or the Dissolution of the Monasteries, but Cobb intended to find out. He might even write a little book, a sort of guide to the area. The story gave a spice of interest to the place, which neither Spire nor Eastminster could lay claim to. There was all the bird life too, about which he knew nothing, but was quite prepared to learn from one of the chaps at Number 4 – a couple of poofters, but pleasant and harmless.

He thought about his neighbours as he went in and bathed and put out his garb for the party Number 4 was giving that evening. Of his neighbours, he liked best Miss Kant and her lodger, whom he thought of as 'young Susan Swann'. Miss Kant reminded him of someone; he couldn't think who it might be, probably some teacher he had once had at his grammar school, but she was only about ten or twelve years older than he was.

He looked out of his window now at the green and the old duck-pond. Originally, it might have been a fish-pond for the monks, he thought sagely. He wondered what was missing from the place. Something was missing – not just hills, nor some natural feature – rather, something human. As he glimpsed Anthony Smith washing his car – the fellow was always washing his car – he suddenly knew what it was. Children! That was what was lacking. The Smiths, his youngest neighbours, had none. Patrick Dawson at Number 5 probably had grown-up children, though nobody seemed to know anything about his wife, or even if he was divorced. Mrs Maitland, in the next house to Dawson, didn't look as though she had ever had any offspring, but the Whitwhams had a daughter, Valerie, married to a vet. She visited once a month in a red Audi. They all knew about *her*. Mr Whitwham disagreed with his son-in-law on most subjects. 'But Valerie agreed with me!' were words constantly on Whitwham's lips. Cobb supposed there might be grandchildren somewhere, though he had never yet seen any.

It was silly – the place was made for children – all that pebbly beach, and the estuary, and the trees for climbing. Ridiculous that a pack of middle-aged and elderly people should be the only ones able to afford houses here. Yes, the Smiths should have children, he thought. Then, close upon that thought came another: I would not like to be Anthony Smith's son. Trouble was, in the Force he had been so used to collecting information about people, he couldn't stop. His greatest regret was that he and Edna had not been able to have children. No one's fault – they had not pursued it as folk did nowadays with all these fertility drugs. Not as if there weren't already too many children in the world, born to parents who didn't always care about them; often the wrong people had

15

children, and the ones who would have loved them were denied them.

He sighed. He must not start to think about Edna tonight, must appear genial and interested in other people. He tied his tie and then looked out again at the green, wondering whether to have a banana to fill him up in case the food was a bit late. There was always plenty to drink at Number 4, but he hardly ever touched alcohol now. His stomach was rumbling. He would have a glass of milk and read the paper. Wouldn't be good form to arrive too early, as though he had nothing else to do. The curtains were drawn at Number 6, he noted, as he drew his own bedroom curtain against the westering sun. Mrs Maitland was probably having a nap. There was a bicycle outside Mr Dawson's at Number 5. Gossip had it that he had had his licence taken away, for driving under the influence. But perhaps he preferred a bike. Cobb could not bear to think about it. It came too near the bone.

CHAPTER TWO

As is often the case both before and after a party, the hosts, Sandy Robson and David Fairbairn, had been discussing their neighbours, all of whom had been invited to their house that evening, among other friends. Sandy, who was the cook, had sharply declined the idea of a barbecue.

'Too, too suburban,' he had said, so David had left him to it, and all morning he had been preparing salads and shellfish and seeing to the Petit Chablis and the Muscadet *sur lie* along with the Frascati Superiore he had bought in Colchester. There was also a side of cold roast beef, a few bottles of Chianti Classico, and some Roquefort. He knew about wine but he wasn't going to waste rare vintages on the neighbours. Just the best *vin du pays*, from Italy or France would do. He and David loved both these countries and hoped one day to retire to south-west France.

'I don't know why we bother,' said David, as he surveyed the splendid spread all ready on and under two crisp, white linen cloths. Sandy liked to give himself time for a shower, shampoo and meticulous shave before a leisurely change of suit, but was now ready.

'That Mrs Maitland is a dark horse,' he replied. 'She didn't come last time, but she promised she would tonight.'

'She hardly ever goes out, does she? She scuttled indoors yesterday evening when I passed by her. She was outside in her garden for once. Perhaps we frighten her.'

'Well, it's a good place to be a hermit,' replied Sandy, 'though she's probably quite well-heeled or she couldn't afford Spickhanger. They say she's a widow. Susan said she thought she was suffering from some nervous trouble,' he went on, munching a piece of celery and contemplating his table with pride.

'Oh, Susan Swann is full of theories; she probably thinks *we* have come to the country to pass our declining years in an idyll.

17

She's *such* a romantic!'

'Well, we did come for peace and quiet, didn't we? We're all retired, or free-lances, except for Susan and the Smiths. I think he's a bit of a horror, don't you, Tony Smith? Not that he's ever done anything but eat our food and drink our wine. Little Lisa is all right though – a pity such a nice little thing had to marry that boor.'

'Well, it's none of our business if Mrs Maitland is bonkers or Lisa Smith is miserable or that husband of hers is a creep – we only have to entertain them all once or twice a year, whatever people say about loving your neighbour.'

'How right you are,' said David.

Susan had changed her clothes, brushed out her shoulder-length light brown hair, applied a little make-up and sprayed herself moderately with her favourite scent, Rive Gauche. She was rather looking forward to the party. The two men's guests might include interesting unknown quantities. In addition, the wine was always good at Number 4 and they had a garden at the back as large as Mr Cobb's, with comfortable outdoor chairs. She looked forward also to a peaceful guzzle, one evening at least when she might forget her work, and Richard. Teaching was certainly not boring, but she had enough noise and excitement in her job to make her need a restful domestic background during the holidays. It was partly why she had chosen to live in a place mostly inhabited by people much older than herself.

Miss Kant had taken a bath, if the splashes and gurgles to be heard downstairs were anything to go by. Perhaps Miss Kant could fall in love with Mr Cobb?

Susan immediately ticked herself off for wanting to pair people off like mating birds, though in this elderly case it hardly had to do with mating. If you taught 'free expression' and were an avid theatre-fan, you tended to see action where there was none. Both Cobb and Miss Kant had many interests to keep them happy. She must resign herself to the fact that most of the Heron Closers were respectable and a little boring, cut off in their own little enclave from an increasingly violent society, and mainly interested in living comfortably. Like the amateur yachtsmen at the marina round the point, or the birdwatchers, or the Conservation Society people, they were there for genuine reasons: for peace and quiet, and to enjoy the spectacular sunsets over the estuary which stained the sky gold and pink and vermilion.

She loved having leisure just to enjoy life, not having to commute to the Smoke, unlike many of the younger inhabitants of Spire who often travelled to work in the City to earn their daily bread. Many of her pupils' mothers worked locally in shops or cleaned for their living, whilst their fathers worked for the big agricultural businesses that owned much of the land around. Rural wages were low and people were pleased when their children went off to work at sixteen on the train to London fifty miles away, where they could earn twice as much.

She opened her window and heard the zooming noise of speed-boats towing their wind-surfers, which rather spoilt the peaceful idyll. Her thoughts turned to one of her pupils, Linda Swift, whose mother worked for Miss Kant and the Whitwhams, coming twice a week to clean. She didn't doubt that Linda too would leave Spire eventually. It was inevitable. One day there might be no original inhabitants in Spire at all. All the old families would have died out, replaced by 'incomers', as Mr Cobb called himself, people who did up the little cottages in Spire and spent their weekends 'in the country'. Some further house-building had begun this year in Spire itself.

Miss Kant had told her that a hundred years ago the rural aris-tocracy disappeared for their 'real' life in town. There was no rural aristocracy left here. The big new landowners were all these agri-cultural companies, making great mountains of money from the yellow rape and the beans and cereal crops. The mortgagors of the new executive type houses in Spire all thought themselves lucky to live in a proper village.

It was not a particularly pretty one, but in the right kind of weather, the low-lying estuary land and its hinterland of small villages, with their churches and their fields reached by winding roads, had a certain charm. The hedges were already full of black-berries, there were mulberry trees belonging to some of the farms, and delicious mushrooms could be found in August all over the place in damp spots. There were worse places to live, thought Susan.

'I'm sure he's got a violent temper,' said Mrs Whitwham, inter-rupting her husband who had been reading an item from his *Daily Telegraph* over their tea and cake.

'Who?'

'Tony Smith.'

19

'You weren't listening, Vera, to anything I was saying,' protested Bill Whitwham plaintively.

Mrs Whitwham, who said little in public, apparently agreeing with her husband on all topics, persisted.

'I said, I'm sure he has a temper – I heard them just now – you know I've got very good hearing.' But I can be deaf if I choose, she thought.

'Vera, I was reading to you about that dreadful bank robbery yesterday in Chelmsford. Don't you realize what a terrible world we live in?'

'Now, Anthony Smith – I'm sure *he*'s a violent man – wouldn't surprise me if he got in the news one day,' she replied.

'But you've never seen him do anything violent, have you?' asked Bill, somewhat nonplussed, putting down his *Telegraph* and taking up the local rag. The trouble with Vera was that, like most women, she took no interest in general problems, was interested only in people, in gossip. He tried to educate her by reading her selected items from the papers because she never got further than the crossword or the gardening pages.

'No – not really – it's just a feeling I have, that's all. You're always talking about nasty things happening and I know all about that, Bill. I don't want to hear about people I don't know. I just said I think Tony Smith is an unpleasant kind of man and that he could be violent. He's very unkind to his wife.'

'Women's intuition,' groaned Mr Whitwham. 'You'd better not come out with that sort of remark. Have you forgotten where we're going tonight?'

'No, of course I haven't. I've put out your nice clean shirt. Now you won't eat any shellfish, will you? You know what happened last time! You were quite poorly.'

'It was the strawberries,' replied her husband, putting his glasses away neatly in a monogrammed case.

'They're good cooks and I'm sure it's very kind of them to invite us all – very neighbourly, I must say,' said Vera, clearing away.

'Pansies can always cook,' muttered Bill Whitwham, but this was one of the remarks his wife chose not to hear.

Percy Thrush was hosing the rose-bed in the middle of Spickhanger Green at six o' clock. The green was a lofty title for the expanse of grass around the old farm duck-pond. The farm had gone, the pond had shrunk, but several barns remained. As she looked out of her kitchen window, Dorothea Kant was thinking how odd it might seem to have so many people in this area called after birds. But it wasn't really odd. Centuries ago some of the same old families had been around in the Hundred and to each family had been apportioned the name of a bird. There was the Swift family, the Wrenns, the Finches, the Martins, the Pheasants, the Crows – and Percy Thrush, who did not seem to belong to a family, but who doubtless did.

'Heron Close' must have been the inspiration of the builder, more elegant, she supposed, than a Goose or Duck settlement. Astonishingly, even two of the 'incomers' had the names of birds: Susan Swann, and James Cobb, their next-door neighbour, though Bill was from Yorkshire. An amazing coincidence!

She pondered on Percy Thrush, who was just leaving in the direction of the sailing club. He worked both for the Heron Closers and for the management of the marina, just round the point of the eight-acre field, where he did odd jobs. She hoped the marina would not expand; some of the young men who hung around at weekends were rough-looking types, not yachtsmen themselves. But she ought not to begrudge them their pleasures; they had as much right to them as anyone else.

The breeze had gone and it was still warm, even a little stuffy. The rest of the late summer evening stretched before Linda Swift, who was cycling down the two-mile lane from Spire and was feeling hot. The earth looked parched. In order to feel cool, Linda tried to imagine it was a snowy winter evening, but the effort was beyond her. The heat haze still half-hid the island in the estuary with its row of poplars behind the foreshore. The birds were silent. Not that many sang at this time of year: robins and wrens mostly. The derelict barn and the old coastguard's cottage round the point next to the marina seemed to give off heat vapours from their lichen-covered roofs, though it would not be long before sunset. The occasional drone of a motor boat could be heard in the distance.

Linda, an intelligent girl who needed to escape from time to time from her cramped council house in Spire, was a birdwatcher, often cycling to the saltings of the estuary to observe rare species. She kept a little notebook to record her observations in the fields too, and had so far gathered the names of forty-five birds there. Soon there would be more, for they were going to let the sea come over part of the seawall further on towards Spire.

There were already hundreds of migratory birds who fed on the mud-flats. In June she had seen terns and heard skylarks but soon the Brent geese would be back from Siberia: she had read that a quarter of the total world population of these geese was in her county. There'd be many different kinds of ducks too; she liked the pretty teal best. On the mud-flats later on there'd be the waders: oyster catchers and dunlin and curlews in enormous flocks. Birds of prey too: peregrines and harriers.

Linda gave far more attention to this hobby of hers than to her school-work, which she found easy, but at present there were just the more ordinary birds to see – linnets and finches, with the ubiquitous wood-pigeons as a constant sound accompaniment. Last week she had seen through her binoculars what looked like a flamingo. It must have escaped from a private zoo. Her cousin in Woolwich had told her that parrots were now found flying round there in a park.

Her plans for next winter and spring were to listen for a wheatear in the fields, and to see redshank on the salt marshes. Linda was always the first to hear the cuckoo in spring. She was glad her name was Swift and felt she belonged to the place because of it.

The swift was one bird she had never seen, though swallows still visited the same barn every year, and house-martins lodged in the ruined eaves of the old farmhouse, though fewer than two or three years ago.

Like Miss Kant, Linda was interested in names and enjoyed attaching birds' names, for amusement, to the people who didn't have them. She had named the Smiths the Blackcaps since they were both dark-haired, and Mr Fairbairn was a Goldcrest because of his fair hair. The Whitwhams and Patrick Dawson and Mrs Maitland were as yet unknown quantities to be renamed in future. Try as she might she could not find an appropriate name for Miss Kant – you could not call her a grouse or a warbler. She was perhaps more like an eagle – being tall and proud-looking.

Linda got off her bike and left it in the hedgerow. People were usually honest in Spire, and the sailing-club people round the point beyond the derelict barns always came by car, their boats perched on roof-racks or towed behind them on special trolleys. The amateur sailors were a nuisance when they interrupted the birds.

She found a comfortable place to sit at the top of a slight rise, looking over the estuary to the island, and unhooked her binoculars. From here she could see Heron Close with trees sheltering it, though the elms her grandfather had remembered were now all long gone. In the distance she saw some small dinghies pulled up on the marina hard. There would be a wonderful sunset tonight at about a quarter past eight. Vast capes and bays of pink and gold would stretch out beyond the coastline into the enormous sky above. Shortly after that the rabbits would venture out to feed. She hoped one day she might spot a cormorant with its purple-green shine, but she would probably be content with a few reed-buntings.

She might walk round in the direction of the sailing club soon to see if the owl was in the old barn. It would be half-light till about nine and she had her sandwiches with her and a flask of tea. She was happy doing her 'birding' alone. She'd go back later to the lane where she had left her bike, and cycle home in the dark.

Her evening mapped out for her, Linda turned with a sigh of satisfaction and turned her binoculars once more to the further reaches of the estuary until the light began to fade.

Not surprisingly, the Whitwhams but, unusually, Patrick Dawson and Eva Maitland, were the first arrivals at Number 4 at eight o'clock where Sandy and David awaited their guests.

Whitwham was always very gruff till he got going, but his wife probably knew more than she let on, thought Sandy, wondering why it was necessary for her to have brought an umbrella for the few hundred yards or so which separated the garden-gates of their houses at the back. But formal invitations meant front doors. Still, perhaps it was going to thunder. It *was* very sultry. David busied himself with arranging and helping the guests on to white wicker chairs in what Sandy grimly called the 'patio'.

Eva Maitland, a woman of medium height with medium-heeled shoes and a medium head of ashy-coloured hair, was remarkable only for her freckles and the extreme whiteness of her skin. After staring around her like a frightened rabbit, she spoke in a jerky way that either betrayed extreme shyness or extreme terror. Pat Dawson sat himself down beside her with his cranberry juice, and Eva seemed to relax a little. Mrs Whitwham sat down on her other side and beamed vaguely around before she got up again to inspect the third flowering of some Gloire de Dijon.

Mr Whitwham had been left with Sandy, with whom he was

23

trying to have a conversation about Brent geese, when another arrival was ushered in by David. Mr Cobb seemed to settle them all down. He listened with every appearance of enjoyment to Whitwham's long recital about a bank robbery, asking intelligent questions as he sipped his tonic water. Pat Dawson lit a cigar, after ascertaining that nobody objected, and listened to David who was recalling a mutual friend at the BBC. But he still appeared to keep a watchful eye on Eva Maitland. Of the Heron Closers, only the Smiths and Miss Kant and her lodger were yet to arrive, Sandy calculated, as he took round his canapés, which everyone pronounced delicious.

The doorbell rang and David opened his front door to Anthony Smith, from Number 3, followed by his wife in a pale-yellow silk dress, looking like some rather rare night moth who had ventured out before her usual time. Anthony Smith was tall and swarthy, with deep-set dark eyes. He was what people called a ladies' man, with hairy wrists and the sort of shave which looked blue round the chin, the faint scent of expensive men's toiletries in his wake. Lisa was dark too. She had really coal-coloured eyes with smudgy shadows underneath. When her husband joined the others, she seemed, like Eva Maitland, to relax. Mr Cobb moved over to talk to her, aware that Tony Smith knew he was talking to her and was ready to move in on them if he felt like it. But then Tony turned back to discuss business with Mr Whitwham, and Lisa gulped down a glass of Muscadet, ready to listen to James Cobb who was asking her about her work as a school secretary.

Other friends of David and Sandy arrived from further afield and the guests mingled. Susan and Miss Kant had come in rather late and got swallowed up among strangers, so it was not until everyone had been provided with a plate of delicious fish mayonnaise, and brown bread, and the Muscadet and the Frascati were circulating and the summer dusk deepening that Susan was able to have a word with Patrick Dawson, whom she had earmarked as the most interesting person there for her purpose, which was to discuss her production of *Twelfth Night*. She had known she would break her original promise to herself not to talk shop. He had been talking to Eva Maitland and she went on sitting by him as he talked to Susan, who had the impression of a sort of magnetic force stretching between Eva and Patrick. Well well, she thought, I've never noticed that before. But now she recognized the unmistakable signs of two people who were close.

Meanwhile Dorothea was stuck with Mr Whitwham, abandoned by Tony Smith who was making up to a girl who had come
over in a small party of people from Chelmsford.

I am bored, Miss Kant was thinking. Yes, I am very bored. I
should not be bored, but I am, and because I am bored I must not
drink too much or I shall have a headache tomorrow. I should like
to talk to David, but he is busy with his host's duties. Pat Dawson
is bored too, except when he is talking to Eva Maitland.

Here we all are, respectable people in a quiet little place, yet I
feel a slight unease. Am I imagining it? Ah, here is James Cobb
come for a chat. He is the oldest person here except for me and
Mr Whitwham, and Mr Whitwham has never been young.

'How did you find the Archaeological Society, then?' she asked,
looking up at Mr Cobb with grey eyes under a fringe of thick hair,
also now grey.

'That's what I wanted to tell you about.'

Soon they were off, ignoring the rest, discussing their shared
passion for the past. Dorothea hardly noticed what she was eating.
A pity one could not really concentrate on both eating and talking
at the same time. Still, she was no longer bored. Cobb was a kind
person, she felt, a man with a quick mind, yet humble, seeking for
information which she might be able to supply.

The heat had been retained in the high back-garden walls,
though it was now quite dark. An owl hooted and someone
mentioned bats, someone else moths. The party had become
animated after the cold roast beef and Chianti, and Sandy was
beginning to circulate with coffee, whilst one or two voices were
already raised saying they really must go, it had been delightful.
Suddenly everyone heard a loud moaning outside the gate to the
lane that ran behind the garden wall.

'What on earth is that?' asked Miss Kant, breaking off her
conversation with Cobb.

The noise was now like the howl of a wounded animal.

'Sounds as though one of your guests has over-indulged,' said
Anthony Smith facetiously to David.

David swept down the garden path, which he had lit with
Chinese lanterns swinging from bushy shrubs, and opened the
wooden door in the back wall. The noise increased as those of the
guests still in the garden stood petrified, their coffee-cups half-way
to their lips.

David reappeared with his arm round a dishevelled young

woman who was now whimpering.

'Somebody throw some water at her,' suggested Mr Whitwham.

'No! Let me,' said Miss Kant and advanced towards the two figures.

'Sit down, Linda,' she said briskly, recognizing the daughter of her cleaning lady.

Susan came up too – she liked her pupil, Linda Swift, a clever girl. Sandy steered the rest of the party tactfully indoors and David left Linda to the women's ministrations whilst he went for a glass of brandy.

The whimpering slowly stopped and turned into hiccups. 'I'm sorry,' Linda tried to say over and over again.

'Tell us what has happened, Linda,' said Susan, feeling she ought to know how to treat hysterical females. Linda was not usually hysterical. David came up with a glass and Dorothea held it to the girl's lips. Linda was now shaking violently. Susan took her hand. Linda coughed but sipped a little brandy which made her cough again.

'Take it easy – just tell us,' said Susan.

'A man must have followed me into the barn, or he was there already. I'd gone to see the owl and I was looking upwards . . . it was dark. Then I felt someone stand behind me – he put a hand over my face. I screamed and he pushed at my back and got me down to the floor. I thought he was going to . . . I smelled something musty and I went on screaming.' She gulped. 'Then I think something interrupted him because he suddenly let go of me and there was a sort of shuffling noise. He must have walked away. I waited a moment, and then I managed to sit up and look and just for a second – it wasn't quite dark outside – I saw a – a *shape* at the barn door . . . wearing a long sort of – I don't know – a kind of long *gown*.'

She stopped and blew her nose.

'You thought he was going to rape you?' asked Susan.

'M-murder me,' whispered the terrified girl. 'When I was sure he'd gone I just ran and ran. I'm sorry . . .'

The girl looked up, dazed.

'Did he never face you?' asked Dorothea.

'No – that was what was so awful – he'd pushed me down and kept a hand on my mouth with his other hand. I couldn't see him – only he smelt like mothballs. Yes, like mothballs,' she repeated. 'I thought he might come back, so I ran round to the back-garden walls of the houses. I didn't know it was my voice making that awful noise. I'm sorry,' she said again, humbly.

Mr Cobb, who had been listening by the french window that opened into the garden came up.

'Who's going to take you home? Shall I get a taxi?'

'No – my bike – I left my bike down on the lane. I . . . d-don't think I could ride it.'

She was still shaking.

'You must inform the police,' he said.

'But he didn't *do* anything – perhaps he just meant to frighten me.'

'He certainly did that,' said Miss Kant.

'I'll take you home if you like,' Susan offered, 'unless you can find someone to give you a lift.' She had had three glasses of wine and would be over the limit. One of the other women had said she was pregnant and hadn't drunk anything. Perhaps *she* could . . . ?

The party was breaking up. People had decided it was time to go. Dorothea was talking to the pregnant lady, and then she and her husband, friends of David, approached Linda and Susan.

'I'll drive you, drop you in Spire, see you right to your door,' said the young woman. 'We're going back home. It's on the way.'

'I could pick up your bike tomorrow or Monday if you tell me exactly where you left it. Better not hang round here,' suggested Susan.

It was all settled, and Miss Kant went out to see Linda into the helpful couple's car.

The rest of the guests preferred not to get involved. They'd talk about it all tomorrow, thought Susan. She went out to join Dorothea and say goodbye to Linda. Then she came back in.

David was clearing away the glasses. Sandy appeared from the kitchen.

'All right now?' he asked pleasantly.

'Who could it have been?' asked Susan, lingering with them for a minute. Miss Kant had gone back home.

'Not many people come down here. Perhaps from the marina? Or some yob?' David said.

'The marina lot are usually all right. We've never had any trouble with them before,' Susan said.

'Depends what you mean by trouble,' said Sandy, not elaborating, but he had heard rumours of drugs.

'She'll have to tell the police,' said Susan. 'I mean – it could happen again.'

'What could they do that we can't, except warn other girls, make them scared of going bird-watching – scared of everything?' replied Sandy.

She looked at him in surprise, but said no more and walked back to Number 2, a little frightened herself. Her car was standing in front of Dorothea's garage where she had left it the night before. On an impulse she looked in as she passed. A back window was open – she ought to have locked the car – you never knew. As she leaned over to secure it, she saw on the back seat a crumpled-looking black gown. The gown they'd used in a form pageant about St. Joan that she'd produced at Easter! She had left it on the back seat since the beginning of the holidays when she'd brought it home to mend.

It had been moved. She had left it neatly folded. Linda had said a 'gown', hadn't she? Whoever had attacked Linda could have taken it and put it back. There was a cowl attached, with slits, rather like Ku Klux Klan. They'd used it for the prison scene. Could the attacker . . . ? With a sick feeling Susan resolved not to touch it. She locked her car up.

She decided to tell Miss Kant about it in the morning. It was late, and she'd be tired; the light was already on in her bedroom window.

Next morning was Sunday, always slow to start at Spickhanger. Susan was usually a late riser, but this morning, after her first cup of coffee, she went out at about half past eight to collect the papers from the box at the end of the path that led to Spire Lane. It saved the paper-boy several separate deliveries at eight o'clock, all the newspapers being put in the one basket and left at the end of the close. She took her *Observer* and Miss Kant's *Sunday Times* and *Sunday Independent*, glancing wryly at the Smiths' *News of the World*.

She went upstairs to read the papers and eat a croissant – her Sunday treat. Whilst she was drinking another cup of coffee she heard Miss Kant go downstairs. She'd better broach the problem of the gown. She went downstairs.

'Linda got back safely last night. Bill came round very early this morning with some damsons from his garden. I couldn't sleep and was already up, about to take my bath. He'd already cycled to

Spire! He's very keen on the girl going to the police. Her dad will be, too, when he gets to hear of it, I'm sure,' said Dorothea.

'She *was* shaken up,' said Susan, feeling even more guilty.

'Her parents will have been told all about it by now. Jim Cobb thought he might go round to see them again. Mrs Swift will be anxious – she won't want Linda coming round here. Such a pity because she loves getting away – absolutely mad on bird watching, I gather. I hope it won't stop her mother coming to clean, though. How selfish I am!'

'The back window of my car was left unlocked last night,' said Susan abruptly. 'An old costume I brought back from school at the end of term and forgot to bring in – a monk's costume we used for a play – was on the back seat. But I didn't leave it all in a heap. Someone has been fishing in my car.'

Dorothea said nothing for a moment, then:

'You mean – whoever attacked Linda?'

'Exactly. It's horrid, isn't it? Someone who was around here, saw the habit—'

'But we were all at the party.'

'All the time? Everybody?'

'I think so. I'm *sure* it couldn't have been anyone at the party,' Dorothea said.

'No, I suppose it couldn't. It wasn't *completely* dark when she was attacked,' said Susan. 'Did she have no idea of who it might have been? Did she tell you last night when you took her to the car if he said anything?'

'No. That was what she found so uncanny. She says he never spoke – just grabbed her and was about to pin her down when something happened to stop him.'

'It's *gruesome*. It could have been a woman, I suppose. She doesn't know for sure it was a man, does she?'

'Women don't usually attack girls in barns, Susan. Not unless they know the person – have some grievance or a jealousy over a boyfriend. Mr Cobb asked her and she said that she hasn't got a boyfriend and as far as she knows no one has any grudge against her.'

'It *was* someone from the sailing-post then – it must have been,' said Susan.

Miss Kant looked thoughtful, but then changed the subject.

By noon, another fine day saw various neighbours washing cars, weeding gardens. Susan, however, was not prepared for Lisa Smith's turning up later that afternoon to tell her she was fright-

ened of going out by herself in future. Tony said there were mani-
acs around. They sat sipping tea in Susan's room upstairs.

'You don't think she was making it up, do you?' said Lisa, lifting to Susan dark, troubled eyes, now with mauve rather than grey
smudges round them. 'I mean, she's a nice girl . . .'

'Nice girls get attacked,' replied Susan, and then wished she
hadn't said that, for Lisa looked even more scared. 'The police
have been informed,' said Susan. 'Miss Kant was telling me that
Mr Cobb was very firm with the Swifts. He went down to Spire
again before lunch and took them to the police station. He's been
round here to tell her about it.'

'But the maniac might strike again! I'm glad she's gone to the
police. I'm scared stiff. Tony says I mustn't go out at all – except
with him . . .' her voice trailed away.

'Whoever it was – unless he's mad – will know that we're all
aware of the attack, so he won't try it again in the same place.'

'That's what makes it so awful,' wailed Lisa. 'He could attack
anywhere – but perhaps it was one of those motor-boat men, on
drugs or something. Hasn't she any idea who it was?'

'No, apparently.' Susan considered mentioning the robe, but
thought better of it. It would only scare little Lisa the more.

'Tony says she was asking for it,' went on Lisa.

Really! thought Susan. But something seemed to have unlocked
Lisa's tongue. Susan had never known her so agitated. Usually she
was quiet and rather depressed, except occasionally at school
when she looked faintly content, certainly less hunted, as she typed
away in the office.

Mr Cobb had advised Linda to make a statement just for the
record, but Mr Swift had been very angry, as though it were
Linda's fault for what had happened.

'She's to do no more bird-watching,' he had stormed, as Linda
sat silent, holding a screwed-up hankie which she kept twisting
round and round, her usual calm manner having deserted her. She
was feeling embarrassment more than any other emotion.
Embarrassed at making all that fuss on Saturday, and shy about
talking to Mr Cobb, though he seemed nice. In the end, Cobb had
persuaded them to report the incident together.

'But, Dad, it was only just near the houses – near the marina –
lots of people are down there. It's not deserted.' She had begun to
feel a little better, just thankful that the horrible man had left her

alone. Who it could have been she could not imagine. The smell of the stuff he was enveloped in was the most potent memory. She tried to pull herself together. On Tuesday morning she had her part-time holiday job in Eastminster where she worked in a chemist's shop. School would begin in the middle of the following week and she must concentrate on her new sixth-form work.

Mr Cobb had smiled at her when they got into her father's battered old van to go to the nearest police station. She had been surprised he didn't own a car, but he turned out to be a great help, appearing quite at his ease in the police station.

After they had reported the incident to a nice young police-woman, who had taken notes, Linda almost felt her old self again.

Lisa had seemed to want to stay talking, and Susan, though long-ing to read the paper, thought she had better be patient with her.

'Just think, she might have been raped – or even killed,' Lisa was saying. She looked glassy-eyed as though she were about to faint.

'Have another cup of tea,' offered Susan. 'Don't worry. I can take you to and from school the week after next and it doesn't get really dark till about half past eight at present. Just don't go anywhere lonely by yourself.'

'Oh, I wouldn't,' muttered Lisa. 'He won't let me go *anywhere* without him, anyway. This'll only make it worse. He means to be kind, of course.'

'Surely you're grown up?' said Susan irritably. 'I mean, he may be your husband, but he's not your keeper – you must have got around a bit more when you were younger.'

'I married very young,' said Lisa. She seemed about to say more, but thought better of it.

When she had gone at last Susan made another cup of tea and thought about what marriage did to some women. What if she married Richard – though that, of course, was now impossible – and he treated her as though she were his property? But Richard was not like Tony Smith. It was surprising that Tony allowed his wife to work, but they probably needed the money for the mort-gage. They said his business was not doing too well.

His garden centre, Smith's Nursery, with its rows of conifers and shrubs and horrible leylandli, was out on the Tollesbury Road, and sold other awfully boring things. She had once visited the place and brought back only a bergenia plant. Most people now seemed to grow their plants in packaged-up clumps which they planted straight away. She was more adventurous and was determined to plant some unusual old roses in Miss Kant's back garden, even though the estuary air was not kind to many plants. She'd have to find them elsewhere than in Tony Smith's dump. Miss Kant loved roses too, and had encouraged her to write to a specialist rose-grower.

Her thoughts reverted once again to Linda's attacker. She hoped there was not going to be a general panic in the village. But you couldn't be too careful. Such attacks were getting more and more common nowadays, even down here, away from towns, away from London. She was uneasily aware that the old robe had formerly been kept in a cupboard full of mothballs.

CHAPTER THREE

The Saturday attack on Linda Swift was followed on the Monday by the late summer bank holiday. Nobody at Heron Close took much notice of bank holidays, whereas the marina had a busy day.

Both the Whitwhams said they were relieved that Linda had been prevailed upon by Mr Cobb to make a statement to the Eastminster police, Mr Whitwham opining that Cobb had been helpful 'beyond the call of duty'. Susan told Miss Kant of Tony Smith's chauvinist reactions to Linda's attack, and said she was feeling more angry than worried on Linda's behalf. None of the other Heron Closers said anything further about the matter to them, and Miss Kant spent the Monday indoors cleaning out cupboards.

A lot of the junk she had kept when she retired was still unsorted, for she never seemed to have had enough time to throw away old teaching-plans, catalogues, theatre programmes, photographs, holiday mementoes, files of her own history notes, old OS maps, letters – even lists of books she'd once sorted to give to Oxfam. She confessed to being a hoarder and had kept putting off a final 'uncluttering'. She'd intended one day to get it all on to a computer but then realized she'd need a hundred years to do so and would not live for ever. The computer had so far not been purchased. She managed, however, to make a pile of the books she would either never read again or had not liked in the first place.

The rest of that week was uneventful, after all the unpleasant excitement of the attack on Linda. Susan had to go into school two or three times to prepare for the autumn term, since school proper began on Thursday, 9 September. The holidays would soon be really over.

Miss Kant was feeling it was about time she had a day out, and decided on Tuesday, the seventh. For some time she had been intending to make a new will, and needed to visit her solicitor who lived in a part of London where she had once taught. It gave her the excuse to get out of the house and to see a bit of the world.

She had never really missed her old London life and even less her last post of lecturer in a college that had been swallowed up in a new 'poly' in the Midlands, now part of a new university. The retirement sword had fallen on her and they were in any case 'downsizing' on numbers of staff. She was relieved to have an extra year's freedom.

Retirement suited her well – there was still so much to read, to learn, so much she had never had time for when she was working full-time. She had begun a study of the stories of women mentioned through the centuries in memoirs or letters or diaries about whom little was known, and had also researched a good deal of her own family history.

In order to be sociable, now that she was supposedly retired she had thought she might join an evening class in Eastminster, the nearest town, in a subject that interested her. Pottery, flower-arranging and a little mild art appreciation were not however in her line. There was a university extra-mural centre further away, or she might even go to a daytime class in London.

She was still looking for a suitable class and sat scanning a syllabus in the train to London, having left her car at the station. There was so much going on at the larger centres: advanced classes in family and local history, for example, but she knew enough of the techniques for studying these. A philosophy class interested her more: *Philosophical Issues of the Next Century*. They called it Applied Ethics now: animal rights, abortion, general medical ethics, euthanasia, punishment, feminism, censorship. . . . Yes, she would like to attend that course, but it was in the evening and she preferred not to drive at night in the winter.

She flipped over to the literature classes. She ought to make an effort to understand new – now rather old – literary theory, but fiction itself interested her more, and she could always read about it in library books. She was at present rereading Victorian novel-ists, enjoying them hugely, with their clear ideas of right and wrong. To think that forty years ago she had dismissed many of them as writing for the bourgeoisie! Well, that was what *she* was now – an elderly *bourgeoise*! Ah, here was a course given in the French language – that would be good for her. She smiled as she leafed through the prospectus, but wished she had many more years in which to read and learn.

At Liverpool Street she took the tube to the part of East London where she had once lived years ago, and made her way to her solicitors, never having bothered to arrange matters with a new one. Things had changed in the High Street; it was full of Asian shops and shoppers, all so much more colourful than the drab old shops she had once known. She thought about the Asian girls she had taught at the college, all so bright and polite and hard working. A pity so many had to buckle down prematurely to the fate their families had arranged for them. Still, marriage being such a lottery, it was perhaps no worse a system than the one that precipitated two people into lifelong companionship – and mother and fatherhood – on the flimsy basis of sexual attraction?

Mr Potter was amazingly still there in the office, white-haired now, but after an initial look of blankness – she knew he had forgotten her face – he instructed his secretary to bring Dorothea's file for updating. Her brother, to whom she had been going to leave the bulk of her capital and her house, was doing nicely in Canada, having become a real estate agent in Ontario, and she had decided that charities and persons other than family were more deserving of her house and savings.

'Oh, you've brought a draft with you,' said Mr Potter, peering at Dorothea's typescript under his half-moon spectacles. 'Of course we shall have to word all this legally – they insist, you know,' he said, as though it was nothing to do with him and he would choose to modernize the legal system.

It was absurd, she thought, the entire preamble that was required and all the obfuscation to express a few simple requests, but he had his expertise as she had hers and it was, she hoped, money well spent.

When the details had been sorted out and Potter had promised to have the new document sent to her in a few days, he sat back and ordered her a cup of coffee. He seemed disposed to talk.

'How do you like country life then, Miss Kant?' he offered. 'Glad to have left the Smoke? Of course, though, you didn't go directly from here to – er . . .' he looked at the address again, 'Spickhanger . . . is it? Charming name . . .'

'Oh, no – I was in the North and the Midlands for several years training teachers,' said Dorothea, answering his last question first. 'I decided to . . . put myself out to grass,' she said, and he smiled faintly, obviously thinking, lucky for some, with their index-linked pensions and their lump sums.

'It's quiet where I live now,' she went on, thinking, as soon as she said it, that's a lie! A girl attacked by a man dressed in a dark robe! Still, it was *usually* quiet.

'You knew East Anglia before then?' he hazarded. 'I always thought Norfolk and Suffolk were pretty.'

'No, I didn't know it,' she replied. 'Where I live happens to be near enough London if I want to do some research or to go to galleries or museums. Norfolk is vast, but too far away and the transport is bad.'

'Yes. I hear that villagers there have returned to driving ponies and carts!' he said, looking interested. 'Local bus services have almost disappeared and ponies are cheaper than cars to get to stations.'

Dorothea thought it a charming idea and said so.

'I hate driving,' she said. 'I only learned because I had to. I used to have to visit lots of schools to see students teach.'

He made a few remarks about the appalling standard of spelling and punctuation evinced by the girls he took on as clerks or secretaries in his office as she finished her coffee and rose to go. They shook hands and she went out, a whole afternoon before her if she wasted no time over lunch.

She might buy a sandwich and eat it in a City churchyard. She could take the tube there and then walk back to Liverpool Street before the rush hour. But first she wandered along the market stalls that were set up all along the pavement near the underground station. She was a tall, striking figure among the small Indians and fat East-Enders. She looked at bright cottons, admired gaudy jewellery, bought two cups and saucers – slightly imperfect but half the price they were in Eastminster – and studied a stall of potted plants and herbs, wondering whether to buy some rather sweet purple-and-white winter pansies which she could pop in her front-garden urn. There was also a dwarf hebe which would be very suitable for wintering indoors and then planting in her little rockery, and she was hesitating whether to commit herself when her attention was caught by some large pots of end-of-season hardy annuals, tall droopy plants in fading purple flower which she recognized as 'love lies bleeding', here with the label 'prince's feathers'.

'Like a pot?' said a voice from behind the stall, where two women were shouting their wares now and again, but mostly sitting down chatting to each other. Dorothea looked up.

'Why – Lisa!' she began, but then stopped. The woman wasn't Lisa, but bore an uncanny resemblance to her.

Dorothea's smile faded as the woman stared at her, 'I'm sorry, I thought you were a neighbour of mine, but of course she couldn't be here: Lisa Smith – you look so like her.'

The woman was regarding her suspiciously.

'And her husband is a landscape gardener. Perhaps you're related to his wife?'

'Lisa, did you say? My name's Brenda,' said the woman in a rather aggressive East London voice. 'Did you want to buy anything?'

Dorothea hesitated – she really did need new glasses! The woman was older and coarser-featured than Lisa, but there *was* a resemblance. She intended to restock with some perennial and biennial seeds, but there was nothing suitable here. Her own garden seemed to grow massive amounts of valerian – it must be the salty air? Dorothea loved flowers but was only just beginning to understand gardens.

'I'll take the hebe, and perhaps a herb – a pot of thyme,' she said. 'I can't carry anything more. I must say your prices compare well with country ones.'

'Yeah, well – I expect we sell more here,' replied the woman grudgingly, wrapping the plants in newspaper. 'Wouldn't you like a 'prince's feather' now? It's easy to grow – for your border or your greenhouse?'

'No, thank you. I have some of those already as a matter of fact,' replied Dorothea. She stowed her purse away and put the pots of hebe and thyme along with the cups and saucers into her capacious canvas bag.

There was something unpleasant about the woman, who looked wary.

'Sorry I mistook you for my neighbour, Mrs Smith. I ought to wear my glasses when I'm shopping!'

'They say we've all got a double,' said the woman. Her eyes were hard, not like little Lisa's soft dark ones, but Dorothea walked away, feeling rather stupidly upset by her error and her fumbling over her purse. She really did need her reading-glasses on when she went shopping, she thought, but the woman *did* look like Lisa, she really did.

'Funny, Tony Smith sells plants too,' she thought. She had not bought any from Tony, feeling he could easily have given a few plants to his neighbours. Like Susan, she was not keen on those she had seen in his nursery anyway.

She felt thirsty, and abandoned her plan to sit in a churchyard. She boarded a bus back to Aldgate and looked out on London from the top. She could have a sandwich at the refurbished station and browse through the magazines at the W H Smith's to see if they had anything interesting. She remembered the station in the past; it was so different now, but so was everything. Time was getting on, but she could get a train back and have tea at home in Spickhanger. She was already tired of London with its dirty streets and general air of neglect and crossness. She'd save a visit to the West End for another day, visit her favourite cheese shop and the London Library and perhaps look in a Cork Street gallery. She'd missed the last week of the summer exhibition at the Royal Academy where, she had heard on Saturday at the party, David had had a painting accepted.

No, she did not regret leaving London. About thirty-five years ago, before the swinging sixties had got going, it had been a pleasant city. But now she felt she no longer belonged there except as a visitor, in spite of the improved railway stations and the certainly improved cups of coffee. She realized it must be because she was older. Later, as she sat in the train, gloating over several old paperbacks, reduced in price, which she had found on a special rack and had not been able to forgo, her thoughts reverted to Heron Close and the attack on Linda and then to that woman who had looked so like Lisa Smith. The East Ender had looked at her so curiously. Did she herself look odd nowadays, out of place?

She opened the autumn study programmes again: the extra-mural daytime course at the nearest university; another at the City Lit. She was soon back to thinking about the subjects she might take up, as the train swayed along through north-east London and then into the country, past wheat-fields with hedges now removed, dead elm trees still standing sentinel at old borders, looking like the witches from Macbeth. It was better than London, though the blight of rubbish-strewn streets and vandalism had begun to reach Eastminster. How far would you have to go back in time or place to escape the approach of the twenty-first century? The Highlands, perhaps? Southern Ireland? Spickhanger would have to do. She felt a little depressed. What she needed was a course in how to live at the end of the 1990s. She looked at the novels she'd bought, bestsellers of the thirties, set in a distant time when, in her opinion, the English language had not yet degenerated.

She found she was still thinking of the market-stall woman. Perhaps she really was a relative of Lisa Smith. But she would surely have said so if she were, or asked for more details of whomever it was who looked like her. There was nothing else to connect the two women except the fact that Tony Smith sold plants.

Dorothea Kant had always had an insatiable curiosity about people and their motives. Her long years as a teacher had brought her into contact with many hundreds of girls and young women and, as time had gone on, she had begun to feel a little like Miss Marple, finding parallels across the years in faces and characters. Lisa Smith already intrigued her, remembering as she did one Bunny Corrigan, whom she'd known many years back when she had just begun teaching in the East End.

Bunny had been very quiet and withdrawn and always looked hunted. Several of the staff had agreed that Bunny was probably beaten at home by her stepfather, but no obvious bruising or other marks of physical punishment had ever come to light, even when they had asked Miss Williams, the gym teacher, to urge the school nurse to look very carefully at the child during her next medical inspection. *Something* had been wrong with Bunny Corrigan but no one ever knew what, and she had vanished into the world of work after her O levels.

She ought to look Bunny up in the deaths' register next time she went to the Family Record Centre to pursue her research. She came across all sorts of interesting things there. It was true that families sometimes threw up second or third cousins who looked more like each other than brothers and sisters. All to do with which genes you'd inherited, she supposed. She and her brother in Canada, for example, were not at all alike, but her brother's daughter looked very like her, Edmund said.

This reminded her of the old family photographs that Edmund was always pestering her to send, with details of names. He wanted all his ancient relatives marked up for him. Not that he had ever bothered with them when he lived in England. She had been the one who made family trees, from the received wisdom of their Aunt Muriel, another spinster like herself. All her notes must be among those she had been trying to sort yesterday.

Dorothea was soon miles away in thought, retracing obscure

patterns of naming, and tenuous links with the Kant family who were said to have come from Germany in the eighteenth century. If the station in Eastminster had not been a terminus she might very well have missed it. She got out, looking forward to a cup of tea at home, and a good read. She pushed the Lisa look-alike to the back of her mind. The trouble was if you had been teaching young women for years you tended to connect people who had no connection.

When Linda Swift got home from her job at the chemist's that same Tuesday afternoon, her last work-day before school started on Thursday, her mother was waiting for her in the kitchen with a cup of tea. Linda had scarcely opened the door when Mrs Swift stood up from the table and shrieked:

'Thank God! You're back!'

'What on earth's the matter, Mum?'

'There's been another attack! I've just heard from Mrs Pheasant. Last night – a woman down Spire Lane before it turns into the private road to the marina and the close. Oh, Lindy – I thought it might be you – and then they said no, it's an older woman – some camper—'

'Mum, of course it couldn't be me. I've been at the shop all day! Anyway, he never *did* anything to me.'

Linda had managed, in her father's words, to 'get her head round' the happenings of ten days ago. Telling it to the police-woman had done her good.

'But this woman – she was raped! It *could* have been you! It must be the same man. They say she was walking back to the field where the boat people camp when – Mrs Pheasant says – he followed her. A man just returning from a sail saw her sitting by the gate to the marina about eight o'clock last night. Hardly able to walk, she was that terrified. He stopped his car – it was John Bertram from Spire – you know, he has a dinghy down there – and she recognized his van 'cos he'd done some painting down at the boathouse. Otherwise she'd not have dared to go back with him. He brought her straight into the police station – that's how I know. . . .'

Mrs Pheasant was married to a constable who had used to patrol the village of Spire, but who now spent most of his time chasing motorists in Eastminster. He'd told his wife some of it late that night and she'd wasted no time telling everyone in the village.

'Poor woman – how horrible!' Linda shivered. She herself had been lucky, then.

'Mrs Pheasant said she didn't know her name. We've all got to take care, she says. It might have been you, Lindy!'

She began to cry and Linda sat down, trembling, suddenly able to project herself into the mind of this unknown woman who had not been as lucky as her. It must be the same person who had attacked them both. Mrs Swift poured her a cup of tea and then one for herself.

'I expect the whole village knows by now?'

'Must do. They've got to find him. Stringing 'em up's too good for them – wait till your dad hears. No one's safe round here – he won't be letting *me* go down the close on my bike – you wait.'

'Then he'll have to take you in the van – you can't miss your work.'

Linda's dad was a TV repair man and had the use of a van; most days he'd gone out before his wife in the opposite direction and so could not give her a lift to her job at Heron Close. He usually collected her on his way back from jobs.

'We'll have to see,' Mrs Swift said, and poured another cup of tea.

'Then they've no idea who it might have been?' asked her daughter.

'No. He might do it again. No woman'll dare to go out after dark.'

'It'll be getting dark earlier soon,' said Linda. 'No one told you what she said about him? I mean they might want us to compare notes. Did she *see* him?'

'I've told you – that's all I know. Mrs P said enough – she wouldn't have been told any details, I don't suppose. Her hubby's probably wishing he'd said nothing. She's an alarmist.'

Linda forbore to point out that her mother was acting in the same manner. But you couldn't blame mothers for being scared for their daughters as well as themselves.

After his tea Mr Cobb had a phone call from Eastminster.

'That you, Jim? Jim Cobb?'

On being told it was indeed, the caller went on: 'Chief Inspector Graham here – George to you. We thought you'd like to know, off the record like, there's been another attack. You knew? Who told you? All round the village, is it? We might have known Fatty

Pheasant wouldn't keep his mouth shut. Well, keep your eyes open. By the way, does anyone know you were once a copper?'

'No,' said Mr Cobb shortly.

'Keep it that way then – you might pick something up for us. It was very wise of you to bring the girl round the other Sunday – not that it seems to have scared Chummy off. Still—'

'Were the details the same?' asked James Cobb – ex-Chief Inspector Cobb (retd), South Riding police.

'He wasn't wrapped up in a dust-sheet or whatever. She says he had jeans and sneakers and there was no particular musty smell. He just came up behind her from the ditch at the bottom of the hedge, dragged her there – she thought she was going to be murdered. Not a timid sort of woman though. It was dusk so she couldn't see his face, but she was sure he was a young man. She's a lot older than the Swift girl – about twenty-seven – she'd been camping near the marina with her girl friend over the Monday. Husbands had gone back to Witham after a sailing weekend and the wives had decided to stay on because the weather was still good.

'I was going to ring you anyway,' said Cobb. 'I was just having my tea. It's about the "robe". A young teacher who lives here thinks Chummy took it out of her car, which she'd left unlocked that Saturday night. It was an old prop belonging to the school over at Eastminster – a monk's habit. She's a teacher there. Thing was – it was all in a heap on the back seat of her car, not neatly folded as she'd left it. Told her landlady who told me, when she came round for a gardening catalogue that I'd promised her. But it isn't really my business, is it. It may mean nothing. Perhaps I should have told you before.'

'Too late for prints – still there might be traces on it. Where is it now? I'll have to report it.'

'Still in her car, I expect – now locked, I hope. She used the car to go to the school for some meeting today, so she probably took it back to school. She wasn't sure about it – just thought it had been disarranged – and it *did* smell odd, she said. It had been hanging for years in a mothballed cupboard at the school.'

'Tell her to bring it round to us, then. Just as it is. We might find something.'

'You think it's the same chap?'

'No comment. Rape is – still – rare enough round here to think it must be. Two in ten days – not good. Cheerio, Jim. Thanks for the info.'

42

'Cheers.'

Cobb put down the telephone and sat for moment thinking. He didn't like this at all. He hadn't come to Spickhanger to start amateur criminal investigations. It was only chance that, accompanying Linda and her father that Sunday to the station, he'd glimpsed George again, who had worked with him years ago before leaving the South Riding force for the south. Cobb did not wish to advertise the facts about his previous employment. All that was over, had ended when Edna had died. He'd left everything, taken early retirement, gone away to forget.

It was his own fault that he had been the officious one who'd forced the Swifts to the station to report the attempted rape – if that was what it was. George had seen him there but had only raised his eyebrows, not greeted him. Gossip spread news like wildfire in a development like Heron Close. Damn his own officious – or interfering – mentality. But in a minute he'd go along and ask Susan Swann if she wouldn't mind taking the robe to the station. Then his responsibility would be over. He had been neglectful.

'On Spire Lane it was – just before the turning to Spickhanger, about a mile along – what the devil are the police doing? This is getting disgraceful,' said Mr Whitwham to his wife as they drank their after-supper coffee and prepared for an evening's viewing, or Mr Whitwham did.

His wife was already sorting out her knitting-needles to begin on a lacy bed jacket for her daughter.

'Well, they can't be patrolling everywhere – and anyway, it could have been anybody, even a motorist from somewhere far away. He might just have seen the girl and stopped.'

'No, they say he wasn't in a car. He came rearing up from the ditch. Must have been someone who uses the lane regularly.'

'What time do you say this was, dear?' enquired his wife, beginning to cast on a creamy, silky mixture.

'Yesterday evening, about eight o'clock, the woman – a camper – was walking back from the off-licence in Spire – the bar at the marina only opens on Saturdays.'

'Who told you all this?'

'In the shop at Spire – everyone was talking about it – and then I met Mrs Swift as I was walking back to the car and got some more details.'

'Well, I expect they'll ask where all the men were last night. You were here with me so you've nothing to worry about,' she said placidly.

'Vera! It's not funny.'

'No, I know it isn't. But they're sure to ask. It would be awkward for anyone who wasn't at home, wouldn't it.'

'But it isn't anyone from here! We were all at the party on Saturday when the Swift girl was attacked – they know that attack couldn't be anything to do with us.'

'No, but what if it isn't the same man, dear?'

He looked at her in amazement.

'Not a lunatic *and* a villain in a little place like this – don't be silly.'

'It only occurred to me it *might* not be the same man. But I'm sure you're right.'

'I'll lock up extra carefully tonight,' he promised.

Pat Dawson was saying much the same to Eva Maitland, the Woman Who Hardly Ever Goes Out, at that very minute. So was Tony Smith to Lisa Smith.

In the latter case, though, it was accompanied by a good deal of shouting, whereas Pat Dawson, bicycle rider like Cobb and Linda, was in bed with his neighbour and they were murmuring rather sleepily. Then he sat up, pulled on his shirt, which he had dropped on the floor and had to fish up rather woozily, and added:

'Would you let me stay with you at night till this beast's discovered? He might strike again, taking a chance. I shan't sleep if I think you're worried.'

'This man attacked a young women on a country lane,' said Eva Maitland. 'Anyway, the house is very well secured. It isn't staying at home that worries me – I feel safe inside.'

'Yes, yes,' he said soothingly.

He wouldn't press her, but he was sure that in the end he and Eva would eventually make a go of it together, help each other, one day spend their lives together, not just an hour or two in the evenings, with the curtains drawn. He gave her a kiss and lit a cigarette and when she'd got up, she made them bacon and eggs before he returned to his own house and his own bed, a narrow one ever since his wife had left him for a younger and soberer man.

'You won't go out without me unless it's in the car to school – you can go with the Swann woman but there's to be no walking around by yourself – even in the day, even at weekends. Otherwise you'll come with me to the nursery all day Saturday. There's a Johnny Madman around and I'm not taking any chances. You'll do as I say, Lisa.'

He was squeezing her wrist so hard it hurt.

Later, he made violent love to her. Half-terrified as she cowered beneath him, she thought: what's the difference? This is rape too.

'I left it there on the seat this morning,' Susan was saying to Miss Kant on Tuesday night. 'I took it back to school when I had the staff-meeting. During the meeting I thought, after this I'll take the beastly thing to the police. But when I went back to the school carpark and looked on the back seat of my car, it wasn't there!'

'You must have left the car unlocked again,' said Dorothea mildly.

'I know – and now I feel so guilty. I should have taken it to them before. Now what will they think of me?'

Cobb had telephoned that afternoon and asked Miss Kant to tell Susan to take the offending article to the police in Eastminster.

'If I were you I'd lock your car everywhere you go. I always do myself – in the station carpark, outside a shop, even here in the drive – and I'm sure it's even more likely to be broken into at the school.'

'But who would use a mouldy piece of theatrical property? It doesn't make sense. Unless ... what if the man who attacked Linda was around the school? But how would he know to find my car there unless he knew *me*? I understand why you felt I should mention it to James Cobb.'

'Look, Susan, apparently this new attack they're all talking about wasn't done by anyone dressed up as a monk or anything else. Remember, the attack on Linda didn't come off; it could be another person. I'm sorry, I should have asked you before saying anything more to Mr Cobb.'

Susan was off on another tack.

'Linda's attacker must have come from the marina, and the man who attacked this other woman did so as she was walking back to the field behind it. I'm sure the police will be looking at the boat-owners – or anyone who worked down here regularly. It's horrible.'

'Let's hope the police will soon find out who it was,' said her landlady sombrely. 'There are heaps of people who come to sail, but they mostly know each other. I am puzzled about the robe. It doesn't make sense, as you say.'

'Unless there's going to be another attempt,' said Susan. 'I wish I'd never brought the bloody thing home at all in July. But I'll call the coppers with my story; perhaps then I shan't feel so guilty.'

'That's what Mrs Swift says Linda feels,' said Dorothea, preparing to go up to her study. 'Guilty. Women always feel *guilty*, don't they? When they've done nothing at all – when in fact someone has attacked *them*, or someone has stolen something from them.'

'You're right,' agreed Susan rather wearily. 'Of course, I suppose that Linda's attacker *could* be a woman – with a down on her.'

Miss Kant gave a short, sharp, dismissive snort and Susan was left to wash up after her supper and reflect upon her own deficiencies in the matter of feminism.

CHAPTER FOUR

It was early Wednesday evening and David and Sandy were sitting nursing glasses of single malt. They had drawn the blinds and there was an envelope and a letter on the Regency card table before them. Now that their house was empty of guests, the simple, stylish elegance of the furniture of their joint sitting-room was more in evidence. Over the years together they had picked up many bargains from provincial auction rooms. The grandmother clock ticked away in one corner; in another there was a plain corner cupboard with glass doors, which boasted their small collection of china. There was some Wedgwood, a twenties assortment from the Omega workshops and part of a mid-Victorian tea-set, china roses splashed on white glaze with a thin gold rim on each cup.

The firescreen was of Victorian tapestry – Berlin work, which Sandy did not like but David did. They had had an old fireplace and grate put in especially for Sandy, who liked open fires in the winter.

In the dining-room recess of the sitting-room stood a Georgian circular table with a vase of late roses. The walls of the sitting-room were covered in David's watercolours of birds and waders. A Welsh dresser stood in the kitchen, and along the staircase wall were Sandy's photographs, mounted by him and framed to cover one whole side. The long pier-glass half-way up the stairs reflected them and the second vase of roses on the landing.

For the present, however, they were not concerned with their surroundings, or even with what the other inhabitants were discussing, but were staring at the letter on the table. Then Sandy got up and began to prowl up and down. David went to the window and raised the blind a little to look at the evening sun through the slats that had earlier caused the light to fall in bars on their pale Chinese carpet. The misty ball of the sun was rapidly sinking behind the estuary, but he knew moonlight would soon be coming through a cloud shaped like a galleon, to shed bands of silver over Spickhanger. Why should all this be spoiled for them? He let the blind fall again.

'Read it again,' he said. He went to the sofa, crossed his legs and folded his arms.

'You know what it says,' said Sandy irritably. 'There's nothing we can do about it.'

'Except go to the police,' suggested his friend.

'I suppose the police in Eastminster would be delighted to help a couple of gays who have had allegations made against them.'

David took the envelope. It was addressed in crude block capitals to Mister David and Mister Sandy.

'Illiterate,' said David, unnecessarily.

He took the letter up between his finger and thumb and read it aloud.

TO WHOM IT MAY CONSERN. WE KNOW WHO IT WAS THAT GAVE KEVIN AIDS. WE ARE WATCHIN YOU, SO DON'T THINK YOU CAN GET AWAY WITH ATTACK-ING GIRLS AS WELL, BECAUSE YOU ARE DIRTY MURDERERS AND WILL BE DEALT WITH.
SIGNED – NO FRIEND OF YOURS.

'Who do you know called Kevin, Sandy?'

'The only Kevin I know of is that son of Mr Black down at the sailing club.'

'*I* don't know anyone else called Kevin either. Only that young chap, as you say. I may have once said good morning to him. Anyway, neither of us has ever been HIV positive.'

'So?'

'So someone doesn't like us and thinks he can scare the shit out of us. *We* know there's no truth in it. Kevin, whoever he may be, couldn't catch anything from you or me even if we knew him.'

'Maybe it *is* that Kevin Black. How old is he?'

'He looks about seventeen, but he may be older.'

'You know where I think it comes from? Or who might be influ-enced by a little suggestion from him?'

Sandy was pursuing the same train of thought.

'Which young men at the marina sailing club might know our names?' he wondered. 'Heron Closers don't mix with them, but I've seen Tony Smith down there once or twice. Could he have put somebody up to it? He's machissimo and not too nice with it. As well as being a sadist.'

'But why should he want to? We've done him no harm.'

'He wouldn't need a reason. He just doesn't like us, even if he comes to our parties. Probably mixes us up with paedophiles. He might have got something on one of the lads who works down there,' Sandy gestured in the direction of the club, 'and "persuaded" him to do it.'

'Do you think it's got anything to do with those people who've been attacked? Could it be Smith knows who it was and is playing about with him?'

'Smith's been the one most vociferous about catching rapists. I heard him only this evening talking to Whitwham at his gate.'

'Men like Whitwham are the ones who make the most fuss about crime,' said David. 'He might have written our letter.'

Sandy objected. 'Whitwham talks a lot, but I can't see him writing any letters except to the *Telegraph* – *Yours Disgustedly*. Also, he can spell and doesn't have the imagination to pretend to be other than himself.'

'But it's made us victims,' said David, thoughtfully. 'It's the same sort of thing, isn't it? "They" think we rape little boys, *ergo* we rape anybody and we're filthy etc, etc, so they hound us out.'

'Why not go to the police?' said Sandy again. 'They've got nothing on us.'

'You forget – Marcus,' murmured David.

'That's long past. It wouldn't count against you now. Not since the 1998 Bill. '

'You'd be surprised,' replied his friend. 'The English in a fit of morality, frightening the horses. The fact that I once had an affair with a willing sixteen-year-old when it was still a criminal offence.'

'I know. Have another drink.'

The letter lay between them like a magnet which attracted to the pleasant room echoes of a distant past along with the smell of persecution. They put it away in the rosewood desk when they went to bed, David having counselled against burning it, just in case.

The school term proper was about to start on Thursday for Susan the teacher and Lisa the secretary. Like all the other inhabitants of the close they were seething with speculation, worry or fear.

'You know what I think?' Miss Kant said to Susan. 'That robe of yours was just a red herring. We don't even know if it really was what Linda's attacker was wearing. The other young woman – according to the local radio – swears her rapist was dressed in jeans and a T-shirt.'

'Does it say how old she thought he was?'

'I think they said she had the impression of a young man – I believe she thought twenty to twenty-five.'

'And he didn't demand money – or hold a knife to her or anything?'

'No, just jumped on her from behind. She glimpsed his face only when he was getting up afterwards. He never spoke either. It was too dark for her to see him clearly.'

'Miss Kant thought she saw you in London the other day,' Susan remarked to Lisa as she drove her into school on Thursday morning.

Lisa gave a start.

'Of course it wasn't you – just someone who looked like you. I think she should wear glasses for middle distance, or bifocals. She wears specs for reading but she doesn't like to admit she needs stronger ones for distance.'

Susan felt a little disloyal saying this.

'Where did she see this girl?' asked Lisa in a tremulous voice. Everything seemed to start her trembling nowadays.

'Oh, I think in some market in the East End when she was up in town, near where she used to teach years ago. She thought it might be a relative of yours – a sister or something.'

'I haven't *got* a sister,' replied Lisa.

For the rest of the drive Lisa was silent.

'Well, it hasn't turned up,' said George Graham, Detective Inspector, Eastminster police, over the phone to Jim Cobb. 'There's been nothing further on the second woman's case either – Patricia Simmons. You'll doubtless read all about it soon in the *Eastminster Gazette*. She's back home in Witham – in a right state, I don't mind telling you. The local papers will be too: *What are the police doing to protect our womenfolk?* etc. Do keep an eye on your neighbours, Jim – there's something a bit "off" going on at that marina near you. Nothing we can put a finger on, just a few suspicions about a little boat from Holland that comes over rather too regularly.'

'Drugs?'

'We think so – a dealer. You could be very useful to us. All off the record and not a word to anyone, even my own coppers. Better keep you under covers, if you don't mind?'

'I do mind, rather. I did my duty as a citizen when I took the Swift girl to give you a statement, but I don't intend to get involved any further. Besides, it may be "unofficial", but HQ wouldn't like it. I've no professional position now – nothing so dead as a dead policeman, you know.'

Even as he said it he knew it was not quite true. He didn't want to be involved any longer in criminal investigation, but he couldn't restrain an old CI's curiosity about people and their odd ways.

'Come off it, Jim,' said his old mate.

At least one inhabitant of Heron Close felt the failed rapist of Linda Swift might be close at hand. This person had been sitting one night that week leafing through several files and scrapbooks with a sort of disbelieving horror. The files contained pages of cuttings from tabloids, reports from broadsheets and lists of radio and TV broadcasts, each one under hand-written headings. Certain extracts were paused over:

'I couldn't care whether she was five or fifty, right?' (*Evening Standard*).

'If I'm pissed I've got to give it her. Know what I mean?' (It was attributed: *Local radio*)

The hand turned over a page and hesitated, before its owner read on: a newspaper report of another young woman, this time in a seaside resort:

'Having been asked for her rings at knifepoint, Mrs Jackie Bermondsey handed them over to the attacker, a youth of about fifteen. Before he ran off he slashed Mrs Bermondsey's daughter of twenty months across the forehead with his knife.'

Another told of a boy thrown off a moving bus by his schoolmates: 'If I pierced my ears, wore the right trainers and swore all the time they would probably leave me alone, but I don't.'

The hand turning the pages trembled.

Headlines this time, over and over again:

'Nurses attacked in casualty . . .'

'Estates too dangerous for ambulance men to enter without police protection . . .'

'Milkman has not delivered for 2 years . . .'

'WW2 veterans tremble before thirteen-year-olds armed with baseball bats . . .'

'Hit and run driver kills three-year-old.'

'Ornamental ducks slaughtered by youths. . . .'

The paragraph under this headline was too disgusting to pursue. Strange how cruelty to animals could rouse even stronger anger than cruelty to children. Even children felt that.

Some extracts had been cut out and pasted into a book. 'Toddler 4', 'Boy 6', and 'Girl 8' were next to: 'Boy pushed off bicycle by motorist dies in road under lorry', followed by: 'Baby thrown into canal rescued by philosophy student.' On the next pages the repetition of events became wearisome, a turning inferno of evil: Woman of 76 . . . woman of 86 . . . woman of 93 . . . raped. . . .

Babies, old ladies, people who just happened to be passing – raped, slashed, mugged; the only motives ones of destruction. Violence not always, seemingly, triggered by booze, or drugs.

A journalist had written a headline above the cutting on the latest page:

'The Rights of Man: to fight, to mug, to rape, to kill . . . ? Do whole sections of the country possess a death wish?'

The scrapbook was closed, the files put back, scores of further cuttings placed back in a box. Once all had been locked away, and the light put out, the figure opened a window to soft country air, which surely, if anything could, might blow away the evidence of man's inhumanity?

Late on Thursday night down at the now deserted marina, where he had several jobs, Percy Thrush was ready to go home. One of his jobs was to crop the greensward at the front of the hut where flew the flag proclaiming SPICKHANGER MARINA in yellow on blue at the top of a white flagpole. He was useful too for carrying boxes of wine and packed crates of lager up the rickety outside stairs of the clubhouse to the bar on the first floor over the members' locker-rooms. Percy had never been averse to a spot of pilfering. They would *expect* him to take half a dozen cans for himself, he argued.

He had been working on at the point quite late, since everyone had now gone home, swabbing down the floors at the clubhouse and checking the moored dinghies, and the beached boats in the field behind. He liked the darkness, liked being alone. There was no one else around and he planned a drinking session on the shingled beach before walking through behind Heron Close down Spire Lane and then across the fields to his 'chalet' on the other side of Spire. He was saving for a car, kept all his cash from his employers under his bed in a tin box.

The Heron Closers were a 'close' lot, he'd decided, though Mr Whitwham, the treasurer of the residents' association, was scrupulous in regular cash payments to him. Alf Black was less regular. Percy had told each of his employers that the other was paying his national insurance stamp, and neither enquired further.

That morning he'd had an offer for the land round his chalet – more of a shanty or cabin in reality – an offer he might not be able to resist. He'd inherited the building and its patch of land from his mother, but had not lived in it until two or three years ago when he had returned to Spire. This offer was from some agents in Eastminster who wanted the land for a few small houses. They'd pointed out that the land round the shack would fetch a good price nowadays, being so near the coast. He realized they'd pull down the old dwelling that had been built by his dad in the nineteen twenties after a little win on the pools and a few other jobs that had gone well. His father had brought his first wife out of Stratford, for holidays 'in the country'. Later, his dad along with Mum, Dad's second wife, and all the children had settled there.

The roof was of tin and there were only two rooms, one behind the other, and a lean-to pantry and outside lav. He'd liked it as a kid and now it was enough for his needs. He didn't want a room in someone else's house. Still, he might sell it if they upped their offer, and then he might buy a caravan – the prospect of a car was enticing. He was on to a good thing too at the marina and the close. One or two queer things had been going on, starting with Alf Black's son hanging round some nights, and a boat that came and went. There might be quite a bit of cash for him if he played his cards right. Information was always useful to blackmailers. *Black*mailers, he grinned. That was dead funny.

He put out the lights in the clubroom, locked the door and bent down to pick up his own box of lager cans; he'd stowed a dozen or so there from different cases he'd opened. He'd go now to drink a few of them on the beach before taking the rest home. He was a night creature; no one was waiting up for him and it was a mild night. An owl hooted somewhere beyond the close in the trees that sheltered the point or in one of the old barns. He laughed to himself again as he made his way down the steps that had been fixed in the sea-wall to the shingle. There was a path going round the point on a highish sea-wall built to withstand flooding after the catastrophe of 1953. He'd been just about to leave school at the time. Percy Thrush sat down under the sea wall and opened his first can.

Lisa Smith could not sleep. Whenever she managed to doze off she would suddenly be wide awake again, frightened that if she succeeded in going to sleep she would die. It had been one of her childhood fears and recently it had resurfaced. Tony had forbidden sleeping-pills – he said they'd make her sleepy for her work. But she knew that nights of bad sleep made her tired at school and wondered how long she could go on like this. Her mind went round and round what Susan had told her about the woman who looked like her. But there was nothing wrong in someone looking like you, was there? It was true she had no sister. She shuddered: if only she'd had a sister, her life might have been easier. She wondered whether she ought to tell Tony about the girl. He was fast asleep, thank God.

When they had first lived at Heron Close she used to envy him his ability to sleep like a baby, and be angry that long hours passed with him snoring whilst she tossed and turned. But lately she'd felt glad that at least for a few hours she had herself to herself, and could lie there with her own thoughts, even if they were not pleasant.

She got up and looked out of their bedroom window, which was at the back of the house. The moon had disappeared and she was disappointed, for moonlight was very pretty. After checking that Tony was asleep, she decided to get herself a glass of water, and tiptoed out of the open door to the bathroom. The curtains of their other bedroom at the front were not drawn and as she came out of the bathroom she went in and looked out from the other side of their house. This room should have been the nursery. She still thought of it like that. But it had only been a dream. She would never be allowed to have a baby.

Looking out of the window now she saw lights go on and off in other houses on the close. It must be the stuffy air. Other people couldn't sleep. It was still very sultry for the time of year. Suddenly the moon appeared from behind high cloud. She saw a light go on and off downstairs at Number 4 on the curve opposite their house. The houses on Heron Close were built in what looked like a random fashion at odd angles to each other so that they did not appear too regimented. Like a child dropping bricks any old how, she thought.

She had heard that Mr Robson often walked up to Spire Creek at night to film bats and other night creatures. Next door at Pat Dawson's it was dark, but further on there was a pool of light from a room at Mrs Maitland's at the side of her house. There was darkness across the pond and she could not see the Whitwham's house. They slept the sleep of the just, she found herself thinking, wondering where the words had come from. She shivered even in the warm air and saw a light go off at the front at Mr Dawson's and then another go off and then on again at Mrs Maitland's and heard the click of a door being shut somewhere. . . .

Lisa was back in the bedroom now, standing lost in thought once more at the window. Suddenly she felt a hand on her shoulder and jumped with terror. Then she turned and saw it was Tony standing behind her. How long had he been there? She must have almost dozed off standing.

'Get to bed,' he said.

'I couldn't sleep. I'm frightened, Tone,' she moaned.

'Shut up – do you want the neighbours to hear? Shut the window.' He put his arm round her waist in a grip that made her wince and she could feel him hard against her. Perhaps it would make her sleep. . . .

It did not, and afterwards she said, as he was falling asleep again:

'Tone, Susan says her landlady saw Brenda – in the market. . . .'

But Tony Smith was asleep again.

She resigned herself to lying awake till dawn. Perhaps it was the pill that stopped her sleeping – they said it could make you depressed, and depression stopped people getting to sleep. She lay on her back as far from her husband as she could get, staring at the ceiling and the shadows cast by moonlight across it.

Percy Thrush woke with a start. He must have kipped out on the beach! He stood, his feet scuffling the empty lager cans on the pebbles, his head still muzzy. He staggered to his feet, groping for the case he'd put behind him, found it and bent down to pull it up. Still some full cans for later. Oh, well, no harm done, he'd get off home. Things were still dancing a bit inside his head in the moonlight and he grunted as he climbed the steps back to the path. He put the case down for a moment. He wanted a pee. When he'd attended to that he took up the case again and began to walk rather unsteadily along the sea-wall. Further on, his route forked into a continuation of the wall and a path across farmland to reach the lane behind Heron Close in the opposite direction from the marina. By the look of the sky he'd been asleep for some hours. He'd take a short cut down the dense pathway locally named the Abbot's Walk which met the lane after about two or three hundred yards. But suddenly, before he could turn down the opening, only a few yards from the sea-wall, he saw something human detach itself from the bushes.

Jesus! It was wearing that bloody robe! A ghost come to haunt him! But before he could run, the figure advanced towards him, and his blood froze in panic.

There was no time even to steady himself or put down the case of cans for, in a split second, he was pushed off the path by a gloved hand. The case dropped from his arms and then he was falling, falling, over the wall, back on to the beach about ten feet below. He heard a name uttered, a name he had cause to remember. Even then he might have saved himself, or suffered nothing but a broken ankle, but as he fell he hit his head on a large concrete boulder that lay on the beach, just under the wall. He knew no more.

Somebody pushed the case down after him, walked down the steps let into the sea-wall, threw the empty cans near him, and stood over the inert body. Then Percy Thrush was scrutinized once more, before a large stone held in the attacker's hand was put down with other stones and pebbles a little further along the beach.

It had not been needed.

A mission had been accomplished.

Even later that night another person bent over Percy Thrush – and exclaimed with satisfaction at what they had found.

Sandy Robson got up early on Friday morning even though he had not been in bed before one o'clock that night. When he was working the ideas came thick and fast; he liked to profit from his mood and get out with his camera. He also enjoyed taking solitary walks. Alone, he could be his natural self, a self which was overlaid by the act he put on for others and even sometimes for David. It had been so long since he had felt 'natural' with people; acting up was second nature to him. It was fun, making a new person of yourself, and David liked his sharpness and occasionally outrageous camping up, which was partly a parody of himself, he'd been doing it for so long.

It was a beautiful morning and he was whistling involuntarily as he walked down to the beach, which lay across the field at the bottom of the garden of Number 4. He paused for a moment, looking across to the island in its September haze. A little breeze had risen to dispel the sweat of the night and the sky was filled with the blue that David tried so often to reproduce, but said he never could. The tide was nearly out. Sandy jumped down the steps and began to walk along the still-dry pebbles.

Then he saw an upturned box with beer cans scattered around it just in front of the piece of concrete that they called the Rock. It was not a rock at all – all rocks had long ago been turned into shingle by the unremitting tides – but a piece of concrete left over from a ramp, built, it was said, in the war when the place had been used by the Navy to practise their D-day landings. He muttered with irritation, stopping his whistle in mid-air. People were filthy. Not even a nice bit of shingle could be left alone, but had to be filled with the rubbish from trippers who left the evidence of their picnics behind them. Then he stopped as he neared the box. Jutting out from behind the concrete was a twisted shoe, rearing upended like a model in a shop window. Surely they weren't going to leave their clothes and boots now? The evidence of a drinking session was scattered around, and he picked up an empty can, then put it down carefully and advanced towards the shoe.

On the other side of the Rock the owner of the shoe lay asleep. Sandy recognized Percy Thrush, the odd job man, a rather unsavoury character, he had always thought, apt to stare and leer at him. But Thrush did not seem to be asleep.

When Sandy approached and bent over the shape, which was twisted on its side, he saw a trickle of blood on the side of the forehead. The man's face was turned halfway into the shingle. Sandy froze. The man was dead. He was sure he was dead. He did not dare to touch him, but turned and ran back the way he had come when the morning had been bright and welcoming.

By the time he got back to Number 4 he was panting from nerves rather than exhaustion. David was not yet up and hated being woken. He looked at his watch: 7.30. Soon the post van would be there, still on its summertime schedule; he could already hear Number 7's dog, Jock, barking. What should he do? Ring 999 was the answer on automatic pilot in his brain. But he hesitated. His mobile had run out; he was always lazy about fixing it. He would go round to Mr Cobb. He was sure *he* would be up. There was an early riser if he knew anything about people. He scribbled on the telephone pad: *Found Thrush dead on beach – gone to Cobb,* so that David should know what had happened, feeling that at least he must write it down to tell himself what he had found. Then he thought, the man had obviously got drunk and fallen the night before. His clothes had looked damp, not from the sea, but from dew. The tide was coming in, though. He had better be quick.

Cobb was up and Sandy was now sitting in his neat kitchen where one porridge bowl was laid and one cup of coffee was rapidly going cold.

'I see,' Cobb was saying. He had not shaved. 'But first we must ring the police. Why did you come here and not ring them your-self?'

Sandy thought of saying that when possible he ignored the police whom he had once regarded as no friends of his, but said only:

'I was frightened. Could you telephone them?' Cobb went into his sitting-room and Sandy waited in an agony of anxiety.

'Go back – stand by the body – stay there till someone comes,' Cobb instructed Sandy on his return to the kitchen. 'I know the place you mean and I'll bring along whoever they send. Here, take this tarpaulin and cover him up – no, on second thoughts you'd better not touch anything. Just stand there, warn anyone off.'

'There was no-one about. I picked up an empty lager can—'

'No, but there soon will be,' Cobb said.

Sandy went off and, having telephoned, Cobb sat by his window looking out for the police car. It shouldn't take too long – they'd probably come more quickly when he'd said who he was and mentioned George Graham.

Perhaps the man wasn't dead at all, had just hit his head and was out for the count. But Sandy, because of his profession, had a photographic memory and had communicated the details of his find in such a way that Cobb was not optimistic. He occupied his time while waiting for the car in writing down exactly what Sandy had said. Often people went back on the first description and it was necessary to refer to the impressions when they were first fixed.

This done, he waited, hoping the police would not use their siren. Why did he feel this was no ordinary accident?

Half an hour later two men arrived in a squad car from

Eastminster, which they parked at the side of his end house before coming up to his doorstep. He did not think there was anyone looking in his direction. Susan had just got into her car and Lisa was running out of her front door. No sign of her husband or of anyone else. He looked at his watch: 8.15. The women were a bit late for their second day back at work Probably overslept after a bad night with the heat. He saw them move off as the detective-sergeant and his sidekick rang at his door. Time enough for statements later. Dead bodies were often the result of heart attacks, but victims of heart attacks did not always hit their heads on rocks. It was better to be safe and sure.

The police lost no time. Accompanied by Cobb, they went down to the shore and strode up to Sandy, who was undertaking his gruesome vigil among the beer-cans. He had already taken photographs, his camera never having left him. The tide would soon be in. The sergeant put a message through his mobile to the station to send a police photographer and the fingerprint and scene of crime officers.

'Tide'll be in soon. How far does it come up here? Would it get as far as the rock?' he asked Sandy.

'Yesterday it was just at the foot of this pebble-line,' said Sandy. 'I remember because I was out early yesterday looking for shells for a montage I'm doing.'

The detective looked blank and Cobb explained. A tarpaulin was placed over the body, once the detective sergeant had ascertained death. They awaited the SOCO as the waves came a little nearer with each slurp.

'Poor chap must have had a heart attack and fallen off the wall,' said the sidekick.

'Probably drunk,' said the sergeant, one Idle, who had suffered so much from his name that he was one of the hardest-working members of the force. Poor, harmless old man, he thought.

'Know much about him?' he asked Cobb when they had left the other man guarding the body and gone back to Cobb's kitchen. Sandy had been told to go home. A statement would be taken from him later.

Cobb poured a cup of coffee for Idle and asked if he'd mind if he ate his breakfast, which had been so rudely interrupted. Then he said:

'Name of Thrush, as we said. Been here a year or two, I think – anyway, before I arrived. Did the lawnmowing, pruned the trees, various odd jobs for residents – and he was cleaner and odd-job man down at the marina.' He gestured with his pipe through the window.

'Suppose that's where the cans came from. He must have been taking some home. Did he work late?' asked Idle.

'I don't really know. I've seen him once or twice walking home on Spire Lane when I've passed him on my bicycle.'

'How old would he be?'

'Oh, in his late fifties or early sixties I'd think. Mr Whitwham at Number 7 might know, he pays his wages.'

'Well, it all seems straightforward. Do you think he had anything to do with the business of the girl a week last Saturday?' he added. 'I mean the one who was attacked in the barn – we're all more concerned with the rape on Spire Lane.'

He was quite bright, thought Cobb. He was unsure, however, whether Idle had been apprised of the "Problem of the Disappearing Gown", so he only said:

'Yes, I heard about it yesterday, but she said he was a *young* man, didn't she?'

'I wonder if the dead man had a record. He always looked a bit shifty to me.'

'Oh, well, we'll turn it up if he had,' answered Idle, thinking: the old boy's sharp, mentioning a record. Wonder whether he's a magistrate or something.

After that, an ambulance arrived with a stretcher and two orderlies, then a van driven by a SOCO, with a photographer sitting next to him. The rest of the inhabitants of the close were all at their windows now and saw the covered body of Percy Thrush returning from his moonlight walk, accompanied by three policemen and the stretcher-bearers.

'Nothing else we can do now, sir,' said Idle. He went out to his car. The ambulance was soon sorted out and bumped back along the lane following the patrol car in the direction of Spire and eventually Eastminster.

Both Whitwhams were at their front door and even Mrs Maitland was peeping out of her window before nipping out and ringing the bell of Number 5 where she suspected Pat Dawson was still asleep. Sandy was in his kitchen whilst David reported from the doorway. Tony Smith was standing by his car. He had been just about to leave when the ambulance had arrived. He had missed the police car, having nicked himself whilst shaving and gone upstairs again for a dab of cotton wool, not having been able to find his styptic pencil. Miss Kant came to her fence and looked over to Mr Cobb, who was now standing in his garden, his pipe still alight.

'What was all that about?' she asked.

'Old Thrush found collapsed – dead – on the beach, by Mr Robson,' he answered. It was no good mincing words with his neighbour. 'Found him on his early-morning walk just before the tide got in. Banged his head on the Rock – perhaps a heart attack. He'd been boozing down by the wall,' he went on.

'What, early in the morning?' she enquired.

'They don't know. I expect the police surgeon will find out how long he'd been there.' He did not mention the dew, or the bruise that Sandy had pointed out.

'He wasn't all *that* old,' said Dorothea after consideration. 'Quite a bit younger than me.' She looked worried.

'He didn't look all that unhealthy either,' agreed Cobb, 'but you never know. He worked quite hard – perhaps it was working in the heat this summer that was bad for his heart – or perhaps too much lager.'

Down at the marina the delivery of cigarettes to the bar was being held up. No one had opened up. Shortly afterwards a police car arrived as the van man was returning to his car with his boxes. The policeman found nothing incriminating, however, and did not see Kevin Black, the son of the treasurer of the club, sitting in a dinghy that was itself sitting in a field, on the other side of the marina.

CHAPTER FIVE

After all the upset of Friday morning Heron Close settled down to another day. It was still pleasantly warm, and Tony Smith went off to his work in his shirtsleeves, with a jacket slung over one shoulder. At Number 4 Sandy took a deckchair out and sat on their back lawn where not very long ago they had given their party and Linda Swift had burst in from the lane, moaning in that weird way. David joined him there bearing the post.

'I don't like it,' said Sandy. 'First, the attack on Linda – never mind this worse one down the lane – and now I'm the person who finds a dead man on the beach. It always seems to happen to us.'

'Well, Linda didn't come moaning especially to you and me,' said David reasonably. 'None else was home that night.'

Sandy made an effort to recover his equanimity and handed his friend the post he had collected whilst David was shaving.

'No more unpleasant letters today, anyway,' he said with a certain bravado. 'I was dreading the postman arriving, but he's only brought two charity appeals and your bank statement.'

'Are you sure?'

'Of course I'm sure. I'd tell you if anything else had arrived.' He handed David the post.

David did not help when he said: 'Still, two attacks taken in conjunction with our letter – it's not nice. And now a dead man!'

He looked down at the lawn, frowning.

'I thought at one time,' said Sandy, dropping his voice, 'that Thrush might just be the sort of man to write a letter like that.'

Now it was out, he waited for his friend to disabuse him. If only someone else had found the body.

It was David's turn to try to sound cheerful.

'Look, Thrush was a tough old chap but he'd been imbibing and fell off the wall. I don't expect he would write a letter to two men he hardly knew – even as part-employers.'

'Someone else might have persuaded him to,' said Sandy, lifting a white face to David. 'Then he dies – and I find him. How's it going to look?'

'But no one else knows about the letter – so why should they think it odd that you find a body on the beach. They know you get up early for your photographs.'

'I promised Mr Cobb I'd let him see the snaps I took of Thrush,' said Sandy. 'He seemed interested in a sort of professional way, though I don't think I saw anything unusual. Do you think we should tell Cobb about the letter? He seems a capable chap. I was thankful, I can tell you, when he took over this morning. I just could not ring the police myself.'

'We mustn't get paranoid,' said David. 'We haven't done anything to be ashamed of. We shall just have to make our own enquiries about nasty minds.'

'If it was Thrush there won't be any more, will there?'

'Let's get away for the rest of the day – try to forget it.'

'OK.'

Sandy suggested they took the car into the town across the estuary to do their shopping. Then they would wait and see what the verdict was on Percy Thrush.

Nobody except Cobb was in fact told about any developments. That afternoon George Graham telephoned his old colleague.

'Getting a bit dangerous down in your place,' he began, and Cobb waited. Sometimes policemen could get very facetious.

'We don't suspect foul play,' continued George after a pause, 'though it seems a bit of a coincidence that you've already had two recent attacks before this at Spickhanger.'

'Has that robe turned up?' asked Cobb, suppressing his curiosity.

'No. Nothing to do with that. But as far as we know Thrush didn't have a heart attack – we think he just fell off the sea-wall. Contusion was consonant with banging a very vulnerable part of his anatomy on concrete.'

'The cans were all on the beach – he must have tripped up climbing the stairs to the wall. But he might perhaps have had a shock – might have been frightened by something?' suggested Cobb, thinking: but then, wouldn't he topple backwards as he dropped the crate of cans. Surely they wouldn't *all* fall on the beach near him.

'Early days for the police pathologist to pronounce, but I get the impression he thinks something had pumped him with adrenaline.'

'Was he drunk?'

'Not very drunk,' answered Graham.

'So fright could account for it?'

'There'll be an autopsy, but I don't suppose anything will come of it.'

Cobb, who had a lively – too lively – imagination, which he had tried to control in his old days in the force, was thinking aloud.

'Could he be a victim of whoever frightened little Linda?' he mused, 'I had the feeling he himself was the best candidate for the attack on her.'

'No sexual interference and we're not looking for a pervert,' replied Graham stolidly.

'Perhaps . . .' Cobb began.

'What?'

'Nothing.'

He was thinking: Could Linda have suspected Percy Thrush all along and, knowing his habits, come along in the night and pushed him over the wall when he was in no state to defend himself? It seemed unlikely. What would you have to do to frighten Thrush so much that he lost his footing? He was a strong man. Then it came to him. If her father believed Thrush had attacked Linda he could have dressed up in the clothes her attacker had worn to frighten him . . . Linda went to Eastminster School and would know Miss Swann's car.

He dismissed the thought as far-fetched, unworthy of him, and terminated his conversation with Graham after promising him a game of chess in the near future.

It was probably something to do with drug-pushing. George hadn't mentioned that this time.

But, he kept asking himself, *was* it Percy Thrush who attacked Linda? He was sure the key was somewhere there. He could not get out of his head the sight of the lifeless body of the former odd-job man and gardener. He had an instinct for the fishy, if not the macabre. Once he had been an idealistic youth, preferring always to give people the benefit of the doubt, but even before the beginning of the growing crime wave in the late 1970s, he had become more cynical.

He had begun to sense a growing aura of the non-accidental floating around his picture of the dead Thrush on the beach. He could not put his finger on anything in particular, though he appeared to have fallen too far if it was just down from the steps. Perhaps Sandy's photographs would help – the police had taken their own and did not appear interested at present in Sandy's.

He began to wonder whether, since his wife's death, he had become unduly suspicious. If George Graham's friends found anything to make them think Thrush's death had not been an accident, he was sure George would inform him eventually. The police would have checked out the angle of the fallen body, the position and timing of the tide and all the other fiddly bits of information that must be sifted through.

There remained his gut reaction. He tried to discount it and scolded himself for perhaps obscurely *wanting* a mystery, though he had not been aware previously of this proclivity in himself. Instinct remained, the same sort of intuition that had made him sure in advance that his wife's hit-and-run killer had been drinking, which was later proved to be correct. He sat down at his neat table with a pad of paper and a pencil and tried to work out logical reasons for his hunch.

If the man had had a heart attack as he walked along the wall supping his lager, an occurrence that had made him pitch over on to the beach, would he have fallen in the way he had? Yet he had not had a heart attack – the pathologist was adamant. What had made him lose his balance, then? Had he been drunk enough to stagger and lose his balance? That must be why? Yet the police-surgeon, according to Graham, had said there was alcohol equivalent to at most only three pints circulating in his bloodstream.

What else would make a man lose his balance? He could have been carrying the case of lager-cans, which was quite heavy, he supposed, and just stumbled as he walked along in the dark on the top of the wall. Unfortunately for him, he then hit his head on a lump of concrete. If someone had pushed him they wouldn't know he was going to hit his head, would they? That must just have been an accident. But if the push had been playful, the pusher would have run to his aid filled with compunction. Even if there had been a fight? No – perhaps not. Seeing the result of the push the pusher would have panicked and instead of getting a doctor would have run away. But even if the push were not accidental, the perpetrator wouldn't have known he would fall on the Rock. There had been no attempt to pick up the beer cans.

Wait a minute. If a man was carrying a case of beer and tripped up, would he automatically hold on to the cans? Not likely. And even if he did, they would not all automatically fall with him. But the cans and the case were all on the beach, as if someone had thrown them there after him. An irate barkeeper? The marina people should be interrogated; doubtless Graham or one of his boys was doing that.

No heart attack then, no tipsy stumble? How long had he been lying there? When had he drunk the beer? What if he had not fallen at all but been asleep? Ah! Then someone could have come up and bashed his head against the Rock to make it look like the result of a fall. That would be murder. There was only the one contusion though, so it didn't seem likely.

Why should anyone want to murder Percy Thrush? Had he seen something going on at the marina, threatened someone and been killed to stop his mouth? More likely. He wondered once more if Thrush had had a record. He had seemed harmless enough, a bit foxy-looking, but a good worker on the whole. Had anyone complained about him? He'd not complained about the wage they gave him. Had he had a national insurance card? Maybe the marina paid his insurance as his main employer? But it was more likely the 'Black economy' – he smiled at his own pun, but tried to stop himself going any further with these shaky speculations.

Thrush's death was not his business. The police would check. But as the day wore on he could not help pursuing his line of thought. What would frighten a man like Thrush? Nowadays, you didn't need much to frighten you when there were so many motiveless attacks. He wondered whether Linda had been asked specifically whether her attacker could have been Thrush, dressed up in a robe he could so easily have taken from Susan's car that night. This notion was not far-fetched: it would just have been an opportunity presenting itself, even if the man was not the imaginative type. He was a bit old for a sex attack, though some men went on doing that sort of thing into their seventies, and beyond, as he well knew from his old job.

Whilst Cobb was allowing himself to indulge in these speculations, Sandy Robson was at the gate of Number 4 talking to Lisa Smith and Susan Swann, who had just got back from school.

'We saw the police car,' Lisa admitted. 'But Susan was a bit late so we couldn't stop to see where it was going. Susan thought perhaps someone had been speeding or something.'

Susan had actually been relieved that they hadn't come for her; she had realized when she saw the car that she had not yet relicensed her own vehicle. She must do so immediately. She had put it out of her mind all day but here was Sandy now telling them the real reason for the police visit.

'Are you sure?' gasped Lisa.

'Quite sure. I found him!'

Susan tried to feel suitably sorry for Thrush and went in to tell Dorothea. But Mr Cobb had already told Dorothea all about it.

'Whitwham called to say he had heard there had been a *stabbing*!' added Dorothea. 'I was sceptical. Mr Cobb hinted to me when I took him some bulbs that Whitwham had made that up himself.'

'Just like him!' said Susan. 'He has to embroider everything.'

Lisa was still outside talking to Sandy. She seemed listless, Sandy thought, and there were even darker circles under her eyes, as though she had not had much sleep. She was wearing a cardigan over her flowered-print dress, but when she moved away to go into her own house he saw her take it off and put her hands up the sleeves in a gesture of self-protection. He remembered he had once seen a large bruise on her arm, and suspected her husband of treating her roughly. Still, some women bruised easily.

Kevin Black had waited on the far side of the marina late on Thursday night for the boat, but nothing had arrived and he had fallen asleep there and gone home on Friday morning to his parents' rather opulent detached house on the outskirts of the next village along from Spire, to beg some money from his mother who was a soft touch. He drove away from 'Laburnums' in an old car of his father's. His father had chucked him out for making no effort to find work when there was plenty around in the district for anyone with six good GCSEs. He'd found new friends after that, gone to London, then returned to squat in a holiday chalet up the coast, along with Darren and Wayne, his new mates.

Kevin smiled. Wayne and Darren were on to a good thing with the *Mevrouw Hanneke*, which came over so regularly from a little Dutch port. A little packet for their own use in exchange for handing over the rest to a chap in Basildon. Quite simple really. They gave him a small share in exchange for saying nothing. Other transactions went on too; he knew the skipper of the Dutch vessel had several other outlets as well as this one.

It had only been by chance last March, when a storm had driven the boat over from its route to Harwich, that he and Wayne had been out near the marina and got into conversation with the stocky Dutchman. The marina had been closed for repairs and there had been no one there but Kevin to help himself to cigarettes and booze with the replica of his father's key, easily extracted from Black senior's pocket. They had made the Dutchman comfortable and he had offered them some 'snow', seeing quite clearly that they shouldn't be there at all and certainly wouldn't tell. That was how it had all begun. Kevin sometimes wondered how it was going to end, especially as Darren was greedy – and also rather violent – and he didn't like the hold over him both Darren and Wayne seemed to imagine they had.

'Going round trying to rape virgins now, Kev?' Darren had said to him when they were discussing the attack on Mrs Simmons.

'Don't be bloody daft,' he had replied. They all knew he was gay, didn't they? At other times this knowledge seemed to be assumed, for they often told him he would get Aids one day, even if he hadn't already.

'Then you could go round *murdering* women,' said Wayne. 'Give 'em Aids – the usual way.' This was his idea of a joke.

Kevin had protested. He had been HIV negative when he'd been tested. They'd laughed.

'If you think I'm infectious, you'd better keep away,' he had shouted. But they had gone on laughing.

'We're moving off soon,' Darren had said one night last week at the pub in Spire. Wayne seemed jumpy and kept looking sideways at Darren.

'You'll be all on your ownio, Kev. Why not go back to your old man?' said Darren.

Now, when Kevin stopped the car at the sandy lane behind the row of deserted shacks and shanties and chalets a few miles up the coast and went round to 'Mimosa' (the name they'd found painted on 'their' chalet) he found no one around. He pushed open the door and was met with the usual odour of rotting rubbish, damp and woodworm.

'Darren, Wayne, I'm back,' he shouted, but there was no answer. He looked for a note, but there was none, only a pile of old newspapers on the rickety table and upstairs only one mattress on the floor in the room they'd taken as their sleeping-quarters. His mates had done what they said they would: scarpered.

He stood there, a forlorn figure in his dyed white hair and studded ears. He took out his last snort – the Dutchman would, he prayed, be back soon with more, and busied himself administering it. His nose smarted and his eyes pricked.

'Got your hay-fever? It's a bit late for that,' his mother had said before giving him some money from her housekeeping, and he had not disabused her.

'I'm allergic, Mum,' he had replied.

'Allergic to work,' she had replied fondly.

Sandy and Susan were not the only people to be worried about Lisa Smith. Susan was discussing her with Dorothea Kant after they had finished picking over the demise of Percy Thrush. Miss Kant was in the kitchen and offered Susan a cup of tea. Susan enjoyed sitting down with it, after the hassle of the school day and the drive back from Eastminster. Afterwards she'd go back up to her room with its slightly less comfortable chairs. Usually Miss Kant said little, and took her tea to her own sitting-room, knowing Susan needed time to herself to absorb the day and collect her thoughts for the evening, but today she seemed to want to talk.

'Mr Cobb told me it was Sandy who found Mr Thrush's body,' said Miss Kant.

'Yes, he told us just now. There was a rumour circulating at school, after Tony Smith popped in at lunch-time to bring some more tub plants from his nursery for the assembly hall – there's to be yet another parents' evening soon.' She sighed. 'Anyway, Tony Smith said Thrush had probably been poisoned by the beer he stole!'

'What next!' said Dorothea, 'James said the police will do a postmortem.'

'Do they think he was *attacked*? I mean, he was getting on. He probably had a heart attack or something. I know he used to go down to the beach sometimes at night. I once saw him there, just sitting, when I went for a walk myself. Of course that was in the early summer when it was light.'

'It seems he'd been having a few drinks. Have the police said anything more about your "prop"?' asked Dorothea.

'No – it hasn't turned up. I'm fed up with all this excitement – not much more than two weeks ago and we were all peaceful, and now we have two young women attacked and a body on the beach.'

'Lisa seems awfully upset,' she added when Miss Kant had taken a cup of tea for herself. 'You know, I think that husband of hers knocks her about. She had a big bruise on her arm and she was really quiet on the way to school and back. The secretaries came into the staffroom for a meeting and one of the other staff was talking about a girl whose father is in prison for assault and Lisa looked quite green. She can't stand people talking about sex or violence. Yet the other day she was saying how she wished she had a baby. I can't make her out.'

'I don't like that husband of hers,' Miss Kant agreed. 'He doesn't fit in here. I wonder why he wanted to come to Spickhanger – it's a remote place for a London type. Still, I suppose that could apply to us all.'

'I told Lisa you'd met her double,' said Susan. 'She said she hadn't got a sister.'

'Oh, well, one of life's mysteries,' said Dorothea, but looked thoughtful.

'I've noticed she never flirts with men,' continued Susan. 'She doesn't seem to like them. Perhaps she's a closet lesbian and only realized it when she was married.'

'I'm sure she's not.'

'Wouldn't you say though, that most men would like to flirt with her? She's very feminine, but I've noticed she doesn't flirt back. One or two of the men staff, you know, come on a bit strong with her – nothing serious, they do it with half the women on the staff and with the secretaries, but she never jokes with them, just moves away.'

'It's her little helpless look that probably attracts them,' replied Dorothea, sipping her tea.

'She's just so stand-offish with them that I think she doesn't *like* men. Of course, she's married . . .'

'She does often appear scared stiff of her husband,' said Dorothea. 'Not just because of the bruises he might inflict, but because he's so jealous.'

'He's paranoid; said Susan. 'Never lets her out of his sight. I noticed at Number 4's party how he always followed her with his eyes.'

'I noticed that too. But of course the same doesn't apply to Lisa – she rather avoids his glance. He's a bit of a womanizer, I would think.'

'How unfair it is!' said Susan. 'You almost get the feeling she's a

70

sort of prisoner, yet *he* does what he wants – chats other women up. He's even tried it with me!'

'I don't somehow think she minds that.'

'You mean she's not in love with him – doesn't even love him?'

'I don't think she does. It must be awful to be married to a man like Smith if you don't love him and are too frightened to escape. No wonder you say the only time she looks normal is when she's at work.'

Mrs Maitland and her next-door neighbour Pat Dawson were also imbibing – a cup of coffee this time – in Eva Maitland's kitchen on Friday morning.

'I tell you, darling, when I left your house last night, I looked towards the end of the close – near where it meets the Abbot's Walk and joins Spire Lane – and I'm sure I saw a figure dressed in some sort of long gown. It was only for a split second though and I was probably half-asleep. Anyway I was tired. What time did I leave?'

'You mean the second time you came round? The first time was around midnight, I think. Then I couldn't sleep and rang you, and you came round. It must have been about two when you went back.'

'Do you think we should tell anybody now that Thrush has been found dead?'

'But he wasn't *attacked*. I heard Mr Cobb talking to Miss Kant this afternoon he said something about his falling off the wall and accidentally hitting his head on the Rock.'

'I heard on the grapevine that Susan's acting-costume is still missing. Perhaps I saw the Hooded Monk again. What fun!'

Eva looked at him sharply and he had the grace to look ashamed when she said:

'He wasn't much fun for Linda. The costume must have turned up again somewhere. Or been hidden by someone.'

If Pat and Eva could have been over later the same day at Number 4, they would have been interested. Both Sandy and David were sitting silent in their own kitchen, their neglected-herbal tea cooling.

'I tell you it was certainly not there this morning,' Sandy was saying for the umpteenth time. 'How could it have got there? I know you didn't put it there and you know I didn't – and anyway not much point in it if *we'd* borrowed it for some hanky-panky. To find it in our garden tool-shed suggests either of us, it doesn't much matter which, is being accused of something.'

'More a joke against us both,' said David.

Sandy had gone out into the patio to find some pesticide powder to get rid of some ants that were merrily scuttering about between two flagstones. The so-called tool-shed was only a large external cupboard under a sloping roof which had been built as part of the house and had on one side space for the dustbin and, on the other, shelves for garden implements. Here they kept seeds and a pair of secateurs and a trowel and the usual clutter. Neither of them had had occasion to open the shed door in the morning and they had been out shopping afterwards, but when Sandy had opened the door to look for the ant powder, there, neatly folded, on a shelf above a row of pots and twine, was a gown. Was it the one that Linda Swift thought she had seen? How long had it been in their shed?

'We were out till four so someone could easily have come into the back garden if they knew we were away,' said Sandy.

'At least,' said David, 'we don't *know* it was the same one. There may be hundreds of similar garments scattered round Spickhanger. But the implication to anyone living here would be that we put it there, and the only costume that would interest anyone here is the one used by Linda's attacker.'

'What shall we do?' moaned Sandy, who had quite lost his head. Coming after the letter, this gruesome discovery made it look as though someone was trying not only to pin a criminal act on them along with sundry 'perverted' practices once prohibited by law, but now the attempted rape of a female as well.

'An unusual concatenation of crimes! It doesn't make sense,' said the more rational David. 'All it proves is that someone has a down on both of us.' They kept coming back to that.

'But since *I* found Thrush's body. . .' Sandy's voice trailed away miserably. 'Do we tell the police now?' he asked.

'Can't see what good it would do – but why don't we ask old Cobb for advice? He's helped you before and he'd know what to do.'

'Better show him the letter too, Dave, and swear him to secrecy. You know how things get around!'

'I mean – where could we put the damned thing,' went on David, still thinking of the robe, 'without it looking incriminating? Someone took it from the car and dumped it on us. It needn't have anything to do with Thrush, I don't suppose, and even little Linda wasn't actually attacked. So, if a missing piece of evidence turns up in our tool-shed we do our duty by mentioning it to a respectable senior citizen. That's all that's required.'

Sandy eventually agreed and they drank their Red Zinger.

'It's all so corny – a monk's robe – I ask you! They've been done to death in every old-fashioned thriller!' said David.

'So we came to you,' added Sandy rather lamely.

They were in Cobb's sitting-room and so far the older man had done nothing but grunt to show he was listening. He was thinking how smart they both looked, David in his cream, button-down shirt and reefer jacket and Sandy with a silk tie. Had they dressed up for him? What the two men had just told him had not surprised him. What if the same silly robe had been used to frighten Thrush? It would explain the shock he had had, especially if he himself had once worn it to frighten Linda Swift. Was he being paid back in his own coin? Or, if he were innocent, would thinking perhaps he was to be attacked by the same man who'd attacked Linda be enough to make him tumble to his death?

But that attack had not been successful and the perpetrator of the second attack, on Patricia Simmons, had not worn any such thing.

'We thought you would know what to do,' said Sandy, sounding rather pathetic. 'Seeing as how *I* found old Thrush, it looks bad.'

'What makes you think the two things are connected?' asked Cobb mildly.

'I don't know. They just seem to us to be too much of a coincidence,' replied David.

'I mean, no one could know it was *me* who was going to find Thrush, could they? It could have been anyone,' Sandy said.

'You are the person known to go for early morning walks,' said Cobb mildly.

'I swear I had nothing to do with Thrush,' shouted Sandy.

'Calm down. I didn't mean you had. Only that once you'd found Thrush, people would be curious, and then, perhaps, someone wanted you to know that you were under suspicion.'

The two were silent as Cobb again filled his pipe.

'Has anything else happened to either of you recently?' he asked.

The two younger men looked swiftly at each other before

saying: 'Yes,' together in the same voice. Then they brought out the letter.

Cobb held it between his fingers and thumb and read it quickly.

'I'll think about it,' he said. 'Don't worry. I won't tell anyone else unless you give me the go-ahead. And where *is* the offending robe?'

'Still in the shed.'

'We didn't touch it – just left it there. We knew it must be the thing there had been such a fuss about. After all, it's not a common occurrence to have someone break up your party with a tale of an attack by a hooded monk.'

'Well, Linda didn't actually *say* that,' said Cobb. 'People jumped to conclusions because there was once a monastery here. I don't know who actually said it was a monk's robe, or gown, or whatever they used to wear. I think you'd better call back one of the policemen who came before,' he went on. 'Let him have a look – take it away for tests. You never know. Say nothing to anyone else. Whoever put it there will be waiting to see what you do.'

'Will you ring them, please, Mr Cobb?' asked Sandy. 'You were so kind before – you seem to know your way round the arm of the law. We'd rather leave it to you.'

Cobb wondered whether either of the two men might have misbehaved in the days when the Davids and Sandys of the world avoided policemen like the plague.

'It's not a crime to find something that doesn't belong to you in the tool-shed,' said Cobb. 'Or to find a dead body.'

They had explained to him that they had gone out shopping since noon and had returned four hours later.

'Trouble is, *anyone* could have popped it into our garden. If it was a Heron Closer they'd know where to put it 'cos all the houses have the same sort of attached shed,' said Sandy.

Cobb lit his pipe. 'Consider who might have a down on you,' he said. He was getting too involved for his own liking. 'And if anything else occurs, you must ring the police yourselves. As it happens I know one of the bods down at Eastminster Station. I'll tell him about it. Meanwhile, I hope you've locked your tool-shed door. I expect a sergeant will be round if he can spare the time from chasing stolen cars. I won't mention the letter for the present.'

They looked relieved, thanked him and went back to their house a little cheered. Sandy had just remembered that when he had been out with his flash camera up Spire creek about midnight on Thursday he had thought he had heard the oyster-catching boat in the distance over the estuary. Now he wondered whether it had been something more sinister. Perhaps Percy Thrush's body had already been lying there? Asleep, or dead? Still, they agreed, Cobb inspired confidence.

CHAPTER SIX

The Whitwhams were gratified rather than aggrieved when a PC Dixon called round on Saturday with some enquiries – perfectly routine of course – about their movements on the night of Thrush's demise and the afternoon following. As well as being asked how well they had slept on the night of the death of Percy Thrush, they were asked what they knew about that gentleman. Constable Dixon was working his way round the close after orders from on high that the place might need a little looking into.

A Sergeant Wilson was sniffing around the marina. Never mind one attempted rape, one successful rape and a dead body – which might or might not have died as a result of natural causes – there was now talk of boats arriving at the marina in which the excise officer might be interested.

He had been over to Percy Thrush's shanty, which was surrounded on three sides by nettles, and found a chap from the estate agents in Eastminster nosing around, with some story of a projected purchase. They'd surely have to see if old Thrush had made a will, but his shack or shanty, or whatever it was, couldn't be worth much, was Wilson's opinion, quite ignoring the derelict land around it.

The Heron Close houses were scattered almost in an S shape all set at angles to each other. PC Dixon thought it an odd arrangement; not very neighbourly in his opinion.

He had ascertained from Cobb at Number 1 that he had been in bed, but not asleep till after midnight; from Susan at Number 2 that she often read till late up in her bedroom but could not remember what time she had put her light off that night. 'Reading in bed is one of my luxuries,' she said. From Susan's landlady PC Dixon had noted that she too often read in bed and also listened to the World Service if she could not sleep. Number 3 had an insomniac young woman who said she had looked out of the

76

window and seen lights on 'in the middle of the night' at practically every house on the close. One of the men at Number 4 had been out late photographing bats and night-owls as well, but his friend had gone to bed early with a headache. Numbers 5 and 6 had been taking late night coffee with each other. (Coffee? thought the constable. Didn't they want to go to sleep?)

None of it so far appeared to add up to much so, after noting down all these items of information, PC Dixon had been glad to take a cup of tea with the Whitwhams, his present victims, who were at home and ready to chat.

They had gone to bed at a respectable hour and fallen asleep immediately, they said. They seemed pleasant people, of the sort he understood. He found Mr Whitwham's observations on his neighbours quite enlightening too, though he knew he ought not to listen to gossip. Still, policemen were always being told to use their imagination and you never knew what details might come in handy. It would be a feather in his cap if he could, single-handedly, discover the assailant of Linda Swift, the raper of Patricia Simmons, and whether Thrush might have been 'pushed'.

'Popular, was he?' he asked Mrs Whitwham.

'Oh, I wouldn't say that. He did this job quite satisfactorily, didn't he, dear.' She turned to her husband.

'He saved his wages, that I know. I notice people's attitude to money – my previous profession.' Mr Whitwham coughed delicately, adding: 'I wouldn't have said he was a heavy drinker.'

'Bill was a bank manager,' said Mrs Whitwham in explanation.

That was why he was the one to dole out the wages then, thought Dixon. He had already ascertained that Thrush had been paid in cash.

'Thrush told me he was saving for a car – mind you, he didn't usually say much. I paid him weekly from the residents' fund for the mowing and the clipping and any bits of maintenance work we thought too simple to put to tender: fences, clearing the bushes, cutting down the deadwood – a lot of our dead elms had had to go.' He sighed. 'He told me the marina paid his insurance card. I'm afraid I didn't check. . . .'

'And this dressing-up thing Miss Swift said her attacker *might* have been wearing. Did you ever see it – in Miss Swann's car or anywhere else?'

Mrs Whitwham shuddered. 'No. I don't look into people's cars unless I'm offered a lift. I've never been in Miss Swann's car. Bill keeps our old Austin going and we shop once a week in Chelmsford, so we don't go near Eastminster very much.'

'Do you think that Miss – er – Swift could have been . . . well . . . romancing a bit?' asked PC Dixon. 'You were there at the party at Number 4 when she came rushing in.'

'Oh, she didn't come rushing in, did she, Bill. We heard an awful sort of moaning noise and Mr Fairbairn went to see what it was. We were all in the patio at the back – like ours it has a back door and you can't see into the back lane unless you go up to the bedroom.' She gestured to the high wall. 'It was an awful noise – hysterics really. She said that all she'd actually *seen* was this man's back when he was disappearing through the barn door. She didn't know what had disturbed him. . . .'

'Good thing he was disturbed,' muttered Mr Whitwham ponderously. He found talk of attempted rape embarrassing in spite of spending a good deal of time contemplating the horrible things that happened in the world and considering his next letter to the newspapers.

'Susan says she left that robe in the car and found it the next morning all crumpled up. Then she went into school on the Wednesday and forgot to lock her car again – and when she came back it had gone! Well, you know all that,' said his wife.

'It may have nothing to do with the man who attacked Miss Swift. Susan Swann is rather absent-minded and might have taken it into school and forgotten,' said Mr Whitwham severely.

'She says she definitely left it there,' said PC Dixon. He had not yet been told the latest news about the robe, which Cobb had phoned in, that whoever had taken it from the school carpark must have put it into Number 4's tool-shed.

'Anyway, that other poor girl – the man wasn't wearing a robe then, was he?' asked Mrs Whitwham.

PC Dixon thought perhaps he was giving too much away – this 'tame' couple knew as much as he did. He knew for a fact that his superior officers were stumped.

'As for Mr Thrush,' he added, clearing his throat, 'you would think he could have imbibed one over the eight and fallen off the wall, having the misfortune to hit his head on descent?'

'That's what we all believe,' said Mrs Whitwham. 'But I don't think he ever drank to excess, you know. It was probably just an accident.'

'Your real problem is the attack on the girl at Spire Lane,' Mr

Whitwham added helpfully, reminding PC Dixon that everyone was waiting for some lead from the police. 'Probably some local hooligan, in my opinion,' he continued. 'Drunk or drugged. Hanging's too good for them – if I had my way . . .'

'Don't upset yourself, Bill,' soothed his wife.

But Bill went on: 'I wondered – well, it's only an idea, but I wondered – if Linda's father – we know her mother, she works for my wife as well as for Number 2 – if Linda's father thought it could have been Mr Thrush who attacked Linda. Mightn't he have decided to teach him a lesson? They do say he's going round telling everyone in Spire he wants to get his hands on whoever frightened his daughter!'

'Quite natural,' said the constable, judiciously.

'It's none of our business,' said Mrs Whitwham, but her husband was in full flow.

'What if he threatened him and Thrush was frightened and lost his footing – something like that?'

PC Dixon did not tell the Whitwhams that this had already occurred to the police. They had also interviewed Pat Simmons's husband for a similar reason. But both had strenuously denied paying off the score – though they wouldn't have minded doing so if they found the fellow. But there was nothing to prove Thrush had attacked anybody.

'Surely Linda would have recognized him, even dressed up as a ghost or a monk,' added Mrs Whitwham, wanting to be fair.

The thought of a ghost nagged at the policeman's mind as he took his leave of Number 7. He couldn't quite put a finger on it, but there was something in the idea of a robed figure frightening people. Frightening Percy Thrush? Anyway, HQ were not really interested in Thrush. They were concentrating on the suspicion of drugs being landed on the beach, and on the – alas, successful – rape of Mrs Simmons.

Susan had also been interrogated once again when a policeman came to school the following Monday to ask about the loss of her prop. She was heartily sick of the whole thing. If only she'd put it away in the acting-cupboard at the end of last term. She was sure it had nothing material to do with the attack on Linda, except that it had been handy for someone to borrow it. Would an ordinary villain know to look in her car? She wondered whether it might have been someone she had taught and who knew her habits: some youth from the sailing club at the marina perhaps, who had left the school with some sort of grievance and who wanted to implicate her in a devious way.

Mr Cobb had invited all the Heron Closers to coffee on Monday evening and they had all accepted. Sandy and David were not the only ones in whom Cobb inspired confidence. He seemed to have some secure air of authority about him. Dorothea especially thought he was trustworthy and reliable. They all had their reasons for accepting his invitation; even those who had perhaps something to hide still felt he would be the person to turn to in an emergency, the one who would be the person to instigate a neighbourhood watch scheme if it were necessary, the one who would know what to do if a swimmer got into difficulties or if there were an accident on a neighbouring farm, or if an unidentified aircraft seemed to be circling the local skies suspiciously. Cobb would know how to apply the kiss of life; Cobb would know his first aid; Cobb would be able to say authoritatively that yes, the plane was obviously on manoeuvres from an American base further north and not to worry, the pilot was probably just enjoying himself. Mr Whitwham was too choleric; Sandy and David too laid back; Miss Kant just a touch schoolmistressy, Susan too young, Lisa tongue-tied, Tony Smith unpopular and Patrick Dawson and his lady friend Eva Maitland uncommunicative. It was old Cobb who would deal with things.

He knew this, was used to wielding authority and knew also that they all had their reasons for accepting his invitation. Mr Whitwham wanted to discuss advertising for a new odd-job man. The residents' committee, consisting of Miss Kant, himself and Mr Fairbairn, could accomplish this at a coffee evening.

He had been on the phone again with George Graham and had informed him about the discovery of the robe at Number 4, but no one else yet knew, and Cobb had told David and Sandy just that it would be taken away unobtrusively. He had said nothing to his old colleague about the anonymous letter.

The robe had been removed after being photographed and was at present undergoing tests at HQ. You could see that Sandy and David were still jumpy and the others at the meeting nervous. Speculations concerning Percy Thrush were thrown up and caught one by one. They all claimed to have found him a reasonable, if grumpy, worker, and all pronounced it a shame that he had come to such an end. Tony Smith could not forbear voicing the thought that was uppermost in Cobb's mind: Was Thrush attacked by the same man who had already carried out two other attacks?

Round and round went the talk. Cobb kept quiet; once he had been used to listening and he listened now. Little Lisa was saying nothing. Occasionally she looked at her husband, who appeared to be in an expansive mood. Cobb thought he detected a look of puzzlement on her face mixed with her usual cowed demeanour when, on social occasions, she was out with her husband.

'Oh, I shouldn't think the police think Thrush was attacked by a rapist,' said Cobb eventually. 'People who attack girls in that way don't usually attack middle-aged men, you know.'

Sandy and David looked rather relieved, but Sandy kept thinking about the anonymous letter, never far from his thoughts. Cobb led the conversation back to the marina.

'I expect they'll have to find another odd-job man there, too. It shouldn't be difficult with so many unskilled workers round here without jobs.'

'Young men won't usually do the work,' said Miss Kant.

'I agree,' said Mr Whitwham. 'There's that boy of Black's. He's never had a job in his life.'

'Kevin has some reasonable GCSEs,' said Susan. 'I taught him once – he's an awful worry to his mother and father.'

At the name Kevin, David had blanched, but controlled himself to say nothing. Sandy was looking away.

Mr Whitwham was about to say that the youth, whom he knew as the son of the treasurer at the marina, was a pansy. He recollected himself in time.

Cobb was looking po-faced. 'Well, we'll be looking for a replacement for Thrush,' he said. 'And I thought if we get anyone remotely possible we could also put him in touch with the sailing club, as we did with Thrush.'

'Yes,' said Whitwham. 'I'll convene an official meeting of the residents soon.' And you really should have checked his insurance card, thought Cobb. Patrick Dawson spoke up. He was seated as usual next to Eva Maitland.

'Did that policeman put you all through the mincer?' he asked. 'I was asked what I was doing on Wednesday night and the police johnny seemed to have a notebook full of all your answers.'

Mrs Maitland spoke. 'It's a pity they can't tell us what they're looking for. Pat and I were having coffee together. It was rather

late and Pat thinks – he came round when I was frightened – my
nerves, you see – he thinks he saw . . . You tell him, Pat.'

Any surprise at the acknowledgement by the usually silent Mrs
Maitland that she entertained gentlemen visitors late at night was
cancelled when Pat Dawson said quite cheerfully:

'I thought I saw a monk – well, a sort of gowned figure – coming
out of the Abbot's Walk! Eva tells me it was my turn for imagining
things, but I'm sure I did.' He stopped, well aware of the effect
upon his audience.

'A *monk*,' breathed Lisa. 'You mean – the man who tried to rape
Linda?' She stopped, looking down in her lap when her husband
chipped in with:

'Sure it was only coffee you two were drinking and nothing
stronger?'

Mrs Maitland flushed. Cobb was looking interested, but said
nothing.

'More to the point, the man who perhaps frightened poor old
Thrush,' said Sandy, thinking: and who also kindly deposited his
outer garment in our garden shed, after stealing it from Susan's
car. David was thinking: Could it have been Tony Smith? He
seemed keen to pooh-pooh Pat Dawson's 'vision'.

'All the people are here who were at Number 4 when Linda
came along moaning,' said Dorothea Kant. 'So let's try and get it
straight. One: Someone attacked Linda. Two: Someone must have
taken Sue's robe from her car, and then put it back. Three: Mrs
Simmons is attacked. Four: Susan takes the robe back to school
and it's stolen from her car again. Five: Percy Thrush is found dead
on the beach. What has the robe got to do with Mr Thrush and
where is it now? It doesn't sound as though we have only one
criminal.'

'Perhaps someone else raped the lady from Witham but the
other three things are connected,' suggested Susan.

'We only have Linda's word that her attacker was wearing a
robe,' said Sandy. Dorothea looked a little irritated.

'Why should she lie?' she asked.

'And only Susan's word that she left the offending object in her
unlocked car *twice*,' sneered Tony Smith.

'I wonder what the police are doing. Are they making any head-
way?' asked Whitwham.

Cobb decided now to add his extra bit of information.

'I believe the police are more interested in a little boat which comes now and again to the marina,' he said pleasantly.

'They should concentrate on people who attack women,' said Dorothea crossly. 'If you mean drugs, what has that got to do with us?'

'Only that Linda's attacker may have been under the influence,' replied Cobb, turning to her.

'She said he smelt of mothballs,' said Susan excitedly. 'Don't you see – it could have been some smuggler, high on drugs, someone who was wandering about that Saturday night who also mucked around in my car and thought he'd dress up. Then he came upon Linda, attacked her, but for some reason ran away. Later, still drugged up to the eyeballs, he attacks Mrs Simmons, and perhaps Thrush has his suspicions – after all he saw everyone down here. He confronts the man and the man pushes him over the wall.'

'You mean he *murdered* him?' gasped Lisa, looking up again.

'He couldn't have foreseen that Thrush would hit his head on the concrete,' interposed Cobb. 'He might have wanted to teach him a lesson and it went wrong, so he runs away and – er – Mr Dawson sees him at the entrance to the Abbot's Walk.'

'But,' said Dorothea, 'if that were so, where *is* this robe?'

Sandy and David looked uncomfortable, but Cobb signalled a reassuring lift of the eyebrows to them and they said nothing.

'Whoever frightened Thrush must have taken it again from my car at school,' said Susan. 'So that rules out anyone who didn't know where I worked or that I was taking it back there.'

'Not necessarily,' said Cobb. 'What about Black's son – Kevin, did you say his name was?' He looked at Mr Whitwham.

'That's right,' answered Whitwham. 'An unsatisfactory boy – might very well be on drugs.'

'But not the type, surely, to rape a woman? asked Dorothea. She had heard Susan last year talking about her old pupil Kevin Black and his coming out in the provincial town as gay.

'That's true,' said Susan.

No one wanted to say all that was on his or her mind, except for Tony Smith.

'I heard at the marina, last summer I think, that young Kevin was a queer,' he drawled. He looked suggestively at David and Sandy. Sandy looked away, but David held his glance.

'Know the lot down there, do you?' he asked. 'Perhaps you know about the little boat that comes in and out?'

Tony Smith tried to look indignant.

83

'Certainly not, but they are all our neighbours and things get round in a little place like this.'

Cobb judged it appropriate to move round once more with the coffee-pot. They all looked as though they would like to go, but something was forcing them to stay.

'Suspect number one, Kevin Black?' said Cobb, when he sat down again. 'For the attack on Linda, and possibly the rape of Mrs Simmons? No? You don't think so. And perhaps the manslaughter of our friend Thrush.'

'No! That can't be right,' said Dorothea Kant. 'What do you think, Susan? Is he, was he the sort of boy who would want to frighten poor old Thrush?'

'It doesn't add up,' said Susan.

But who put the robe into our shed, and who wrote the letters to us? Was it the same person who *may* have also frightened Thrush and *maybe* pushed him to his death? David was asking himself. It was all too far-fetched.

Cobb was thinking that there seemed to be at least two separate persons. Leaving the Simmons rape on one side for the moment, was it not conceivable that if it were this Kevin boy, he had only intended to frighten Linda Swift, only intended to frighten Thrush – and was now horrified to find that the latter was dead? Yes, leave out Mrs Pat Simmons, concentrate on Kevin – that would tie up nicely with Thrush perhaps snooping round at the marina and Kevin threatening him. Perhaps he'd discovered something, possibly that Kevin was stealing from the till or had something to do with a little boat. Whichever was true, it was high time the lad was found by the police.

He put aside the vanished robe – there seemed no reason for Kevin, if it were Kevin, to plant it in Number Four tool-shed. Their garden was nearest to the beach though, so he probably just wanted to get rid of it.

The Whitwhams were getting up.

'Time for bed,' said Bill Whitwham. 'We don't seem to have got very far, but I expect the police will be on to this lad sooner or later. I'll have a word with Black about a new handyman. It'll be difficult to replace Thrush, though.'

Cobb's mind was on another tack as he saw the Whitwhams out of his front door. Principally, had Thrush ever had a criminal record? It seemed a bit steep for a lad who had, so far, done nothing – as far as he knew – but smoke a little pot and dye his hair and not get on with his father, suddenly to become the centre of a murder and rape mystery. Still, that was how the conversation had gone. They'd all be relieved if they found that no one on Heron Close had anything to do with the theft of a monk's robe, the attack on Linda, pushing a man over the sea-wall, drug-peddling, or rape.

When he got back to the sitting room, Pat Dawson was draining his coffee and Mrs Maitland was fastening a scarf round her neck.

'We really must go,' she said. 'It's horrible thinking of the things that go on nowadays. We shall all sleep sounder in our beds when it's all cleared up. Perhaps the lad meant nothing serious.'

'I'll see you back,' said Pat Dawson unnecessarily.

When they had gone, Dorothea spoke.

'What was Mr Whitwham – I mean before he retired. Was it an insurance agent?'

'No, a bank manager,' said Cobb.

'Pat and Eva seem very matey,' said Sandy to no one in particular.

'She suffers from a form of agoraphobia,' said Dorothea. 'That's why she doesn't go out of Spickhanger. She told me when I went round to her once with a plant-cutting she'd asked me for.'

'Well, she seems to have found a new friend. Let's hope he doesn't introduce her to booze,' said Tony Smith. 'Come on, Lisa, we have to be up early. I've to go over to Chelmsford tomorrow.'

'See you in the morning,' said Susan to Lisa as she left.

What an odious man.

When the Smiths had gone the others seemed to breathe more comfortably. Cobb looked at his remaining guests, Miss Kant and Susan and the two men from Number 4. He'd nothing against the Whitwhams or Pat Dawson or Mrs Maitland, but he was glad that the Smiths had gone. 'Tell them,' he said to Sandy. 'I think Susan ought to know.'

David looked at his friend.

'The robe – it was in our tool-shed yesterday when we came back from shopping in Witham. I gather you all think this Kevin Black put it there?'

The women gaped.

'And did he also write us a beastly letter?' said Sandy, emboldened by the sympathetic looks of the two women. David looked startled. They had agreed not to mention it yet.

'What do you think, Susan? Would a young man whom we

know to be gay – we needn't mince words now Smith has gone – would he write a threatening letter to us both accusing us of being what he himself was?' He told them the gist of the letter.

'But that shoots the whole of our surmises to pieces,' cried Susan. 'There must be someone else who planted the robe and threatened you. Surely Kevin isn't HIV positive either. He's only young – unless he uses needles for drugs.'

'Neither of us has ever done more than say hello to him,' said David. 'We thought you ought to know.'

'I bet I know who did plant the robe on you,' said Susan. 'Tony Smith! He doesn't like you, does he. And I think little Lisa knows too.' She was thinking: he came to school on the day of the staff-meeting with the shrubs for the assembly hall. *He* must have taken the robe from my car. She wouldn't say anything yet to Cobb.

'Then the whole thing still turns on who attacked the lady on Spire Lane – and we don't know much about that. It's the real crime the police have to solve and they aren't saying anything. As for old Thrush – it could still have been Kevin. But why should Tony Smith try to implicate *you*?'

'It's all making my head reel,' said Sandy. 'But provided there are no more letters and provided no one accuses Dave or me of manslaughter, I don't much mind.'

'Keep it under your hat, will you – about the letter?' said David to Dorothea as she rose to go.

'I expect it will all have a simple explanation,' said Susan sooth-ingly as they went out. She still had some marking to do. It was all very well playing amateur detectives, but she had other things on her mind. It was obvious that Mr Cobb had got them all there for a purpose.

When they had all gone, Cobb lit his pipe. Interesting to see all their reactions. He struggled to make sense of it. Too many leads – were they all red herrings? He knew the Eastminster police were busy looking for Kevin Black and his friends and he believed there'd be no more rapes, or attempted ones. Not that a rape sounded like Kevin from what he had heard of him.

As he made preparations for bed, he was thinking: monks and ghosts – why can I still not get that double idea out of my head? And Lisa Smith – she's frightened of something. Can it just be her husband? And Thrush – there'd be his funeral soon. . . . He wondered idly whether any of the man's relatives would turn up. *Had* he had a record? Nothing seemed to add up, in spite of his having learned a few things about all his neighbours.

Well, he'd done the dirty work for his erstwhile colleagues and now he hoped they would leave him alone and concentrate on pushers of hard drugs who were almost as much of a menace to society as rapists. As for other kinds of possible 'pushers' who dressed up to frighten old men at night, he'd try to work that one out.

He'd better put on his thinking cap now about that nasty anonymous letter. Black capitals and cheap notepaper – not very original.

'I let drop all you suggested,' said Jim Cobb on the phone to the private residence of his old subordinate, George Graham, next morning. 'A lot of interesting things were said, but nobody seems to believe that Percy Thrush had anything to do with the hanky-panky at the marina, though I have my own suspicions about that. Nothing said about boats or drugs to tie up with any of your suspects except for Kevin Black. Susan Swann *and* the two men *and* Tony Smith knew of your prime suspect, Kevin Black, the men only vaguely. There was one piece of news, though. Mr Dawson at Number 5 says he saw a figure in a robe at the end of the Abbot's Walk very late that Thursday night when he returned from a visit to comfort his lady friend, Eva Maitland.'

'We're still looking for young Kevin,' said Graham. 'He's not at his hideout and his two mates – both villains – have flown too. We've had an eye on them for some time, but we'd rather dropped that angle when no boat was seen actually *landing* anywhere on the coast last week. We've begun to look further afield; most of our criminals are Londoners, you know. But it's probable Kevin Black was using something – or his friends were. We found evidence at his dump. We think it was for – er – "chasing the dragon". Kevin probably snorted coke, but it's his mates we're looking for. We think one of them at least was a runner for a drug gang.'

'I thought it was only pot and speed and a whiff now and then of amyl nitrate that Kevin would go in for – if he's anything like the middle-class youths I used to know back home in the North. That doesn't sound too good. Where would he get the money? Hard drugs are not cheap.'

'Getting cheaper,' said Graham laconically. 'Anyway, Jim, don't bother your head any more. We'll keep our files open on the attacks. Somehow I don't think there'll be any more. I'll let you know when we bring Kevin Black in.'

'And what about Thrush. When's his funeral?'

'As soon as we've finished with the body. It'll be our old friend death by misadventure. Nothing to prove anything criminal involved, unless Kevin squeals. Thanks for all you've done, Jim. You can go back to your roses.'

The trouble was, Cobb did not feel like going back to his roses. He was sure that Graham was missing something, and it wasn't nice for two unsolved attacks on women to remain on file. How did Graham think the women felt? They were jittery, and no wonder.

After he'd put down the phone he wondered whether Kevin had ever mainlined. Chasing the dragon and snorting were, at present, the favoured methods of taking heroin and coke, but druggies could get Aids from shared needles. Might his sexual proclivities have nothing to do with anything? Unless he were HIV positive. Surely he was not?

He tried to push it all out of his mind and went out into his garden to clear up some early fallen leaves.

CHAPTER SEVEN

Cobb had not slept well. At some time in the night he had woken up after a nightmare. He was used to this particular one and was aware, even in his sleep, that he had had it before. He always reached a point where he knew he had to endure it to the end, could not avoid it or refuse it, but must pursue it. It was worse to lie sleepless, obsessed by certain thoughts.

The dream always began in the car with his wife sitting in the passenger seat as he drove along a country road. Then suddenly the car began to twist and turn; the steering-wheel failed to respond, the brakes failed to engage. He knew they were going to crash but also knew that he could jump out and that his wife could not. He would open the door, fall into the road and watch the car like a live monster rear up and crush her. Knowing he was unconscious but still in the dream, he would hear a piteous voice, Edna's voice, crying: 'Let me out! Let me out!' He always stood up then and scrabbled through the twisted wreck with his bare hands to find her. At last he would come across her body and mutter: 'I'll find your head. Don't worry.'

This was the point at which he would wake sweating, horror-struck, his hands and arms numb and the sheets twisted around him as he had frantically scrabbled in his dream.

This morning he got up as soon as he woke from the nightmare. It was six o'clock. He did not want to go back to sleep, so decided to make an early cup of tea. He and Edna had always enjoyed an early cup on those mornings when he had had to get up early, and she had insisted upon having a cuppa with him before he left for the shift at the station. Everything reminded him of her. . . . He had led a life so bound up with routine that everything he did now to break the old routine only reminded him of it, and his efforts seemed pointless. Edna had been killed, not in a car driven by him, but walking back home from a visit to her aunt's one November

Sunday, three years ago now.

Cobb had been at work. It was only when the chief had sent for him and had shut the door in an especially discreet way that he had known this was something personal. The chief always moved in the same way when he had bad news to communicate. And so it was. Bad news. The end of Cobb's old life and certainly the end of his official career.

For months after the funeral, he had tried to discover who had killed her. A hit and run driver – but the police knew no more than anyone else. If he could have got his hands on that man, who had certainly known what he had done, for he had stopped and then driven away, he thought he could have murdered him. Who was he to refuse vengeance to the numberless victims he met in his police work, all the innocent sufferers who had no means of redressing the crimes perpetrated against their loved ones, crimes that had ruined their own lives?

Although he had never been a 'law and order' copper, had indeed been regarded in his young days as a liberal, he could no longer stomach the rising tide of violence. Violence called out violence; he knew that very well, and it sickened him. After Edna died he decided to leave the whole caboodle – his work, his people, his home.

The nightmare, which put him at first in control, and then took it away, made himself the guilty driver, the man who killed his wife. He knew it was a way of expiating his guilt at still being alive when Edna was dead. He must bear the guilt over her death; the out-of-control car symbolized only his own lack and the general human lack of control over events. He wanted to be in control of his own life and his dreams told him he could not be. But who was? Being in control was an illusion nourished in the bosoms of the young.

Also, the times were out of joint. In spite of a general human failure to face up to evil, or human impotence when faced with the indifference of nature, when he was a boy things had not been so bad. After national service abroad, he had returned home and found it was still a good place to live.

But now there were new, and worse, dangers. The former play-things of the rich – drugs for example – had become the addictions of the many. Material affluence had brought with it an under-class, some of whom stole what luckier people owned. Cobb had become weary of the thousands of problems, new ones springing up whenever an old one appeared to have been solved, like the Hydra's head.

In his old work he had been able to lift depression by concentrating on the job in hand. But he was no longer the D I Cobb who had enjoyed just being alive, always with something to look forward to: a short trip to the Lakes with Edna, a tot of whisky or the perusal of gardening catalogues. Since Edna's death he had found he had an aversion to any type of alcohol though he kept it to offer to others. Fortunately he had no aversion to gardening but could not help thinking about what Edna would have planted. She'd been a better gardener than he.

He found himself considering the inhabitants of the close as he passed them in review. Some of them might have been born more moral than others, he thought; maybe they had had a better upbringing, kinder parents. But if you could improve Nurture, might it not in its turn react like an enzyme upon Nature and produce more hope for humanity?

He thought through the whole Heron Close events again, ticking his mental list of suspects. . . .

He knew of nothing against Susan except that she was careless. She was intelligent, the sort of daughter he would have liked to have. He was old-fashioned, and thought Susan should get married to a nice man and work part-time. She was clearly fed up with teaching, though she was the sort of girl who'd be good at her job even though it exhausted her. The robe from the props box had unmistakably played a part in the Heron Close drama, so he must keep her in mind.

She had been at the party all the time; he remembered noticing how she managed to have a conversation with everyone throughout the evening, even with Mrs Maitland, who was not an easy person to talk to. He firmly discounted Susan from suspicion, yet if she'd suspected that Thrush had attacked her pupil, might she have dressed up to frighten him, confront him out of some sort of revenge? It seemed a bit far-fetched.

Dorothea Kant was a very different cup of tea but the same argument applied to her as to Susan. She had a powerful intellect and he'd noticed that she was very observant. Perhaps she had suspected who had attacked Linda in the barn, and the others on the lane and on the sea-wall?

All these crimes were outdoor ones, the sort most often committed by men. They *were* dealing with a man he concluded; though you could not discount a woman who might dress up to frighten someone. The most likely crime for a woman would be writing poison-pen letters.

Did whoever had a grudge against Thrush want Sandy Robson to find the body? Was it a person linked with drugs at the marina, as well as the planting of the robe on Sandy and David? But he did not see either Dorothea or Susan as poison-pen writers, and they were the ones who got on best with the men at Number 4.

What about the Smiths at Number 3? He did not like Tony Smith, but who did? His own wife seemed to be frightened of him. Had Tony some knowledge about Percy Thrush – or had Thrush some hold over Smith? Could Thrush have been blackmailing him? Could he have known Smith before when the fellow was working as a gardener? Tony Smith *could* just have slipped out of the party for five minutes, though he didn't think he had. Smith was capable of raping Pat Simmons too, but George Graham had checked that he was at home at the time.

Oh dear, prejudice must not enter a policeman's calculations, even if he were no longer a policeman and was allowed a little more latitude. Smith was the kind of man who might think it amusing to frighten a young woman or a middle-aged man.

Wait! Smith did occasionally visit the school. Susan had told him that he provided the tubs for the assembly hall, so he could easily have stolen the robe. What day had he been in Eastminster School? Was it on Wednesday and Thursday, or both days? If he had written the letter, or got someone else to write it, he might wish to incriminate the men at Number 4. The letter presupposed some knowledge of Kevin Black, and he had once seen Smith talking to men at the marina.

He was his best bet so far – but a lot of his supposition might be prejudice. There *was* something odd about the Smiths, not that he had anything against Lisa. She was just rather wet, looked a victim type, and was clearly in awe of her husband. But he knew there were no 'victim types'! Linda and Patricia – and his wife Edna – had not been 'types'. Still, it was worth looking out for any connection of Tony with Kevin Black and with Thrush. Thrush might be blackmailing Kevin, so that Kevin had panicked and pushed the fellow over the sea-wall.

Number 4 now. Twice victims – through the planting of the robe and the letter. Three times if you counted Sandy's unpleasant discovery on the beach where people knew he often walked early in the morning. And Sandy had, by his own admission, been out late that Tuesday night with his camera, owl- and bat-hunting. Could he have had something to do with the Thrush accident? His shock had appeared genuine enough and he and his friend had offered the information about the letter and the robe.

Sandy had come to him too, for help, surely not realizing that he was an ex-copper? He might not have come if he had.

In the past, men like Sandy and David had often had things to hide, and it was still a crime for a man to have relations with a youth below a certain age. But even if their sexual proclivities might once have landed them in trouble with the law, he was sure they were essentially law-abiding.

Perhaps, though, one of them had been sent down years ago for some other relationship. That might be a lever for a blackmailer. He was off again! Yet whoever had a down on the one seemed also to have a down on the other, which made it more likely that general unpleasantness was intended. The letter and robe had been planned more to annoy and upset than to blackmail. Neither of the two men had been out during their party, and neither would rape a woman. Unless an HIV positive man who disliked women wanted to give a woman Aids. It was not unknown. No, it was out of the question here. Cobb would stake his professional reputation on it. He was running too many hares at once.

What about Thrush, though? Had somebody wanting to pay off an old score pushed the man over the sea-wall? That *could* have happened. But what could Thrush know?

It came down again to the problem of whether any of these men could have met Thrush before. Someone could have had a fight with him, not intending to kill him. Perhaps Sandy had had the opportunity whilst out walking late at night. But neither David or Sandy looked the type to pick fights. They would hesitate to employ physical violence, would be far more likely to blame Thrush for bad work or negligence or to start up a whispering campaign against him.

The trouble was that he knew nothing about Thrush. Why should he assume he might have a record? He was hampered by no longer being on an official inquiry. He could ask Graham but he rather resented the police's assuming he would snoop for them. He might, even so, take a little stroll soon to the marina to see if he could pick up anything there about Thrush.

He reviewed once again his mental list of motive, opportunity and method for the crimes assumed to have been committed, and was left with little to go on. Motives? Too many! It might just be that Thrush fell to his death after no more than a stumble in the dark. If his death was the result of malice, the perpetrator might have intended only a short, sharp shock, was not to know he would hit his head on the concrete. He might even have felt like doing something like that himself if the driver who had killed Edna had been discovered and let off with a fine.

Perhaps the attacks on Linda Swift and Pat Simmons had had nothing at all to do with the death of Thrush and he was barking up the wrong tree.

What about Pat Dawson, who had been over *twice*, on his own admission, to his next-door neighbour, that Wednesday night, ostensibly because she was frightened? He and Mrs Maitland gave each other alibis. Dawson could easily have nipped down to the beach, wanting to get his own back if, for example, Thrush had been blackmailing *him*. Could Dawson himself have been prose-cuted for drink-driving?

Cobb turned his mind off the subject that obsessed him. He had nothing against Dawson. The man really was on the wagon and would hardly, when sober, go round pushing old men on beaches to their deaths. Yet he claimed he had seen a hooded figure coming out of Abbot's Walk about 2.30 a.m.! He must have felt sure of himself to mention it at all.

That left Eva Maitland and the Whitwhams. Eva had never left the party, and said she had not been out at all on the night of Tuesday. Too frightened to sleep, she would be far too frightened to go for a walk on the beach.

Unless she was also a whopping liar and the agoraphobia was a blind. What had caused her fear? Had she always been like this?

He was beginning to feel sure that Thrush had mistaken his footing, and that his demise was nothing to do with the marina or Kevin Black or drugs or monks' robes or attacks on girls. Unless Thrush himself had been Linda's attacker, had taken the robe, given her a fright in the barn, seen a light on, or someone coming from the landing-stage – which you could just see from the barn – and let her go.

If Thrush had raped Patricia Simmons as well as attacking Linda he might have been pursued – by Linda's father who might suspect him, or by Mr Simmons who knew something about him. It might seem to be another promising line of inquiry, but Mrs Simmons had said her rapist was a *young* man. The pathologist said Thrush was over sixty, and nobody could have mistaken him for a young man.

Cobb lit his pipe and, lastly, considered the Whitwhams. Neither had left the party. Mr Whitwham looked an unlikely rapist, but he had a car, and he was a law and order man, fanatical about bringing criminals to justice. If he had suspected Thrush of either attack on the women, would he have acted to punish him? A one-man lynch law in Bill Whitwham, retired bank manager? But they always said that those who talked most about things never did them, and Cobb suspected it was Whitwham's natural timidity that led him to fear and be obsessed by violence. Mrs Whitwham had declared that her husband had never left her side that Thursday night, adding somewhat gratuitously, but with quiet humour, Cobb remembered, that he snored and she would have noticed if it had stopped.

Cobb liked Vera Whitwham, who was more intelligent than anyone gave her credit for. Neither of the Whitwhams seemed good candidates for attacks on either men or women, unless Bill Whitwham's opinions were a blind for violent impulses. No, too pat an explanation.

Cobb turned all these thoughts over and over again in his mind and came to the conclusion that the attack on Thrush, if it had been an attack, made sense only if it were connected either with something going on at the marina or with the previous attack on Linda or Mrs Simmons, of which someone suspected him. These were two clear lines of inquiry – and at this point he would have sent off his sergeants and put a call through to the computer for criminal records. But he had neither expedient at his disposal, and must use only his own brains for the time being.

CHAPTER EIGHT

Dorothea was still intrigued by the Lisa problem. Young Mrs Smith had once again been confiding in Susan. Sue had reported the evening before that Lisa said she wished she need not work. She'd always wanted children. Susan had pointed out that she was good at her work and seemed happier when she was working than when she was not – and that surely there was time enough, She was only twenty-seven.

'You're younger than I am, and I'm only just beginning to feel that *perhaps* during the next five years I *might* have a baby!' she'd said with a smile.

'You haven't got a husband,' Lisa answered.

Susan was surprised but had refrained from pointing out that being married didn't seem to matter, for Lisa had gone on to say in a rather bitter tone:

'That's what marriage is for, isn't it? To have children.'

Susan had agreed quite sincerely that it probably was the main reason many women of her age got married, or at least cohabited with partners. Men were rather different, and needed to be persuaded about babies, if not about someone doing their ironing for them.

'Nowadays,' Lisa replied, 'you don't get pregnant unless you make a mistake, do you? I mean, the pill and everything. It makes it harder for women to know when to have a baby.'

'Too true,' replied Susan, the same thought having often occurred to her.

'Do you think lots of women cheat on their husbands because they want a baby? I mean, tell them they're taking it and they're not? If they're married there's not much they can do about it, is there, unless their husbands force them to have abortions?'

'Oh, I expect lots,' said Susan comfortably, ignoring the last frightening statement. 'Men usually like their children when they arrive, unless they're very immature – the husbands, I mean.'

She was thinking: Tony Smith wants his wife to himself. That must be Lisa's problem. He can't imagine being displaced by a baby, even his own.

Then Lisa had surprised her again, saying:

'Oh, Tony sees to it that I never forget the pill – he stands over me whilst I take it.'

Susan could not help but feel rather horrified. The pill was supposed to liberate women, not put them under some further diktat.

'Sometimes I feel it would be easier for some people if the pill had never been invented,' she replied carefully, trying not to show her distaste of Smith's bullying. 'But, of course, most couples want to wait a bit before having children, so as to have a bit of time together. Being parents must be *so* different.'

It had been one of Richard's constantly reiterated sayings. 'Thirty-five,' he had used to say. 'That's a good time to start a family, when you've got a well-established career and more money. Then you can fit in one or two.'

She had pointed out to him that women's fertility took a sharp downward turn after that age.

'How long have you been married, then?' she asked Lisa, who for some reason looked haunted once more.

'Oh – seven years,' she said.

'I thought, you know, that you'd been married only two or three years. I mean, Tony always looks so wrapped up in you.'

That's a lie, she thought, but she had thought they must have been married only a year or two for him to be so jealous of his wife.

'So, you were only twenty?' she went on. 'It's young, isn't it, to decide on a partner for life?'

She nearly said a life sentence.

'I've only ever had Tony,' said Lisa.

The conversation lapsed after that, but she had retold it to Dorothea because she felt indignant on Lisa's behalf and indignant also on behalf of so many of her own pupils in the past who had seemed to feel they were on the shelf if they were not at least with a male partner before they were twenty-one. Marriage would come later, many of them still fondly hoped.

'Imagine, she's never had anyone but that pig,' said Susan crossly. 'It makes me feel really rebellious. Lisa could only have

been a child if she was married seven years ago – and, say, court-
ing two years before that. She'd only have been eighteen. She must
feel trapped.'

'She'd be trapped even more with a baby,' said Dorothea drily.
'I still feel she doesn't love her husband. I suppose she thinks a
baby would help her put up with him.'

Dorothea added that she had found the same phenomenon
years ago when she'd first taught in a secondary school. Many girls
would give their eye-teeth for a 'steady', and, probably their eyes
themselves for a husband.

'Blindfold to the scaffold!' she said now. 'A few years later they
realized what they'd landed themselves with.'

'Some people do mature young and there are some still happily
married to their first boyfriend,' Susan objected. 'If not so many
nowadays,' she added.

'I would never want to stop people from doing what seems right
to *them* at the time. If you are in love, nothing else seems to
matter. Society used to say that "love and marriage went together
like horse and carriage",' said Dorothea.

'Well, I suppose it may still be like that for some lucky people.'
Not for Lisa Smith, though.

'Tony Smith appears perfectly happy, provided he can flirt with
other women when it suits him,' said Dorothea.

Susan knew the tide was changing. It had even surprised her,
and she was still in her twenties, that more young women now
actually *preferred* careers. Was it the money? Lisa Smith, however,
did not appear to be one of them.

I quite like my work, Susan was thinking, but I'd leave it for
love. If I had the career I really wanted, I suppose there would be
a conflict. She had always wanted to act, or even direct, but a
change of career now would be impossible without a private
income.

'Tony is just the sort of man to give men a bad name,' she said
aloud, trying to imagine his face if his wife were ever unfaithful, or
left him. The mind boggled. He might very well murder her! She
upbraided herself; they knew very little about him really, and must
not imagine too much.

She went upstairs to do some marking.

When Cobb got round to ringing his old mate George Graham to
see if the police were any further on with their inquiry, DCI

Graham was rather cagey and Cobb had the impression that he did not really need any more 'help'. George said he had seen the photographs of Thrush taken by Sandy Robson which Cobb had sent on.

'Mr Robson's snaps don't appear to add anything new or different,' he said. 'We're concentrating now on the drugs angle.' He would say no more except that the attacks on the two women might also be connected with drugs. As for Percy Thrush, he opined he'd had an accidental fall. 'We're still looking for Kevin Black. He's disappeared for the time being, along with his erstwhile friends, Darren Bogworthy and Wayne Spitt. You might keep a look-out for Kevin,' he said, less grudgingly.

'So the birds have flown?'

'Seems like it.'

Cobb might be of some use after all. He was feeling even more strongly that he would like to solve part of this muddled investigation himself. Drugs might be involved, but he believed they were not the nub of the whole case: a conclusion reached by sheer instinct. He'd said nothing to Graham about his earlier musings. Once the inquest had been held the police would probably close the Thrush case.

The funeral would be next week and he'd a good mind to attend it. Other Heron Closers might also feel that they should attend. He wished he'd asked Graham about Thrush's background, and whether he had ever done time, but his old friend was not interested in Thrush. He would find more out for himself. Let the force spend its time tracking down drug-peddlers.

He decided for the present to go for a walk down by the sailing marina, by the path which led round from the back of the houses on the far side of the close. There was another longer path that led off the lane to Spire, past the barn, but he preferred to have the sea by him all the way.

As he walked, he lit a pipe. He knew it was a stupid habit, but after Edna died he had gone back to it and it had kept him sane. He thought about the boulder on the shore – the 'Rock' behind him. The tide was up and it was only just visible, not a rock at all, just a piece of abandoned concrete. He supposed the police had gone into all the tedious business of tides last Tuesday to check the earliest and latest times when Thrush could have been sitting on the beach. The tide had been out 8 a.m., so the night before it must have been high tide at about 2.30 a.m. Thrush could have been down there as early as 10.00 p.m. until 1.30 a.m. Pat Dawson says he saw a gowned figure about then at the entrance to the lane. Yet Cobb did not believe Thrush had been as early as that. What time did he usually lock up? He could ask at the marina, if there was anyone there, which he doubted.

He looked over the other side in the direction of the marina, where he could just make out another barn, a deserted great whale of a building that must have housed a large harvest many years ago. He passed the old coastguard's hut, which was boarded up now. It had not been a coastguard's hut for years, and the tenant, an amateur sailor and City banker, had not come at all last season.

He walked down the wall that sloped towards the hard where the dinghies were beached. It was a large expanse of concrete and continued for about 300 yards, joining on to the plot in front of the clubhouse. Beyond this there was a sort of miniature grassy valley that extended along the bottom of the new sea-wall where many little yachts spent their winter. Today was dull, and the sound of masts tinkling in the slight wind was the only reminder that man-made objects were not far away. There was no car stationed in front of the clubhouse. Graham must have decided his quarry would not return there. Cobb sat down on a bollard and puffed at his pipe.

Graham had said that Thrush knew Kevin Black. He must have known Kevin's friends too. What were their names? Cobb had an excellent aural memory and soon recalled Darren and Wayne. George had told him they had been squatting somewhere up the coast in a derelict holiday chalet that had been left by its owners. Strange that this Kevin, if he were gay, would want to be associated with youths who, according to George, were not. Drugs must unite them in a sort of parody of friendship.

Kevin must be lonely. There were not all that many men who 'came out' round here; if they were young, Kevin's age, they would go to London. Kevin had stayed. Possibly for the drugs? Now Darren and Wayne had disappeared, along with Kevin. Probably they were all in the Smoke by now.

He walked over to the club house, which was padlocked. The long window on the upper floor covered the whole of one side of the building, giving a good view over the estuary. The flag was not up. There would be only one more club Sunday, he calculated, before the last equinoctial gales began to blow; they were mostly fair-weather sailors. A few stray hardy campers like the Simmonses

100

might be here for a few more weekends before packing up for winter.

He walked across the hard to the dinghies drawn up at the side, their tarpaulins covering the gear.

Then he paused for a moment and looked again at one of them. Was he so obsessed by the discovery of bodies that he had imagined a shoe poking out from under the dinghy at the far end of three?

He went up to it, squeezing between boats parked closely together like cars in a commuter carpark.

Yes, it was without doubt a shoe.

Cobb felt a little nervous, but his old training reasserted itself. At that moment he heard a car in the distance, coming down the lane from Spire over the fields behind. He reached the dinghy, stooped gingerly and whipped off the tarpaulin, which was not fixed.

Underneath lay a man on his back, his mouth open, and one leg in the boat, the other dangling over it.

Not dead, but breathing stertorously. Cobb leaned over him and smelt drink. Better not touch him. Let him sleep it off. He felt the pulse on a thin wrist that emerged from an anorak that had seen better days. Quite steady. No inhalation of vomit, he didn't think. Then he noticed on the side of the dinghy the tell-tale spattering of vomit. The lad *had* been sick, and had then fallen asleep. Was it Kevin Black? He rather thought it might be.

The car he had heard a few moments ago came bumping across the field and he now saw it was a police car. What the hell! Had someone tipped them off? He would have to mention Graham to the driver and he didn't want to do that. He signalled as the motorist, a burly sergeant, got out of the car.

'Hey, Officer,' Cobb shouted.

The man looked up. Cobb came round to the nearest dinghy as the bulky policeman, strolled towards him.

'There's a young man here in one of these boats whom I think you may be looking for. I've just found him.'

'Found him?' echoed the officer, looking immediately suspicious.

'Could you radio your HQ? I think this might be Kevin Black.'

Cobb gestured to the recumbent figure as the policeman squeezed his way round the boat.

'Well, I'm blowed – sleeping like a baby!' he said, after one look.

'Aren't you going to check he's alive?' said Cobb, more curious to hear the reply than for any other reason.

'Are you Mr Cobb?' asked the sergeant. 'I heard from my boss you might be here.'

'From whom?'

'From Inspector Graham. Told me to look out for you. Said you might be taking a little walk in this direction.'

Well, the old bugger, thought Cobb. He hadn't been too clever in covering up his intentions.

'Reckon he's out for the count, wouldn't you say?' said the sergeant gloomily.

'I've only just arrived – I was taking a little stroll in this direction. I believe *you* are looking for Mr Black too?'

'That's right, we are. Down in Pebblehanger.' He gestured down the estuary. 'Young Kevin vamoosed and we'd already looked here. I thought, as Inspector Graham said you might be taking a walk, that I'd look round here again for myself.'

'Well, I've found you something,' said Cobb. 'Shall we wake him up? He can't stay here all afternoon. It might rain. He'd pulled the tarpaulin over him. Been sick, too. Not a pleasant sight.'

'Right, there's one or two matters they would like a little word with him about,' said the sergeant. 'I'm Wilson,' he added.

'Could I come with you, do you think? I'm not sure he'll hold up all the way to Eastminster.'

Why hadn't they sent Sergeant Idle, or even Dixon, who knew the background?

Wilson looked around among the beach pebbles and came across a child's bucket. He marched up to a tap fixed on the outside wall of the clubhouse.

He returned with a full bucket, which he poured unceremoniously over the sleeping form.

'Careful now – he may have been using drugs too, you know,' said Cobb.

There was a sudden groan from the boat and then slowly a form reared up, eyes now open, hair sticking up like hedgehog spikes.

'Whaddya want?' asked the mouth.

'Just a few words,' said the sergeant.

The youth was instantly awake. 'You're a policeman,' he accused him cleverly. 'It's not a crime to sleep in a dinghy.'

'Just in connection with a friend of yours, sonny,' said Wilson.

'Oh – an' who's this then?' asked the youth, looking at Cobb.

'We might ask the same of you,' remarked the sergeant. 'Come on now. Are you Kevin Black?'

'What's it to you?'

'Your mum and dad want to see you – you didn't turn up when you said you would. Your father in particular would like a word with you.'

'Fuck, I'm over eighteen!' said the lad.

'Just give me your name,' said the patient officer, as Cobb helped him haul the boy out of the boat. He left behind a smell of vomit and unwashed body.

'Kevin Black,' he mumbled, looking green now he was on his feet. 'Can't a man sleep off a can or two?'

'We have a few questions about two mates of yours,' Wilson said, taking out his notebook and opening it. 'Darren Bogworthy and Wayne Spitt,' he pronounced.

'Oh, yeah? What they supposed to have done then?'

'I don't know,' said Wilson.

'Who are you? Uncle Tom Cobley?' Kevin asked Cobb.

'Jim Cobb,' answered Cobb politely. The boy might have heard of him, then. Through whom? 'Do you often sleep here?' he asked. 'Must be handy for sailing. I believe your dad's the treasurer at the club?'

Kevin looked mutinous.

'I often kip down here – no law against it, is there? You're always on to us – you and your friends,' he said with spirit.

Kevin must think he was a plain-clothes officer.

'I don't want to interfere with your arrangements,' said Cobb. 'I'm only a civilian.'

'I believe my super is interested in little boats,' said Sergeant Wilson. He winked at Cobb, who wondered what yarn Graham had been spinning about him. To Kevin, Wilson said: 'Come along now, or will it need two of us to put you in the car?'

Kevin, however, seemed resigned to accompanying them, though he made a pantomime of rubbing his elbows.

'Still feeling sick?' Cobb asked pleasantly, but there was no reply.

'I don't want any trouble,' said Wilson, as Kevin accompanied them to the police car.

'Do I look as if I will be? I'm as stiff as a poker. Can I have a cup of tea at the station? I haven't seen my mates for days. Scarpered up West, I expect.'

Cobb noticed that when he did not take enough care, Kevin's accent was almost 'Received Pronunciation'.

'How did you get here, then?' Wilson was asking him.

'I walked down to the sailing club. Dad's car's still up at the chalet – I'd no more petrol.'

Cobb was wondering what the police wanted to know. Was it about Kevin's mates, or anonymous letters – or something worse? He couldn't ask Graham; he would have to return when they'd delivered the young man.

This they did after a stately drive through the lanes of Dillingham and Matchingdon and Layland before arriving in the 1930s 'new' police station at Eastminster. Kevin didn't seem to have any fight in him, and was taken off somewhere by a woman PC. Wilson turned to Cobb.

'Just a statement about where you found him, sir,' he said.

Cobb followed him into a small interview room painted hospital green with last year's calendar hanging on the wall.

Wilson wrote down a quick account of Cobb's walk and his afternoon find, and asked Cobb to read it over and sign it. On his way out Cobb paused at the Duty Officer's desk.

'Compliments to Inspector Graham and could you tell him his old friend Cobb would like a word with him? Would you tell him I'll telephone him tonight?'

'Will do.'

Cobb said, 'I came in the police car. Could you tell me what time the buses go to Spire?'

'We're to give you a lift,' said the policeman unexpectedly. He gestured him to wait on a bench whilst a car was ordered. Red-carpet treatment. Cobb was under no illusion that ordinary members of the public were treated in this way and waited with a certain amusement. He ought to have thought ahead about getting back. He wondered what they were asking Kevin.

Wilson came out and took him round to the carpark at the back where his own private car, a Volvo of a few years' vintage, awaited them. He was driven home in some style. He chanced a question: 'What about the Simmons woman?'

He knew he should not have asked, for Wilson replied:

'I expect Inspector Graham will telephone you, sir, if there's anything more you can do to help us.'

Cobb smarted rather. He really must remember he was retired.

*

104

The day after Cobb discovered Kevin asleep in the dinghy the post-man arrived early for once. He came in the post-van as his walk was extensive, and delivered the Heron Close letters after he had called at the sailing club and the two farms, which lay between Spickhanger and Spire, on each side of the lane.

Lisa was up, getting ready for work, and took in the letters. Tony was shaving, swearing as usual. She looked through what the postman had brought and suddenly her heart turned over. She recognized the writing.

Addressed to Mr Anthony Smith, the letter looked innocuous enough, but Lisa knew better. Perhaps she could hide it, but another letter would soon follow it if this one were ignored. She put it under the circulars and offers of £50,000 prizes from one of the mail-order firms she patronized, and tried to eat her breakfast. But she was trembling too much; eventually she gave up and sat trying to sip a cup of tea.

When Tony came down she was already dressed for school. He looked at the paper for a moment then turned his attention to the post. She went into the kitchen. Soon he was beside her as she watered a plant on the window sill.

'You saw this, I suppose?' He was holding the envelope and thrust it in front of her face.

'No – what is it?' she tried.

'You bloody well know what it is. I suppose your "friend" who takes you to school has already mentioned it, since she lives with the woman it's about.'

'I *told* you Tony, the other night – but you went to sleep—'

'Recognize the handwriting, I expect,' he sneered.

'Yes, it's Brenda's,' she replied in a shaky voice.

'A friend of yours,' he read, *'a tall, elderly woman who said she knew you came up to me not long ago at the stall and remarked upon how like Lisa I looked. Thought you'd like to know, that's all. Funny coincidence, wasn't it? Nothing to worry about, but I do need a bit more money and would be glad to receive £500 next week. Yours Brenda.*
    PS. Love to my 'double'.

'Don't pay her – she can't *do* anything,' cried Lisa. 'She's in it as much as you are – I mean *we* are.' She fluttered.

'I suppose that was Miss Kant,' he added, 'poking her nose in.'

105

'She doesn't know anything about us, Tone! I'm surprised it hasn't happened before. There's no law against looking like someone,' she quavered.

'Don't be a fool, Lisa. We have to go on being careful.'

'Brenda would never split on you.'

'If anyone ever asks, you don't know her.'

'But, Tone – what harm would it do to say we might know her? I . . .' She had been going to say she had told Susan Swann she had no sister, but remembered just in time.

'Get to work,' he said brutally. 'I'll write to put her off. You might be right. There's nothing she can do.'

Except to land us in prison, thought Lisa. Tony had always told her that she was as guilty as he was and she believed him. The cloud always hung over her. At school she might forget it for an hour or two, but once home the awfulness of her situation overwhelmed her. In spite of her attempt to brush aside Tone's fears, she felt sick as she went out of the door to join Susan in the car.

Tony Smith was thoughtful before he too left for work. He knew Miss Kant went to London now and then, and he wondered how well she knew the area where Brenda had her stall. He hoped she would not visit it again. In the meantime, what could he pin on her? He disliked her as much as he disliked the two gays next door. But he couldn't think of anything; her little friend Susan Swarm would be an easier target.

CHAPTER NINE

Dorothea Kant was a woman who never let the grass grow under her feet and who pursued her hunches with energy and rationality. She had gone to London the day Cobb discovered the recumbent Kevin, intending to visit the new Family Record Centre in Islington. In the past, as a regular visitor at the old St Catherine's House, she had occasionally done some family history research on her brother's behalf. She had begun her own research into family wills before they were moved from Somerset House. Now, yet another change had led to the foundation of the new record centre, all the material for research on three floors in the same building.

It was sad; nothing ever stayed the same. She must be getting old to think this, but she had enjoyed going to the well-organized Somerset House and to St Catherine's House to consult the post-1837 births, marriages and deaths indexes, and to the land registry and the census rooms in Portugal Street, though the last of the three had been crowded and tiring. Often, though, she had strolled around Lincoln's Inn Fields afterwards and felt a sense of the past.

This morning, wanting to access some indexes, she found Islington almost as crowded. She knew exactly what she was looking for and had her notebooks and sharpened pencils ready. Naturally, the most recent census might have told her more, but such information was not released for a hundred years. There was the electoral register for 1997 on the ground floor, along with the births, marriages and deaths indexes, but she did not know where Anthony Smith had been living two years previously.

Perhaps she had been wrong in deciding not to have the Internet at home to use the many facilities for family history, but she had decided against the time wasted involved in surfing the Web, never having enough time to read for pleasure, as it was. Here, people came only for specific information, and today she had names to look up.

She had less faith in the International Genealogical Index on the floor above, which was not much concerned with the twentieth century and in any case had many omissions for past centuries. It was not needful for her to know who Tony Smith's great-great-great-grandfather had been; only to go back over the past fifty years or so. It might take time, but she had the rest of the afternoon until the place closed. There was a marriage she had to check, and some births. She would start with the marriage; it was easier and would give approximate dates of birth.

She found the name she was looking for after some time with the indexes, having already ascertained possible registration districts. Then she would have forms to fill in and a queue to pay for the actual certificates.

Susan had said it was seven years ago. She was correct. The easy thing about marriage was that once you got what you thought was the correct entry you could check it against the name of the other party. If the name and reference number were the same – Eureka! you were home and dry!

Nothing out of the way here:

SMITH/LANDON . . . East Ham March 1993. She looked next for LANDON/SMITH, found it, and it matched. She might, if she had time, look up the birth of Mr Smith. But Smiths were a problem. If only he had been called Fotheringham or Featherstonhaugh or something equally unusual. She looked up LANDON, for a woman some years older than little Lisa, a Brenda Landon. She ran though many indexes, but found nothing. She was disappointed.

Perhaps, then, it was true and Lisa had no sister. Then she thought: let's try Lisa *Smith* then. She often had these hunches and enjoyed following them. The woman had looked older than Mr Smith, but you never knew. Lisa appeared very much younger, but that might have been the skilful application of make-up and the little-girl-lost look. After another half an hour checking entries up to ten years before Tony Smith of East Ham's birth, which involved a lengthy search of each year divided into quarters, she had found nothing. She kept her handbag between her feet, having left her coat on the rack.

What a business; the older you were the longer it seemed to take to accomplish all the mechanics of research. But the marriage she was looking for was not in the popular period between 1880 and 1910, where everyone was searching for grandparents' marriages. Formerly there had been notices everywhere telling searchers to beware of theft; lockers were an improvement but she would not let her handbag out of her sight. She would risk waiting to order a copy of the marriage certificate.

'You are nosy,' she scolded herself, but she felt obscurely that she was on to something untoward, unexpected.

She had no idea whether her Lisa Landon had been born in the same district as her husband. She had known the registration district for the marriage, having done her research at home for the volume numbers. The marriage certificate would show that. She looked at her watch. She prayed the queue would move quickly; she had her money ready and had filled in the forms. She'd spent longer than she'd imagined looking at the various years, deflected by interesting names and speculations. Perhaps she had just been amusing herself. But who knew, it might be useful one day to have a little more information about Anthony Smith. It was not a crime to ask for certificates concerning others, even recent wills, once they had died and probate had been dealt with. She had often done that very thing down the road at the old Somerset House.

Dorothea speculated on other matters as she waited. She would have to come again to look for the birth certificates. To whom would Percy Thrush leave his money – if he had any? She filled in the request for a certificate of the marriage of Tony and Lisa, saying she would collect it in a few days, as she would need to return to the centre in any case.

She went into a small snack-bar after that, where she treated herself to a slice of cheesecake. London seemed even noisier and more crowded than last time, filled with miserable-looking people. Everyone was in a hurry going somewhere they didn't particularly wish to go, and everyone without exception looked tired and pale. There must indeed be benefits from living in the country, she thought, but possibly some of these Londoners were also commuters to places as far away as or further than Spickhanger. How tiring to travel every day. Public transport dispirited her. But she had enjoyed her day and now walked into the City. There were still a few buildings standing that belonged to London's past and she comforted herself with this as she joined the rush-hour crowds for a train home.

If she needed many more sessions at the record centre, she would stay at 'Hero', her university women's club, of which she had been a member for many years. At least she had made a beginning; things always took longer than you imagined.

Cobb had a visitor that evening, no other than his old friend George, DI Graham, who arrived bearing a bottle of whisky after he had telephoned. It embarrassed Cobb to explain he would no longer touch the stuff, but it had to be done and he poured a tot out for George and tonic water with ice and lemon for himself.

'You don't, then? Sorry – I'll bring you some flowers next time.'

'Since the accident,' said Cobb. 'Can't touch the stuff.'

'Had he been drinking then?'

'Yes. As you know, they often have,' replied Cobb.

'I came to apologize for not seeing you yesterday at the station, and for my sergeant. You must have thought he was spying on you.'

'Seeing as he expected me to be down there?'

'It was only, we – I – thought that after our chat on the phone you'd have a poke around the place – and I wanted another check. He was told to say I thought you might be there.'

'A good thing I was, as he'd never have found Kevin himself,' grumbled Cobb. 'But it's your case, George. I'm not in business. I shouldn't have gone. Curiosity, you know, and sixth sense. The lad would hardly have died of exposure if we hadn't woken him up, he'd pulled a tarpaulin over himself. He couldn't have been all that far gone, but he'd made enough mess. I thought it might be drugs – but it was just drink, wasn't it? Have you interrogated him?'

'Ay, we've let him out on bail pending further enquiries so long as he stays at his parents.'

'His mother will be pleased,' said Cobb. 'Not his dad though – no love lost there, I expect.'

'Why is it, Jim? He'd a good home. Dad a bit of a snob. Kevin got five GCSEs, even if a year late. Could have gone on to college then, but he left school, would have gone on the dole if they hadn't stopped giving it to unemployed youngsters. Two years ago he just does a bunk. Then he comes back and sets up house with some mates. Hangs around his dad's outfit at the marina. Lets himself in with a copy of dad's key. Pilfers the till.'

'His trouble is that he's gay,' said Cobb, 'and his father won't accept it.'

'Yes – he kept telling us that. I told him it wasn't a crime – he's over eighteen. We were more concerned with what he might tell us about his mates – and about Thrush.'

'He knew him well?'

'Said he chatted to him now and then. Knew the fellow took drink away with him.'

'And the mates?'

'Now *there* is something a little more germane to our investigation. We pressed Kevin – no heavy stuff, just asked him about drugs. First he said he knew nothing about them, but admitted knowing Darren and Wayne, his squatter friends. Then he agreed he'd used a bit, but didn't now. Don't know whether to believe him. He'd shot up once or twice in the past, but was too frightened of the consequences. I don't think he was lying.'

'I think he might use coke,' said Cobb. 'Bit out of his class, though. It's mostly yuppies who use that.'

'No, it's got round to everyone now, George. General improvement in social facilities.'

'What we found at "Mimosa", where they'd squatted, would explain the little boat. There's someone coming in with supplies. Only a middleman, but we'd like to know who else he delivered to, and how much. Kevin confessed he knew heroin users in London who'd caught Aids from needles. His offering this information led me to ask him a direct question. I said it was important for our inquiry – he needn't answer it.'

'You asked him if he was HIV positive – or if he'd had a test.'

'Yes – just whether he'd had a test. He went white, but said yes, he had, and it was negative. He was most insistent.'

Cobb thought about the original accusation directed at Sandy and David.

'There was some gossip, apparently, between Thrush and Kevin's mates. He says there's paranoia building up locally about paedophilia, not gays.'

'Well, there is such a thing as pederasty, but lots of people don't know the difference.'

'His father's very anti-homosexual. Thinks it's the same thing –

that was why he left home. Says that there was talk about the two men who live on the Close – that they might have Aids and that they mucked around with kids. They were going to be told, in no uncertain terms, to leave Spickhanger.'

So someone knew how to play on the men's fears. The letter had been specific, thought Cobb. He said nothing about this to Graham.

'I asked him who else went down there – locals sometimes go to the bar or buy a bottle from the barman there. Here it is for your book: Darren and Wayne were "friendly" with your Mr Smith, apparently. He volunteered the information. And he says Darren is a violent bloke.'

'You asked Kevin about the rape?'

'Yes. He seemed genuinely angry that we might think he had anything to do with that. Said Darren wasn't around at the time of the party at Number 4 – he was with him at a pub up the coast. But on the evening Mrs Simmons was attacked he admitted Darren *and* Wayne acted "peculiar". He thought they'd been using, but there was something else. Wayne picked a fight with Darren late that night – he heard Wayne accuse the other bloke of "going a bird".'

'Mrs Simmons?'

'Maybe. They'd seen her and her husband several times at the club apparently, or, to be more accurate, in the campers' field behind, and Kevin said the two lads had been saying something about Pat Simmons and her woman friend. He had seen Mr Simmons drive away. They all knew the women were alone for a night.'

'You suspect Darren or Wayne of the Simmons rape, but not of the attack on little Linda?'

'Right. We've a patrol out looking for them and a search in Basildon and the East End. Kevin swears they had nothing to do with the other girl – and he knows nothing about a monk's robe, in case you're wondering. 'Course, either lad might have seen Linda's attacker and not told Kevin.'

'Kevin seems to have been very co-operative,' murmured Cobb.

'He was frightened more than anything. I don't think he's a violent man. Only a kid really – young for his age. We hope to tie up the drugs and the rape with Bogworthy or Spitt, and both Spitt and Bogworthy – and maybe Kevin – with selling drugs. Or at least passing them on.'

As he tamped his pipe Cobb asked himself whether Kevin Black's friends were responsible for the letter, and if so at whose instigation? He ought to get David and Sandy to consent to the police seeing it.

Graham sighed. 'There just seem too many motives around. Once we've got Bogworthy and Spitt we'll challenge them with meeting that little boat. They've not just been "using"; as I say, they've been dealing. Far worse criminal offence. Kevin swears *he* hasn't, though. Scared out of his wits. Says he hasn't made a penny.'

'He's probably passed dope on, and kept a little for himself. Aren't you more concerned with the attack on Mrs Simmons?'

'Sure. We're dropping the Thrush thing. The old man probably knew something about them all and told someone. He might have picked up about the drugs, but there's no proof Kevin attacked him; he says the others had left Spire by then. Thrush most likely just fell. It'll all be tidied up by tomorrow, I expect, and they can go ahead with the funeral. We think the second attack on the woman and the drugs are connected, but we don't think Thrush had much to do with either.'

'But the attack on Linda?' Cobb pursued.

'Rest assured, when we find the lads they'll be asked very carefully about that – and pressed in the matter of Percy Thrush.'

Cobb was thinking that the unknown element in it all was any connection between Linda and whoever attacked her and Thrush's death. But there was no proof, no evidence, just his hunch. Did Thrush fall because he was frightened? He did not think it worthwhile to say any of this to Graham who would think it all too fancy. But couldn't someone have got Darren – or his friend Wayne – to scare off Fairbairn and Robson, to implicate them in the attack on Linda and the Thrush death, just as a piece of nastiness? Was he trying to pin down something in the woodshed that just didn't exist?

'I'm sure Tony Smith has something to do with it, though no proof at all. I wouldn't suggest it to anyone but you,' he said aloud. '*Smith* knew those lads all right. *Smith* knew Kevin was gay, and he wanted to scare Number 4 with the robe – just for devilment.

'But I don't think he attacked Linda. I can't remember his going out of the party. He could easily have swiped the robe, though, from the school carpark, and could just as easily have put it in the

113

men's tool-shed. He could have gone in through the back garden gate – they were out all afternoon. As far as the school's concerned, I gather he often goes there with plants for parents' evenings. He has an alibi, I imagine, for the rape of Pat Simmons.'

'So long as we catch Kevin's friends and draw up a charge list – rape and drug-peddling should be enough – I think we can safely leave Percy Thrush out of it, and anyone else on the close for the time being. It's a muddle, I agree, but it's probably one of those concatenations of circumstances you always used to be going on about.'

'Did I?' asked Cobb.

'And I know you'll probably solve this one too,' said his old friend. 'But mind, Jim, we're in charge of the drugs side and of the Simmons rape – we're grateful for all you've done. . . .'

'But now you want me to leave it alone?'

'More or less. Drugs are coppers' business. Does anyone on the close know you were once a chief inspector?'

'Not unless they've got second sight.'

He poured himself another tonic and Graham poured himself the same this time.

'One's enough, Jim. Wouldn't do for an off-duty inspector to be breathalysed.'

'Indeed not,' said Cobb. 'You take the bottle back with you, son.'

Cobb sat on after he had left, trying once more to piece the whole business together. If they caught Darren and Wayne, he felt the case would probably be sewn up as far as the rape of Mrs Simmons was concerned. That was none of his affair. Neither was the drug running. He was sorry for Kevin, being tangled up with it. Sorry for Kevin's parents too. This seemed to be a case of nothing matching – the letter and the robe had nothing to do with Kevin.

There was still, to his mind, a puzzle about Thrush and about the attacker of Linda. And he felt sure that someone else knew something about that. Trouble was to distinguish details that seemed irrelevant to the case Graham was pursuing, but were still important. If no one had been murdered and the rapist was apprehended – as he felt he soon might be – he would still continue to take an interest in the anonymous letter and the mysterious robe.

He was tired, though grateful to George for keeping him up to date. He ought to be relieved they didn't need his help any longer.

114

'Super'-annuated, that was what he was. He ought to be grateful about that, too.

He'd concentrate on his garden.

He went to bed and fell asleep and this time had no nightmares, but dreamed he was promoted to assistant commisioner.

CHAPTER TEN

The following Saturday, Dorothea invited all the women in the close to coffee and cakes at Number 2. It was now almost the end of September, dankly autumnal but not yet wintry. Susan had been amused when her landlady had mooted the idea of a coffee-party. Miss Kant was not the sort of woman whom you imagined enjoying entertaining neighbours. She was not stand-offish, but did not seem to belong to the same world as Eva Maitland and Vera Whitwham. She was not unsociable, but she was self-sufficient.

'You ought one day to give a real party here yourself,' said Dorothea. 'I wouldn't mind if you didn't invite me – you could have all your London and local friends and people from the school.'

'People usually go to parties to meet the opposite sex,' Susan replied. She had met Richard at a party, Richard whom she had seen only once since his return from holiday. It was obvious that their break was final. She tried telling herself it was a good thing, but whilst her head agreed, her heart still felt sorry and sad that what had once seemed to be going to be a permanent relationship should have foundered on their inability to agree over the importance for married women of having some financial independence, and keeping their own name if they wanted to.

Had she been childish to make such an issue of it? She had enjoyed their lovemaking and still found him attractive. They had liked doing other things together too: driving to National Trust houses, and looking in antique shops. But it was not enough. She could drive to stately homes and chase antiques alone. Perhaps it was less trouble to do without a man? Richard had said she put too much energy into her work; at other times, he had berated her for being 'vague'. No, she did not feel like

116

giving a 'real' party at present, though it was kind of Miss Kant to suggest it.

She welcomed the Heron Close ladies, as Richard would have called them, that Saturday morning, and settled them in the long downstairs sitting-room with cups and plates ready on a trolley. Dorothea seemed determined to do things in style. It was not clear whether Lisa would be able to come. Usually, Tony required her presence at the weekend to help in his garden shop, but fortunately this Saturday he was away, had gone up to London to order some equipment he could not buy elsewhere.

Mrs Whitwham arrived first and sat quietly on the comfortable though modern sofa, before asking if they minded her having a look at Miss Kant's garden at the back. The french window opened on to Dorothea's little back garden which was, in plan, like all the patios at the backs of the houses, except for the Whitwhams' at the other end of the S-shaped close. Dorothea, however, had made more of the garden and had more tubs and pots on the flagstones.

'I wonder whether Mrs Maitland will come,' said Susan, who was in Dorothea's kitchen, cutting an extremely delicious-looking coffee-cake into twelve portions before carrying it into the sitting-room. Miss Kant was busy with coffee-filters.

'She said she would. I think she's coming out of her shell a bit. It must be Pat Dawson's doing. She looks quite happy sometimes now.'

The doorbell rang and Susan led in Lisa, dressed in a pale-mauve cotton dress and loose pullover. Obviously she had permission to attend an all-female party without her husband. Mrs Maitland followed a few minutes later in a green shirt-waister that set off her creamy skin. She had put green eye-shadow on her eyes. Very skilfully, Susan thought. She must once have been a less ordinary-looking woman.

Vera Whitwham came in from the garden.

'I've been admiring your late roses,' she said. 'I love those pale creamy ones. Your chrysanths are lovely too. You've managed quite a cottage-garden effect by the wall, and you have several unusual plants!' She was quite loquacious. Apparently it was only when she was with her husband that she kept quiet.

'You must see it in spring or early summer,' replied Dorothea.

Vera Whitwham came back into the house.

'How cosy,' she said, as the guests were all handed their coffee.

'Look – you have another visitor.'

Linda Swift was standing at the door. Susan had invited her to come and borrow a book of old engravings of birds she had picked up herself at a second-hand bookshop.

'You must stay, Linda,' said Dorothea kindly. 'It's only a hen party I'm giving. You know Mrs Maitland and Mrs Smith? Mrs Whitwham I expect you've met.'

Linda, whose last sight of all these people together had been on the night of her hysterics, looked rather shy, but Vera Whitwham soon put her at her ease, and Miss Swann was so friendly, not like a teacher really. But then Miss Kant was nice too, thought Linda. The six of them made desultory conversation for a time over the cake, but soon got down to past events.

'Thank goodness nothing else has happened,' said Eva Maitland. 'Pat felt he might be suspected of being drunk when he said he'd seen a figure standing by the Abbot's Walk!' she went on confidingly. 'But he never drinks now,' she added proudly, as though she expected to be contradicted.

There was a slightly awkward silence, but Dorothea filled it.

'Mr Cobb is almost teetotal too,' she said. 'What a sober bunch.'

'Sandy and David make up for it,' said Susan irreverently.

'He's nice, Mr Cobb, isn't he,' offered Mrs Whitwham.

'Very reliable,' said Dorothea.

'Tony says he must have once been a policeman,' said Lisa.

There was a curious silence.

'He must have retired, then. I don't know him very well,' said Eva, obviously determined to join in.

Tongues were suddenly loosened. It was almost as though they had been sipping gin, not coffee.

'Bill says they've discovered the man who . . .' began Vera Whitwham, but then hastily remembered that Linda Swift was among them.

Linda went a little pale.

'Are you feeling better now, Linda?' asked Dorothea. 'Now your father has decided to let you off the leash a bit?'

'Dad was worried at first, but now I think he doesn't mind so long as I'm not out in the dark. Mum says Mrs Pheasant in Spire – the policeman's wife, you know – told her that they're on to the man who attacked that Mrs Simmons. I really hope they are.'

Dorothea was thinking what a very mature sort of girl she was, in spite of her initial reaction to the attack, which had been an involuntary response.

'It's about time,' said Lisa indignantly. 'There hasn't been anything in the paper about it yet, though, has there?'

The *Eastminster Gazette*, came out on Fridays, but was not delivered to everyone at The Close.

'You bought one, Susan, didn't you, yesterday?' asked Dorothea. They had both seen it but Susan had resolved to say nothing about the item until someone else did.

'Yes, it's there about them wanting to interview two men about Mrs Simmons,' she said now. 'But no mention of you, Linda, or the other excitements.'

'The police came round again,' said Linda in a subdued voice. 'They asked me if I knew . . . well I was asked not to say who, but there are two men they are looking for, I think in connection with Mrs Simmons. They asked again for a description of everything. About the smell, you know.'

'You said it smelt musty,' encouraged Susan, who still felt some responsibility for letting the robe be taken from her car.

'I keep remembering. It was as though it had been in mothballs – or the man was wearing something that smelt like that.'

'I told the police my acting-cupboard contained mothballs,' said Susan. She'd been through this before with Linda. 'Of course it has . . . it's a strong smell.' The others looked puzzled.

'I expect they'll find whoever it was and put them behind bars,' said Lisa. 'Tony thinks . . .' She stopped.

'Yes,' asked Dorothea.

'Oh, he thought it was a young man who goes to the clubhouse. Mr Black's son. He says he's up to no good.'

'I knew Kevin Black,' said Linda. 'He was at school with my big brother, and he's, you know – gay. What would he want with trying it on with a girl? He certainly wasn't the man who attacked me.'

The frankness of the younger generation rather nonplussed the assembled women.

'I think you are quite right, Linda,' said Dorothea.

'I've nothing against gays, myself, or against Mr Fairbairn and Mr Robson,' said Lisa. 'Tony doesn't like them, but he's funny that way.'

'Does anyone know more about this drugs business?' asked Vera Whitwham after a silence. 'My husband is getting very worked up about it. He thinks that men who do drugs are liable to become violent, like some heavy drinkers, but I told him that wasn't always true, it's just that they rob to *buy* the stuff.'

Mrs Whitwham clearly absorbed information better than her husband imagined, thought Susan. But did she realize that she might have been a trifle tactless, with Eva Maitland's being among them?

'I don't think some people need drugs or drink to get ideas,' said Dorothea. 'It's possible some might lose their inhibitions, I suppose.'

'I'm certain my attacker wasn't a *young* man,' said Linda. 'I really must go. I have to shop for Mum. Thank you, Miss Swann, for the book.'

She rose, and Dorothea saw her to the door.

'She's taking it quite coolly now,' said Mrs Whitwham. 'My husband isn't keen on gays either,' she added, turning to Lisa. 'It's a common prejudice.'

'There's still a mystery about the robe,' said Susan when Dorothea came back. If her landlady had set up this coffee party for a good gossip, she might as well help.

'Yes, I'm surprised it hasn't turned up,' said Eve. 'Pat thinks one of your pupils might have taken it.'

'Oh, I don't know about that,' said Susan.

'Kevin used to talk to old Thrush,' said Mrs Whitwham. 'I've seen them down by the sailing club this summer when we've been for a walk.'

Dorothea looked interested but said nothing.

'It was a pity about the old man,' said Lisa. 'Tony thinks someone might have pushed him over, you know. Of course they weren't to know he'd hit his head.'

'I think he was rather a peculiar character,' said Susan. 'Just the way he used to stare at one – I suppose he did it to all women.'

'Yes, that's what Tony says,' added Lisa, glad that someone seemed for once to agree with her husband.

'They don't know him well down in Spire,' said Eve. 'Pat was in the pub down there – fetching my cigarettes,' she added quickly, 'and they were saying he'd only lived round here for about two years.'

'Apart from the native bird tribes, there've been so many newcomers,' said Dorothea. 'Like myself. I come from Northumberland originally.'

'And I hail from Lancashire,' said Susan, 'and Mr Cobb from across the Pennines! Funny to have a Swann and a Cobb who are not natives of the place!' Having seen Linda out she was loyally helping on the conversation.

'We're from Suffolk originally,' said Vera Whitwham, 'though that's regarded as foreign parts down here. Where did *you* live before?' she asked Eve Maitland.

'Norwich,' said Eve. 'After my husband died I wanted somewhere away from Norfolk, but I didn't want to leave East Anglia.'

'And Mr Dawson?' asked Dorothea.

'Oh, Pat is from west London.'

'I believe you are also from London?' said Dorothea to Lisa.

'Well, almost. Tony and I come from Wanstead,' replied Lisa.

'I used to teach near there,' offered Miss Kant. 'Did Susan tell you I was in those parts not long ago and saw a girl I thought was you? A woman, I mean. Your spit image, perhaps a bit older. But Susan reports that you haven't got a sister.'

'No, I haven't. Susan did mention it, but it might have been a cousin, I suppose,' said Lisa looking distinctly nervous.

'Likenesses can crop up generations later,' said Mrs Whitwham unexpectedly. 'For instance, my husband's sister looks just like their great-great-grandmother. We we have an old photograph of her, must have been taken in the 1860s. She looks about forty on it and she's the image of his sister Joyce.'

'And, of course, people can even grow alike,' said Dorothea. 'I've noticed it with dogs – people grow to resemble their dogs.'

'And husbands and wives,' said Eva Maitland. 'There's something about living together that makes people look the same.' She blushed a little.

'Well, we're no nearer solving the mystery of the disappearing robe, are we,' said Susan after a pause. 'When is Thrush's funeral by the way? Does anyone know? Surely now they've done the autopsy, or whatever it's called? I wonder if he had any relatives who'll turn up to claim his money.'

'Shouldn't think he had any,' said Vera. 'Poor old man, speak no ill of the dead, I hope they'll bury him soon. Bill wants to get ahead with appointing someone else to do the gardening work.'

'Perhaps they *do* think there was something suspicious,' said Dorothea. 'They're taking their time over it all. I must ask Mr Cobb.'

'He seems very matey with the police', said Lisa.

'He was once a policeman, I'm sure,' said Vera Whitwham. 'I think he expected the post mortem to be over sooner.'

'Oh, surely Mr Thrush wasn't *attacked*?' said Lisa. 'Who could have anything against him? He might have stared at women – Tony thought he did at me, but he was harmless.'

'I didn't like him much,' confessed Susan, 'but I didn't imagine he was the kind to attack a girl. I'm sure he didn't deserve to fall and hit his head.'

'Many victims have done nothing to deserve attack,' said Dorothea. 'Although most murders are, I believe, family affairs.'

'I can't imagine wanting to murder anyone,' said Mrs Whitwham. 'Unless it was in self-defence.'

'Neither can I,' said Susan.

Lisa said nothing.

'I keep telling Bill that most violence is perpetrated on young men by young men,' said Vera. 'It's true. He thinks I don't read the papers, but I do, and I've noticed. I suppose they just get around more, "clubbing", whatever that is!'

'So if Thrush *were* attacked, it would be very atypical wouldn't it,' suggested Dorothea.

'A-what?' asked Lisa.

'Untypical,' explained Susan. 'I expect that some of the monks buried here could have been killed at the Dissolution of the Monasteries. Perhaps Mr Dawson saw the ghost of one,' she added. 'I wonder which is most to be feared, a ghost or a murderer?'

'Oh, a ghost,' said Eva Maitland unexpectedly, following her own train of thought.

'Are there more women ghosts than male ones in stories?' asked Susan.

'There are just as many men murdered as women but not so many female murderers,' said Dorothea.

'Women take things out more on themselves, not on others,' said Eva Maitland.

'Psychiatrists say that angry people who don't show their anger become anxious, and women are generally agreed to be more anxious than men,' offered Susan. 'At school, the girls are much better at acting anger than the boys but the boys do it more in reality!'

Lisa was looking from one to the other in a baffled sort of way.

'*We* don't always show our real feelings,' added Vera Whitwham.

Or they keep quiet, thought Susan, for whom the turn of the conversation was interesting, though it didn't seem to add much to the solving of the various Spickhanger mysteries.

'Come on now, you must all have another piece of cake!' said Dorothea.

'The funeral is next Tuesday,' said Graham. 'Thought you'd like to know. We have not been able to find any Percy Thrush on our own criminal data base. Of course, things have not always been recorded properly in the past.'

Cobb put down the phone. The little plot he had been building up had suddenly fallen through. He was a meddlesome old fool. This would really be the end of it. For the last week or two he had had fewer nightmares. He supposed the mental activity occasioned by all the various events of the past three or four weeks had given him something else to think about.

On the surface, life was pursuing its even tenor at Heron Close. The days were drawing in; the blackberries still there in early October were no longer being gathered; all the mulberries had long since been put in the freezer, the harvest in the fields around safely gathered in by the combine, and most of the stubble ploughed in. Sandy managed to get good photographs of the last of the swallows lined up on a telegraph wire, and a flock of gulls on a field off Spire Lane. The pond by the old farm half-way to Spire had shrunk from lack of rain; soon it would begin to fill again.

Until the end of September some mornings had still been hazy and golden and Susan had wished that she need not set off for school and could enjoy domestic pleasures for once. But now she felt things dying down for winter, though Linda Swift told her skylarks still went on singing, and leaves were still on the trees. The water-skiers had gone away but the marina was to have one last cold end-of-season Sunday sail. Campers were no longer coming for the weekend, and the field next to theirs had been ploughed ready for sowing. Linda Swift said that this was reducing the seed-food for certain birds and they were dying out.

The electricity meter-man and the gasman called; Sandy and David lagged their hot-water pipes for the winter and Cobb gathered apples and pears from the trees in his garden. His was the only house to possess fruit trees, left from the time when orchards covered much of the area that had once belonged to the ancient monastery. The wood-pigeons slowly stopped the melancholy, monotonous calling that had punctuated the late summer months, and the occasional robin began to mark out his territory.

Susan was reluctant to enjoy the end of autumn because what followed was winter, and she did not like the cold. Last winter they had been snowed up and the telephone line had been down for a week. The winds were biting and it was at such times that she wondered whether she would be better off during the winter in lodgings in Eastminster which, though just as cold as Spickhanger, did have the benefit of proper roads when the weather was at its worst.

Mrs Maitland seemed to have become much more cheerful as time went on. Whatever had been the nature of her own inner problems, they seemed to have had nothing to do with the weather or the season or the climate, and she was beginning to venture out more. She and Pat Dawson were now accepted as an 'item' by the other Heron Closers. It was rumoured that they were actually going to marry, thus releasing one house that would have to be sold to a new family. Nothing had yet been said publicly about marriage, but it was clear they were very fond of each other.

Linda sometimes came round with her mother when the latter was cleaning for the Heron Closers and Cobb had remarked that she looked her old self. She was even going to take part in Miss Swann's new play, she told him. He was planning the course of lectures and classes he wanted to attend in Chelmsford, and borrowed some books from Dorothea Kant. David began to think of writing a short book about the area illustrated with his own paintings, and the Whitwhams had a visit from their daughter and her new baby. Vera Whitwham looked very happy. Her knitting had increased in amount if not in much bulk, each garment being so tiny. Bill Whitwham decided to write to the police in Eastminster with his idea of a neighbourhood watch scheme. It was time he did something about his fears and indignation rather than sit gloomily contemplating the end of civilization as he had known it. Only the Smiths seemed devoid of new interests or plans. Tony Smith snapped at his neighbours and Lisa looked increasingly cowed.

The autumn equinox had passed and it was during the first

week of October that Cobb received the verse. You could hardly call it a poem, he thought, when he saw the block capitals confronting him. The envelope had been printed likewise, and with his heightened policeman's instinct he had opened it with a qualm. He had heard nothing new for some time from George Graham. Thrush had been cremated across the estuary. Only Miss Kant and himself and, surprisingly, Eva Maitland had attended, the others having cried off at the last minute. He assumed that a search was still out for Darren and Wayne for he had heard nothing of their arrest or questioning but the local rag said that the police were about to make a successful arrest. Graham had said nothing as yet about this to him. They were keeping quiet and lying low to flush the youths out. The youths must have gone to London.

As he slit open the envelope that had come that morning and read its contents, he wondered whether all had indeed blown over. The verse, on cheap blue paper, read:

PERCY THRUSH
DID NOT FALL.
HE WAS PUSHED.
'TIS A PITY YEARS AGO
HE WAS NOT DUCKED.

He read it two or three times before putting it back in its envelope. It would now have his fingerprints and DNA as well as the postman's and the post office lady's and the writer's. It gave him a shiver of satisfaction to think his instincts had not been wrong. But if somebody *wanted* him to think that a murder had taken place, that did not mean it *had*. Who would think he was a suitable person to receive such a missive? Why not send it to the police? In any case, Thrush's injury had been caused, the police had proved beyond doubt, by hitting his skull at its thinnest point at the side below the temple. It was a chance in a thousand that he had actually died, a chance in a hundred that his skull at that point was thin. So somebody knew better than the police and/or wanted an investigation.

Somebody had suspected murderous intent, even though the death appeared to be accidental.

Somebody had seen something.

Cobb was also aware of murderers who wanted everyone to

know what they had done, murderers who were disappointed not to achieve fame, who perhaps wanted to be punished, wanted to be discovered, without actually confessing. What kind of mind would write a note like this?

He sat over the problem with another cup of coffee. Had the person who said he knew Thrush had been pushed felt that the case, if it had ever been one, was closed, or had he wanted to cock a snook at the police? *He* was no longer a policeman. He thought that by now they had all guessed he had been one in the past. He had never told anyone down here directly, but had thought it might eventually percolate, in spite of what he had said to Graham. He had no wish to talk about the reasons for his retirement.

He looked again at the last two lines: *'Tis a pity years ago/ he was not ducked.* He turned to his neat bookshelf for his New Chambers Dictionary, which he used for the many crosswords he solved. Was it just a joke? 'Ducked' might mean 'given a shock' or something like that. It could be a cricketing term perhaps, or one natural to a villager from these parts with the names of birds and waders so prominent among local families.

He found *coarse cotton or linen* and then *ducking-stool*. That was more like it: *A chair in which offenders were formerly tied and ducked in the water.* So someone thought Percy Thrush was in some way an offender in spite of the fact that he had no record?

His finger went through the rest of the entry in the dictionary: a bird, a zero indicating no runs, and then various metaphorical phrases derived from the word of which the most suggestive ones seemed to be: lame duck, dying duck, ducks and drakes and sitting duck.

Apparently the word had also been used for a landing craft, and Cobb remembered that Spickhanger had been used for D-Day practice in the last war.

He ruminated over this and over 'sitting duck'. Thrush seemed to have been that. Perhaps also a lame duck. *A defaulter, a bankrupt, disabled, inefficient or helpless.* He certainly had been a dying duck. Cobb found as he read the entry that to play ducks and drakes meant also *to use recklessly, squander or waste*, as well as the usual meaning of skimming flat stones over the water. Well, it was up to him. This was a missive with which, like the first anonymous letter, the police were not going to be entrusted. They had used him when he was useful to them and now he would see what he could discover for himself. There was probably nothing in it – just a piece of neighbourly spite, but it would do no harm to sniff around a bit. He did not regret not having told the police about the letter David and Sandy had received, even though it might have had something to do with those lads down at the marina and the boat. Let the police concentrate on discovering Pat Simmons's rapist and then they could receive additional evidence.

He would take over the Thrush problem! He thought back to the funeral. It had been a dismal affair and he and the two women had gone only out of a certain feeling of duty or responsibility. The man had worked for them, after all. He had not expected to see the Smiths there, but had been surprised that Sandy at least had not attended. But young people – he thought of Sandy as young – disliked funerals, and Sandy probably suspected that Thrush might have got someone to write that nasty letter to Number 4 – or have written it himself. If he had written it himself, it proved there were two anonymous poison pens in the area.

Susan Swann had not attended the crematorium either; she had been teaching. The Whitwhams had been suffering from heavy colds, and the others had made no excuses. Pat Dawson would not put himself out for anyone he hardly knew; though he obviously put himself out a good deal for his new lady-love. Cobb felt that Mrs Maitland had gone just to prove to herself she was overcoming her agoraphobia and that she could go out without Pat Dawson. She now ventured out in a taxi with her lover to shop in Eastminster.

Cobb had been glad when the extremely short service was over. It had been embarrassing. There had been the owner of the marina, one Hammond, but no one from Spire. Funny, he had always imagined that Thrush had once been a Spire man, though nobody in the village seemed to think so. Perhaps all his relatives were dead. He hadn't been married, had no children, and had lived in that awful shack near Spire Creek with not even a dog to keep him company.

There had been no **For Sale** board in the garden when he had cycled past for a look; he assumed that Percy Thrush had died intestate, but perhaps he had not owned the land, just had a long lease on it that would end at his death. Developers would be interested. Cobb was aware of how the price of land was rising in the whole of the old Hundred. He thought he might eventually check that no will had been registered. He wasn't going to ask George Graham for any more information. Did anyone know *anything* about Thrush? Anyone at all? Except perhaps for the writer of this morning's letter?

CHAPTER ELEVEN

'Did you see her then?'

Lisa was waiting for her husband. He swept into the house without an answer. She followed him back into the kitchen.

'Shall I make you a cup of coffee?'

'Don't fuss me, Lisa.'

He didn't seem angry really, more preoccupied, and for this she was grateful.

'Get to bed,' he said shortly. 'I'll be up later.'

She crept upstairs. If only she knew what was going on. Tone never told her anything unless it was to shout at her and tell her it was all her fault. Sometimes she wished she were dead. At least he was not in a bad mood tonight. She undressed and went to bed, but she did not sleep for some time. When at last she did, it was an hour before he joined her and he too lay wakeful.

The following afternoon Linda Swift was given a lift by Susan back from the school to Spire as she had missed the school bus which went as far as the village. Lisa had not needed a lift that afternoon as her husband was meeting her on his way back from the garden centre and they were to have a meal at the only decent restaurant up the coast.

School had been tiring. It always was, but usually Susan could cast off the sensation of accumulated fiddly jobs and obligations once she had left the place, though she planned, and marked, and read round her work in the evenings. It was administrative chaos that irked her, as well as the constant noise and clatter. She was expected to produce a play in the middle of it all! No extra money for all her labours. They assumed she produced plays from a hat like a conjuror, in the same way as the English teacher conjured a magazine of creative writing and managed the library, as well as following a full timetable. They all tried to do too much. The reward was, just occasionally, girls like Linda Swift who wanted to work, had interests in things other than money, make-up, boyfriends and pop music, and who blossomed with good teaching.

Oh dear, she knew she was beginning to think like a middle-aged spinster. Linda at her side, safely wrapped in a seat-belt – for Susan might be forgetful about locking her car, but never about safety – was saying how she had spent all the evening before practising her lines in the garden. She was to be Olivia and was thrilled.

'I suppose it's unusual still to do Shakespeare,' said Susan. 'It'll probably be the last. They want something everyone can join in – a rock opera or a dance display. Mr Johnson and Miss Walpole can do that. It'll be my turn for a rest.'

'Well, you're using music and dance for *Twelfth Night*,' Linda pointed out. 'There must be half the upper school doing something – with all the lighting and the costumes and all.'

Susan knew that was true, but it still left the other half doing nothing: the half who couldn't be bothered. Why should they bother? It was only that the ethos of the school demanded one hundred per cent participation. She often thought she would be less exhausted teaching in an old-fashioned private school, even if it had fewer resources than Eastminster High, which owned a stage and changing-rooms and a swimming-pool. Its library, however, was not impressive.

The school was built in a ghastly Sixties style that gave Susan a headache, concrete in her opinion not being suitable material for the English climate. When it rained, the walls went a dirty stained brown, and when it was sunny the large windows were suntraps so that blinds had to be drawn half the time, and they were always breaking.

She sighed again, and Linda, thinking she was still worried about the play, said sympathetically:

'It'll be fine – everyone's very keen.'

'How did you like the old book of birds?' asked Susan.

'Oh – lovely!'

'Miss Kant has heaps of beautiful books,' said Susan.

'I decided to copy one or two of the etchings, then I can compare later if I ever see a greylag or whatever – they're better than photographs. I should think Mr Robson or Mr Fairbairn would like to see it. It's very rare, isn't it? I was scared I might drop something on it or accidentally put something on it, so I wrapped it up and put it under my bed. I keep all my treasures there away from our Steve.'

Our Steve was the last and very tardy addition to the Swift family. He was three, and a menace. Sometimes he had accompanied his mother when she cleaned in the close and the inhabitants had been glad when a nursery playgroup was instituted three mornings a week in Bardwell.

'Have you heard anything new about that Kevin, miss?' asked Linda. 'I mean Miss Swann,' she added, blushing.

'He was cautioned for stealing from his father – that's not official, so don't spread it.'

'He wasn't the one who attacked me,' said Linda. She seemed absolutely certain.

'Have you still *no* idea?' asked Susan after a pause.

'Well, I've thought and thought and I still don't know, but till I know I can't get it out of my head – know what I mean?'

'Yes, I do know what you mean,' replied Susan with a grimace.

'I had an idea – but it was only an idea and if I was wrong it would be awful, wouldn't it?'

Susan waited.

'I wondered if it could have been Mr Thrush after all. It was something my grandpa said once.'

'Your *grandfather*?'

'Yes. I wasn't paying much attention, but you know how things come back to you later – I've got a good memory. Of course he's dead now so I can't ask him. I don't think Mum or Dad know anything about it 'cos they didn't live in Spire when they were little. Grandpa moved away from here before they were born and went to live in Eastminster, and my parents came back later, you see. It was something about what could have been Percy Thrush's *father*. I mean, my granddad *did* live here in Spire when he was a boy growing up in the nineteen twenties. How old do you think Percy Thrush was?'

'I'm not sure. Dorothea or someone said he may have looked younger than he was. Well over sixty, I'd think.'

'So he'd be born before the war. Granddad was still here then.'

'But you said it was about Percy Thrush's *father* he said something. Your grandfather would be an adolescent when Percy was a little boy, if he did live here.'

'Yes, I calculate Granddad would be fifteen or more years older than Mr Thrush. It would be Granddad's parents who would know Thrush's family. Nobody else in the village seems to remember him, but you see the very old people go to the home in Pilling. My mother says an old woman used to live in that old shack Percy Thrush was living in. She died a few years ago.'

'What exactly did your grandfather say?' asked Susan patiently. Linda always told a story very methodically and there was no hurrying her.

'I'm trying to remember. He died a few years ago when I was about eleven. He was in his late seventies. We weren't allowed to go to the funeral and I saw the grave afterwards, not here – in Eastminster. Mum and Dad came back to Spire after that 'cos there was a council house. Mum doesn't remember any Thrushes there *then*.'

'What exactly did he say?' They were driving now up to the village street past the church. Spire was a straggling place, a one-time one-horse village with little cottages on each side of the road and a clump of council houses up the lane that went towards Bardwell in the other direction from Spickhanger.

'You can drop me here, Miss Swann,' Linda said as Susan slowed down. 'He said something like this: "There was a family I once knew – a bad lot they were – the kids were lousy – wasn't their fault at all. Their dad was always inside – and when he was out he used to beat them something dreadful. Little Perce I can remember – often wonder what became of him after he moved way. They lived in an old shack off the Wickenden Lane up from Spire – we used to call them the Cuckoos 'cos they built in other people's nests!" And he laughed.'

'But he didn't say they were called Thrush?' asked Susan.

'No, but I remembered later that our Thrush was called Percy, and there can't be all that many children called Percy, can there.'

Susan stopped the car before they came to the signpost and she must turn to go down Spickhanger Lane.

'I believe it was quite a usual name in those days, but a bit old-fashioned even then. Why did you think that he must have been talking about Percy Thrush?'

'Well, I didn't *then*. I didn't even think about what he'd said at all except about the Cuckoos. It was only last week that I remembered what he'd said about the shack and then I remembered that last spring I was out bird-watching and heard the first cuckoo. I was sitting on a gate listening and Mr Thrush passed and he said "Hello", and I just said: "Did you hear the first cuckoo?" and he stared at me so strangely – as though he wanted to say something. It made me squirm. But he went on past me. I suppose he was walking to Spickhanger. It was just a feeling I had – that perhaps "Cuckoo" was what they called him as a child. So Granddad might have been talking about his family, mightn't he?'

'It sounds a bit involved to me, Linda,' replied Susan, thinking, if Linda had said something that annoyed him he might have wanted to get his own back by frightening her in the barn. 'I mean, are you sure there aren't lots of families still in the village who would remember him?' she went on, aloud. 'All those Finches and Pheasants – surely there must be plenty of old inhabitants who would tell you if it were true about the Thrush family.'

'But that's just it! People think that the old families just go on living here till they die – that with all the bird names around they've been here for generations. But you know they *don't*. Those who do live a long time go to live with their children away somewhere else or they give up their cottage for development or, as I told you, they go into the old people's homes. There's no one really old left. But the younger ones sometimes come back if they can get housed. Even where we are,' she gestured towards the council houses, 'they're all young families – younger than Mum and Dad – and all those cottages we just passed in the car – they're all owned by "incomers". I can't find anything at all about Percy Thrush, though I've tried.'

'Perhaps they didn't like the family and don't want anything to do with them.'

'Yes, but when I was attacked – not then, but a week or two later, I remembered about the way Mr Thrush had looked at me when I mentioned the cuckoos, and suddenly it came to me that it might have been him getting his own back on me for something. He might have thought I was taking the mickey or something? It sounded daft so I didn't say anything.'

Susan felt excited.

'But you've absolutely no proof?'

'No, none at all. I expect it's just my imagination.'

'Well, if it was him, he's dead now, so you needn't worry any more.'

'I know, but it was the *way* Grandad talked about little Perce and I had the impression he was ill-treated or something – his sister and brother too – I'm not sure. Grandma was alive then and she shut him up. Perhaps he was going to say something she thought was not suitable for my ears. She died last year, so I can't ask her either.'

'Wouldn't your mother know anything?'

'I've asked her again and again but she says she knows nothing about the old days in Spire. She never listened to Granddad's stories anyway. *I* like stories about the olden days – it's not so long ago, is it.'

'No, only sixty or seventy years or so. I expect the place was pretty poor then.'

When Linda had gone, Susan sat for moment thinking before she started the car up. It was true that nobody seemed to know anything at all about Percy Thrush. The only link with the past was the disreputable old shanty – and perhaps the memories of a generation now in their eighties or older who might remember his parents. Might it be possible to visit the old people's home? But what excuse could she give? It was none of her business. The idea had probably occurred to Linda too.

There was one very nicely kept home about three miles inland where the surviving 'Spirants' sometimes went to spend their last days. There might be someone there. Still, Thrush was dead and it had been accidental death on the coroner's report – she had read it in the paper. If he *had* been Linda's attacker, he might also have attacked other people. Funny, he'd looked such a nondescript, unmemorable sort of man, muscular but pasty-faced. Not what you'd expect from an outdoor life. She might mention it to Dorothea, who knew so much about local history and legends, though this was hardly a legend.

She decided not to take the Spire Lane turning, but to drive along past the hill with the church at the top and to take the sandy path down to the beach a mile or so further on, where Thrush had lived. Sheer curiosity. Of course it would have been quicker to go there from the fields but you couldn't take a car that way. It was bad enough here, though there were ruts made by a lorry or something big.

She was surprised to find when she got out of the car opposite Thrush's shack that the land was being cleared on one side of it and there was a billboard bearing the words **Site for Development**. In her mind's eye she saw them already rising like mushrooms, or rather toadstools, where there had been nothing but mud and marram grass. She walked past the shack, which was set a little way in from the lane and stared for a moment at the door, which was padlocked, and at the tin roof and pile of rubbish waiting for collection. Someone had been round, probably the police. The window was boarded up. It looked as though no one had lived here for fifty years, yet Percy Thrush had!

She did not open the gate, but made a note of the telephone number of the house agents in case she might find something out from them. The scrubby land round the shack would be earmarked for development, she felt sure. She got back in the car. Then she saw a workman piling up rubbish at the side of the shack, so she put the car into gear and drew away quickly. There was a queer air of desolation around the place that new buildings would do little to alleviate. She felt depressed, would be glad to get home. She'd mention the story to Dorothea. They ought to discover who possible developers might be in the future.

Dorothea was out when she got back, and the matter was to slip Susan's mind for some days, preoccupied as she was with *Twelfth Night*.

That afternoon Dorothea was once more at her Mecca, the Family Record Centre. She had collected the marriage certificate that had interested her. Nothing of great interest to be seen there at first:

Anthony John Smith: bachelor aged 27. Occupation: Nurseryman. Father: John Smith of East Ham, deceased.

Lisa Mary Landon: aged 20, spinster, daughter of Ronald R Landon of Wanstead, deceased, market porter. Witnesses: J Thorpe and Anne Hunter.

The only item of interest was that neither of the witnesses was apparently a member of either family. But Lisa, being over eighteen, would not have needed to have permission to marry. Maybe her mother had objected to the marriage for some reason. Also the wedding had been at the town hall, Wanstead, not in a church, and Dorothea considered this for some time. Of course, more and more people had been getting married at registry offices for some time. Still, Lisa seemed just the sort of young woman who would have wanted a white wedding with all the trimmings.

Neither of them had, of course, been married before. There would hardly have been time for Lisa to have been married before, but Dorothea had earlier wondered whether Tony Smith, with his obvious interest in women, might have been married at some juvenile age, a shotgun wedding, perhaps?

She folded the copy of the marriage certificate and put it in the zip-up compartment of her capacious handbag. Now to find more about Anthony Smith, now that she knew from the marriage certificate the year within which he must have been born: 1965 or 1966. The wedding had been on 12 June 1993 and he had been twenty-seven so he must have been born between 13 June 1965 and 11 June 1966. She went back into the search room and applied herself to the indexes, finding a seat before she went to the registers necessary to establish his date of birth. Soon she discovered he was born on 17 November 1965, which made sense. Still in East Ham. She wondered when his father had died, but to search all the registers for the years before 1993 for a John Smith in East Ham was rather out of the question. Why did she want to know anyway? She could look for his parents' marriage, probably in the early 1960s, but there didn't seem much point.

As she was there among the births, she decided she might as well look up Lisa Mary Landon around 1973.

Fortunately there were fewer of them than Smiths. People did sometimes marry on their birthdays. She had checked with her date calculator and 12 June 1993 was a Saturday, as she had thought. It was always possible that Lisa had married around her twenty-first birthday. She searched all the indexes from 14 June 1973 to 12 June 1974. Nothing. Strange. Still, people did sometimes register late and she went forward and consulted the September quarter as well. Still nothing.

Puzzled, she wondered whether Lisa had perhaps been born abroad. There would be no indication of that, of course, on her marriage certificate if she were a British subject. The certificate stated only where the bride was resident, didn't it. No – she looked again at the marriage certificate. Place of birth was quite clearly stated as Wanstead, Essex. Perhaps Lisa Mary Landon was under age, only sixteen or seventeen, when she married and the information on the certificate was false.

She became thoughtful. Once more she consulted the files, this time going both forwards and a little backwards in time. Perhaps Lisa was *older* than she looked – but why pretend to be younger on your marriage certificate? It didn't make sense. She worked away, her eyes smarting a little with all the print. Someone else wanted her place; she had been here long enough.

She was frowning once more over the birth indexes for East Ham, thinking of returning to Smiths, when Cobb noticed her. He had come in a little later and been absorbed also by a computer file, much further back in time, and then he had begun to scribble in his notebook. Then he had put that away and looked around – and seen his neighbour on the further side of the room. She looked puzzled.

He wondered whether to make himself known, but decided against it. He hugged the piece of information that he had discovered to himself. Miss Kant was probably doing some family history researches. He had often discussed that sort of research with her. She would not want to be interrupted. The room was full of keen family historians – some of them brute beginners, who had only just begun their searches and were usually accompanied by husbands or wives to whom they would give delighted squeals of discovery, or gloomily ponder the lack of anything pertaining to their grandfather. Others were professional researchers who accomplished their work swiftly and departed to more difficult assignments.

Cobb decided to go to the National Portrait Gallery before returning home. He needed a change.

Dorothea, on the other hand, had already passed into the room where one applied for certificates. She wrote another cheque for the new copy she had requested. Almost another week to wait, unless she could get away in two days, or paid for an express item. Two visits to London in a week – a nuisance, but possibly necessary. An unusual story was forming in her mind and one, which, if it were true, might help at least one unhappy soul.

Lisa Smith was sleeping worse and worse, in fact hardly sleeping at all, and was going to plead a headache when her husband got into bed with her that night. But Tony was preoccupied too, turned on his side and was soon snoring away.

Did she still love him a little? Where was it all leading her? She had not really looked ahead at first. Tony had always been so masterful. Recently, though, he seemed to have become more and more irritable. Perhaps he didn't love her any more. But if he didn't, what was she doing here? She thought of old friends whom they never saw now, even thought of her parents who had both died when the plane had crashed on the way to the Costa Brava. She had been so lonely afterwards, though Tony had taken her under his wing.

There had been a piece in the local paper about the tragedy. It seemed so long, long ago. She tried to think of something more cheerful, but could not think of anything. She thought of school where that nice Bob McAlister, the physical education teacher, would come into the office and talk. She thought of Susan Swann, with her chat about women's rights, which didn't make much sense to her really, for men would never change, would they, and you were lucky if you had someone to look after you.

Tone had said about Susan: 'We don't want that sort of woman around here – filling your mind with rubbish.' But Susan was nice and kind – and she didn't hate men. She had confided that she had had a boyfriend, well a man friend, she supposed, but they had quarrelled. Lisa couldn't understand why, and now Susan was alone working at her career. Lisa was glad *she* wasn't a teacher. They had an awful time on the whole, though they tried to keep cheerful. Some of the boys were dreadful and some of the girls not much better. She liked her work in the office where people seemed to accept her.

Now once more there was all the trouble over Brenda. Tony wouldn't say much except: 'She'll go too far one day,' and that made her frightened. She knew he had been to see her again last week in London. Lisa turned over carefully, so as not to disturb Tony if he were in a wakeful patch. She herself slept so lightly. What was there to live for really?

Two tears ran down her cheeks and she sniffed them away. She had got over crying long ago, surely. She often wished she could go to sleep for ever and ever. It would save all the worry and the fear, both of which were her constant companions, wherever she went, whatever she did.

CHAPTER TWELVE

The weather changed for the worse before the last meeting of the sailing club and suddenly it was almost wintry. The boat-owners had arrived late on Friday afternoon and parked their cars in the field behind the sailing club. These were the long-distance addicts; others from nearer at hand arrived early on the Saturday morning. By then it was, of course, raining, with that peculiar insistence of English rain, and specifically East Anglian rain, which tries to reduce land to sea as quickly as possible. It was not actually freezing, and the wind, although strong, was not too strong for the experienced sailors who were already racing across to the other side of the estuary by breakfast time on Saturday. There were several motorized speedboats too, chugging away.

Dorothea decided to go for a stroll to look at the boats, and found, once she had reached the hard, that another Heron Closer was already taking a constitutional. Jim Cobb had walked round from the beach end on the top of the sea-wall whilst she had come the long way round by the field of campers and the clubhouse.

The clubhouse was full. There seemed to be more spectators than sailors congregated on the first floor and looking out at the island, binoculars in hand. Several children were running about shouting. Their fathers all looked the sort who enjoyed uncomfortable sports, in which Dorothea included standing around on beaches looking at specks of boats. 'Scott! Gary! Samantha!' rang in the air from their mothers who had nipped into the clubhouse to warm themselves up and who kept popping out on the first-floor balcony to check that their offspring had not been spirited away by the wind and rain.

Several little dinghies were bobbing up and down a hundred or so yards from the shore and in the far distance a brown-sailed Thames barge, now used as a pleasure-craft, could be seen moving in a stately way, soon to be laid up across the estuary for winter.

Occasionally, some people would get into the dinghies, only to capsize.

Owners of much larger boats did not often come to Spickhanger, preferring a more up-to-date yacht marina that could cater for them. It might therefore appear that this expanse of water was for the amateur, but it could be quite dangerous around the northern point of the island. Dorothea counted at least eighty other boats, mostly white-sailed and mostly with only one mast, although there were one or two with a jib and following dinghy. There was a red-and-black striped sail, a green one, and a cluster of bright laundry-bag blue, with one or two of orange and yellow, already a long way away out across the estuary and she realized that the race must have begun. As she could never tell in such contests who had won, who had lost, or whether indeed anyone had won or lost or just disappeared, she thought she had done her bit and had enough fresh air for the day.

It had almost stopped raining but more wind had blown up. Rather bored, she was halfway back home when she saw Cobb being approached by both Sandy and David, who had stopped their car on the lane for a chat, on the way home from their Saturday shopping. They were evidently not intending to get out and walk across to the hard.

'Aren't you going over to come and look at the boats?' she shouted.

They did not reply till she came up to them.

'I'm afraid we're *persona non grata* at the marina, or whatever is the correct plural,' said David. 'Ever since little Kevin and his mates were found to be playing around here, we have been politely warned off. The "sailors" have heard we have the plague.'

He sounded very bitter and at first she did not understand what he was talking about.

'Sandy and Dave had a nasty letter some time ago,' said Cobb, his eyes on her.

'You mean . . . ?'

'That we were responsible for Kevin, for whatever is wrong with him – nothing much, I don't think, except for injudicious sniffing of coke. We don't do that, but we might have done something worse: entice Kevin on to the paths of unrighteousness.'

'The letter mentioned HIV positive,' said Cobb shortly.

'Kevin is?'

'No, I'm sure not. But certain citizens thought it their duty when

140

we were down here last week to warn us off. They didn't want their children catching anything, was what they said.'

'That's preposterous. Who could have spread such a thing?'

'Whoever wrote the letter we had,' said Dave. 'There must have been some common misapprehension in process of fomentation.'

'Why not ask Kevin?' said Dorothea.

'The clubhouse is out of bounds to him,' said Cobb, 'since he was charged with raiding the till. Also he's on bail, and lying low.'

'What has been happening?' asked Dorothea. 'I'm all at sea. Have they found the other man, then?'

'It was in the paper this morning – the local one. One of Kevin's mates, a certain Darren Bogworthy, has been located and brought in. He is suspected of the rape of Patricia Simmons.'

Dorothea caught her breath. 'They don't connect Kevin with that?'

'People like Kevin will all be tarred with the same brush,' said Sandy. 'If they accept *we* didn't attack poor Mrs Simmons, we'll soon be drug-pushers instead. It's all very unpleasant.'

'But you and David had nothing to do with Kevin or his friends or with drugs or Mrs Simmons. It's absurd. This can't be all that recent. Whoever spread rumours must have started them long ago. *Did* you know Kevin?'

'No, we did not, except to pass the time of day when we went for a walk sometimes. We weren't even sure of his name.'

'Well, thank goodness they've found the rapist,' said Dorothea. 'I suppose Kevin shopped his friends about the drugs?'

'You'll read all about it in a few months when they find his other friend, and one of them – or both – go on trial,' said Cobb. 'Why not all come in for a chat when you've stowed your shopping away,' he said to the men and smiled at Miss Kant, including her in the invitation.

'We all ought to feel safer now,' said Dorothea, 'if they've got one of the men and the other is on the run.'

'And Kevin won't be darkening the clubhouse with his presence any more,' said Cobb.

'Yes, I'd love to come,' replied Dorothea. 'Thank you.'

'Count us in too,' said Sandy.

Dorothea and Cobb were sitting in his comfortable chairs waiting for the two men to unpack their Waitrose items and come over.

'Kevin is gay,' said Cobb, 'as you have probably guessed.'

'Is that enough for Sandy and Dave to be accused of being HIV positive – never mind pushing drugs and raping women? I don't think David or Sandy do more than smoke pot – if that.'

'Whether Kevin took drugs is immaterial. He is gay and he was a mate of a man who may be a rapist. Dave and Sandy are gay and may have said "Hello" to Kevin, *so* – Dave and Sandy could be rapists and not safe for your children to meet,' riposted Cobb.

'Really? Is that how people's minds work? How ridiculous!'

'That's how it is. The letter they showed me some time ago was really nasty. I've a good idea who wrote it, though, and who was behind the writing of it.'

'But you're not saying,' replied Dorothea. 'I think anonymous letters which try to put the blame on the innocent are almost as bad as people who are violent towards others, don't you?'

'We ought to ask Susan round too,' said Cobb, after giving a sigh, which might have meant he agreed with her or might not.

'I was talking to Bill Whitwham last night. We've found someone, by the way, to do the gardening, but he doesn't want to work at the marina, because of the druggy reputation.'

'Have they actually caught a *smuggler* at the sailing-club then? Is that what this Darren youth is? Were other people in it too?' asked Dorothea.

'Oh, I don't think that the place is very important. What I should think happened is that something went wrong at the larger dumping ground on the other side of the estuary up the coast and the boat may have come in here to investigate a possible courier. The skipper met Kevin and his friends and thereby found another small outlet. The police will be looking for bigger fish. It'll all come out in the wash – or the Wash!'

She winced at his pun, then went to the window and opened it and waved to Susan, who was out in the close in front of their house next door, locking her car for once.

'We're in here. Come for a chat,' she called. She turned to Cobb. 'What do the fear of Aids and the persecution of gays, have to do with the rape of that poor woman on the lane – or even with Linda's attacker?' she asked.

'Thrush interests you?' asked Cobb in reply, handing her a vermouth and bitter lemon, which he knew she liked. He was amassing quite a stock of drinks for neighbours. He sipped at his own lemon.

'Yes, Thrush – and that robe – yes, he does. And why Tony Smith treats his wife so badly and she puts up with it. And why *you* are interested in it all too.'

'I saw you the other day at the Family Record Centre,' said Cobb.

'Did you? I didn't see you! I was busy doing a bit of research. I didn't know you had already started on family history.'

'I'm interested in the past,' said Cobb.

'You seem to take an interest in many things,' she said, smiling. 'Personally, I think we could unravel most mysteries if we understood character.'

'At bottom, it's always the old sins. In modern dress, of course.'

'If I were David Fairbairn, I'd be very angry,' she said, and then changed the subject as the men came up the path.

Susan joined them and Dorothea wondered if Cobb were going to reveal anything further. The information that the robe had been found in the men's tool-shed had eventually leaked out. Cobb had evidently had their permission to mention both items, for she saw a look pass between the men when Cobb said:

'Well, are you any further forward with a theory as to your hidden enemy? Now that it appears Bogworthy has been apprehended, not to mention Kevin Black being still suspected for possession of drugs and drug-pushing, it looks as though you might be able to ask them a few questions – and their pal Wayne, who is still missing. I don't doubt he'll turn up eventually.'

'I hardly think any of *them* was responsible for the little present in the tool-shed,' said David to Cobb. 'Or the little missive we received. You know who I think did that – and Sandy agrees.'

'And by the time this Bogworthy is actually sentenced – knowing how long people spend on remand nowadays – they'll have forgotten. The letter, of course, may be another matter.'

'Bogworthy – what a name! No wonder he may have turned to crime!' said Susan.

'If a rumour was going round the marina, it must have been started by someone,' said Dorothea. 'Kevin would be the ideal person to prevail upon if some nasty-minded person wanted a rumour started – but I don't know what your letter said.'

'Take it as read,' said Sandy. 'The police have it now. I'm sure you can imagine it.'

'Perhaps Kevin knew nothing about it?' she suggested.

Susan was looking from one to the other in puzzlement.

'Too many different things have happened – too many loose ends!' she said.

'Don't you think that if your suspicions are the same as mine,' said Cobb to David, pursuing the letter, 'that our deceased friend Thrush might have had something to do with it? After all, he was familiar with Kevin, and also worked here, so he could have been worked upon by the person you are thinking of.'

'This is all Greek to me,' said Dorothea. 'Does it mean there might be an additional reason for supposing Mr Thrush was found dead on the beach?'

'Well, what do you think of this?' said Cobb. He went to his bookshelf, extracted a book and slid out a piece of paper. He put his glasses on and read aloud as if it were written in prose: 'Percy Thrush did not fall. He was pushed. 'Tis a pity years ago he was not ducked.'

'Well, well,' said Sandy. 'Who on earth wrote that?'

'Someone who wants me to pursue enquiries,' said Cobb, biting his pipe.

'Probably for a nasty reason – or just to make trouble,' suggested Susan.

'You mean that if the person you are thinking of is Tony Smith – which I presume you are – he might have also written that, as well as the letter to Dave and Sandy?' asked Dorothea. 'But why?'

'Have you any ideas?' asked Cobb.

'What do we know about Smith? I must admit I do feel there's something fishy about him.'

She was not going to reveal all her own Smith researches yet, but went on: 'I suspect Smith of worse things than giving a push to Thrush – if anyone did.'

Cobb took out his tobacco tamper and busied himself poking out pieces of burnt tobacco into a large ashtray. 'Suspicions are not enough,' said David wryly.

'I *can* see him writing nasty letters to you two,' said Susan. 'He is not a very nice man. Poor Lisa is always so miserable. I don't know how a girl would want to marry such an unpleasant specimen.'

'I suppose this is just gossip,' said Sandy, 'so doesn't count, but I must admit that when the letter came, Dave's and my own thoughts immediately leapt to him. And when we discovered the robe lying in our tool-shed . . .'

'But what was it *for*?' asked Dorothea. 'I can see why he might spread rumours about you – though that would be difficult to prove. And I can see why he might want you to be worried, but surely if you hadn't pushed old Thrush or attacked Linda – both highly unlikely – so long as you told no one about the robe or the letter, no one could do anything anyway? It just looks like a rather senseless practical joke.'

'Yes – that part of it,' agreed David. 'But the stories about us are much worse – slander really, aren't they.'

'Yes, they would be actionable,' said Cobb.

'And he must have just wanted to go on being unpleasant. He knows Sandy often goes out at night to photograph, and that he walks early in the morning on the beach, so if he did do anything to Thrush there'd be a double reason for incriminating someone else – put the suspicion on to others and—'

'Yes, but that's not logical,' said Dorothea. 'It would only make you want to know who had actually attacked Linda wearing that silly gown, or who might have been out when you were at night. I think he just didn't think – if he is the one. I don't suppose he's very bright.'

'And all it's made us do is rally round you two,' said Susan. 'But if he *did* push Thrush, why call attention to it with a letter?'

'Just to tantalize?' suggested Cobb.

'Oh, I think the whole thing is too far-fetched,' said Susan. 'Granted he might spread rumours, granted he might just want to put the wind up you – it's all for nothing, since we know you were both at your party every minute of that evening when Linda was attacked. By the way,' she added, 'I didn't have time to tell you, Dorothea, but Linda thinks she remembers something rather funny-peculiar that her old grandpa once said about a family in Spire, and she thinks he may have meant old Thrush's family!'

They all looked at her questioningly.

'She remembers his saying something about a family who used, when he was a young man, to live in a cabin or chalet or something. That could be the one where Thrush ended up. Something about his father.'

Cobb looked alert now.

'She says there was a family the children used to call "cuckoos" and that once last year she quite innocently said to Thrush that she was listening to the first cuckoo and he looked at her strangely. She wondered whether he thought she was taking the mickey out of him and that was the reason for the attack on her.'

'My goodness!' said Miss Kant. 'Things get even more complicated.'

'But just imagine if he did attack her – and if her father knew –
and revenged himself on him by pushing him over on to the boulder!'

'Well, we shall never know. Personally I was sorry for the old
bastard, but we'd nothing else against him, had we?' said Sandy.

Cobb was looking from one to the other stroking his chin. 'Did
you hear an oyster boat at about midnight the evening before you
discovered Thrush?' he began, turning to Sandy.

'Yes, what of it?'

'I don't think it was the oyster man. I think it was the little boat
that had intended to go to the marina and for some reason did not
land there. Perhaps they expected Darren or his mate to be there
to receive and he wasn't.'

'He must have vamoosed after taking fright if he was the one to
attack Mrs Simmons,' said Susan.

'Well, I think Thrush may have known about the drugs, though
they weren't his line,' Cobb went on. 'Sandy, I think you nearly
discovered the drug-dealers. I wonder what they thought when
you took a flash photo? Probably thought they'd been rumbled.'

'Is nowhere safe?' asked David dramatically. 'Soon I shan't
believe anything that goes on here has an innocent explanation.'

'Even Mr Whitwham and his letters to the papers,' said Cobb.
'Or Mrs Maitland, she-who-hardly-ever-goes-out.'

'Oh, she's going out a lot more now since the funeral,' said
Dorothea. 'She's getting quite adventurous. Pat Dawson's done her
good.'

'His good deed for a lifetime,' said Sandy.

'I worry more about Lisa,' said Susan. 'I'm sure there's something wrong with her or with Tony. Or with them both.'

'Possibly nothing is what it seems,' said Miss Kant, gathering up
her handbag to depart.

'Soon I shall start to suspect *everyone*,' said David.

' "Guilty creatures sitting at a play".' quoted Susan.

'Hamlet,' said Miss Kant, and rose to go.

'I'll come along with you now,' said Susan. 'Thank you, Mr
Cobb, I did enjoy the drink. I'll tell you if Linda remembers
anything else.'

'It's not likely she will,' she said to Miss Kant as they went in
next door, 'I really am more worried about Lisa Smith than Linda.'

Sandy and David took their leave soon afterwards.

'It seems a pity to worry more about what people think of us than about poor old Thrush,' said Sandy as he left, 'but we feel sure Smith had something to do with the gown *and* the letters.'

When they had all gone, Cobb sat quietly for a full twenty minutes trying to sort things out to his satisfaction. Later that afternoon he decided to take another walk on the beach with the intention of visiting the marina once more. The wind had whipped the waves up to a minor frenzy and the foreshore was almost deserted. Where the sailing boats were was anyone's guess. He had no idea whether they were supposed to return to base or whether some of the crowd was waiting on the distant island opposite to cheer them on or time their arrival.

Cobb decided he knew nothing about boats and was determined to remain in ignorance. He had been a mountain climber in his youth and preferred to holiday in Austria where he could go for long walks; he felt no longer nimble enough, alas, to dare anything very hazardous, though he wasn't in bad shape for his age.

Edna had never accompanied him, pleading a fear of heights. He thought of her tenderly. She would have liked this low-lying land. He found it tame, and wondered, for the hundredth time, why he had decided to settle here. He reviewed the morning's conversation once more and wished he could talk to Tony Smith. If the chap really had slandered the fellows at Number 4 so as to make their lives miserable, and prevent them enjoying ordinary pleasures, like watching boats from the hard, it was a serious matter. Could he take the bull by the horns?

He took up a flat stone and skimmed it, but the water was too disturbed. He thought again about ducks and drakes and about Susan's report of Linda's grandfather's remarks. He ought to have a word with Mrs Maitland and her paramour too. They might know more than they were saying.

But what exactly was he investigating? Was it *only* an old copper's inability to resist mystery? He was relieved that Darren Bogworthy had been apprehended – *if* he had been the perpetrator of the most serious crime, in his opinion, that had taken place at Spickhanger.

Anonymous letters, however unsavoury, were not in the same category as rape. Kevin must have told them it was not Wayne Spitt, who was still at large.

'Hi!'

He turned and saw the Whitwhams staggering along the pebbles in sou'westers and macs.

'Thought we'd come for a breather,' said Bill Whitwham. 'Sea air good for you too, I expect?'

Cobb made some innocuous comment. He would have to invite the couple in soon or they might think they were being discriminated against.

'Why not pop round for a coffee?' he said genially. 'I'd thought of asking Mr Dawson and Eve Maitland.' He almost said: *If you've nothing better to do* but stopped himself just in time.

'This evening?' asked Mrs Whitwham.

Perhaps he ought to have given them more notice.

'Yes, thank you,' she said. 'Bill often watches telly on a Saturday – but if it's just for half an hour or so?'

Her husband looked rather sheepish.

'It's a detective drama,' explained his wife. 'Bill likes them. They're always too quick for me, or completely incredible.'

Cobb changed the subject. 'Think the race must be over?' he asked. 'The weather's none too good.'

'The ones who made it within an hour to Westsea Island will come back to settle the winner – it's a time race,' explained Whitwham.

'Bill used to like sailing,' said Vera Whitwham. 'He wanted me to go when we were young, but I was no swimmer and was always sea-sick, too.'

'These things are all right when you're young,' said Bill. 'The bank had members in the old club over in Mardon.' He gestured across the estuary.

'I like the look of the barges,' offered Vera. 'More like real boats, aren't they?'

'I believe there are families living on some of them, and others are hired out to tourists,' said Cobb.

'Fancy wanting to *live* on one,' said Vera. 'Our son-in-law's a keen sailor. But of course now they've got a family he hasn't the time.'

'Women's Lib, you know,' said her husband.

Cobb said goodbye after the exchange of a few more commonplaces and walked back the long way by the field next to the marina. Several families were packing up.

The few remaining tents looked cold and uninviting. The

148

masochism of the active young, he thought, and then: by God, I wish I were young again!

On his way back, he knocked at Dawson's door, rightly surmising that if the two were in bed together it would be at the lady's residence. But they were both in at Dawson's and eating a cherry-cake, of which they offered a slice to Cobb, somewhat shame-facedly.

'Thanks – no – trying to get rid of the tum,' he replied.

'Would you both like to come round this evening for coffee?' he asked genially.

'Coffee would be excellent,' replied Dawson. 'My favourite drink.'

'You're very kind. We could just pop in for half an hour,' Mrs Maitland added.

Nobody seemed very keen to stay chatting for too long, he thought. They're all wondering what really happened to Linda and who wore the robe and who stole it and whether it really was the Bogworthy man who raped Mrs Simmons. Their little world has been turned topsy-turvy. Dave and Sandy's parties were always an event, but coffee with old Cobb was probably an ordeal, especially for someone like Dawson with his old life spent at BBC bars. But Mrs Maitland obviously enjoyed the occasion drink. He ought to buy a bottle of Chardonnay for the women, who all seemed to prefer dry white wine.

They came at eight o'clock as they had promised, and Cobb wheeled out his new coffee-pot and distributed the ginger biscuits he had bought at Eastminster Sainsbury's on the Thursday, the day he did his shopping. The wind was a faint moan in the distance now as they sat in the dusk.

'Isn't it peaceful,' said Mrs Whitwham.

'Yes, I always like October,' said Eva Maitland rather dreamily.

'Hope all the boats are back,' said Dawson more practically. 'By Monday there'll be no more sailing. It can be quite dangerous round the point.'

'I used to sail,' confessed Bill Whitwham to Pat Dawson. 'Used to like taking out the little ketch with the other lads at the bank. Long time ago now, of course.'

'The trouble is that at our age,' said Cobb, flattering Bill Whitwham, 'everything seems a long time ago. Did you ever know the old families round here?' he asked innocently. The question was a general one. Only Whitwham answered at first.

'Before the war, I was what they now call a teenager and we lived over in the Goldhunt area. Then I was in the Marines. Then after the war I came at first to Colchester when my parents died, and met Vera It was a different world then, though it's only fifty years ago. Of course, for a young chap at the time, banking was a very respectable occupation.' He looked round at the assembled company as if to challenge them. 'Not like now – chits of girls, hardly able to add up – everything done with calculators. Things changed a lot even before I retired. Got their calculators of course. Now it's borrow here and borrow there. Even the banks – above all the banks – encouraging debt! In my young days it was as much as your life was worth to run into an overdraft, even of a few bob.' He sighed.

There was a short respectful silence after this outburst. Then his wife spoke.

'I didn't know round here very well either,' she said. 'But we used to come near here for picnics when the children were little. There was no sailing-post then. Just the old coastguard's hut. The boats used to go up to Pebblehanger and in winter the whole place was shut up. Still, it was nice.'

She sighed as if remembering the times when others, not just her husband, had needed her. She smiled affectionately at him however.

'Bill left sailing and took up golf,' she said. 'I never thought I'd actually live here. I like it though. I don't mind the isolation. You can have too much of other folk.' She sipped her coffee, having delivered herself of her speech.

'I never knew Essex at all well,' said Pat Dawson. 'I'm a Londoner – Hammersmith. We always went abroad for holidays. France was my Mecca.' He smiled reminiscently as though remembering the vintages he had tasted. 'Of course, after working at the BBC, where work was always frantic, it's a relief to live in the country, though I'd have been as surprised as anyone if I'd been told there'd be a day when I'd had enough of London.'

Good heavens, thought Cobb, how expansive he was being! He must be feeling out of the wood at last. Or was it that he had got away with murder?

He decided to tackle Eva Maitland next.

'Were you a Londoner? Oh no, you come from Norwich, don't you,' he said, offering a biscuit to Dawson's girlfriend, though that seemed a rather silly appellation for a woman who was possibly in her mid-fifties. She was sipping decorously at her Vermouth.

'Yes. I really prefer Norfolk,' she said. 'Though round here is quite pretty. I was ill after my husband died. I'd had a job in a charity shop, but I gave it up to nurse him. I was used to never going out,' she added, before Cobb could say anything.

The coffee and the Vermouth and Cobb's friendliness seemed once more to have unlocked all their tongues. Eva Maitland looked much better than she had a month or two before. Her creamy skin was glowing now and the freckles on her face were intriguing rather than ugly.

'Thank goodness I'm a reader,' she said. 'There's always something to do when you like reading.'

Pat Dawson smiled benignly at her. He was clearly quite besotted. At his age! thought Cobb, and then suppressed the thought. Here was a man whom life had buffeted but who now appeared set for a happier existence. He envied them both.

'Did *you* know Spickhanger before you came here, Mr Cobb?' asked Vera Whitwham.

'No, I wandered round a bit looking for a place near the sea and not too far from London. Sussex was much dearer, and you couldn't get much for the sale of a house in the north at the time. They were still building here when I drove around. It looked suitably sited and I put my name down for a house.'

'You were the last to come,' said Mr Whitwham. 'We ourselves and Miss Kant were the first.'

'True. I can't make my mind up whether I shall stay, though. These events have rather unsettled me,' Cobb lied.

'But surely now that's all over as far as *here* is concerned?' said Dawson.

'I keep telling my wife – there is violence everywhere. Only today I saw in the paper . . .' Whitwham was off. Cobb rescued the conversation again by turning back to Mrs Maitland.

'Rural East Anglia has a low incidence of crime, if that's a comfort,' he said.

Mrs Maitland looked as though she had once had big problems, he thought. Had she been frightened of herself, or of rapists or murderers? He wondered about her background. But Pat Dawson answered for her.

'Yes, we both like East Anglia. You must be the first to know. Eva and I have become engaged to be married.'

Everyone looked suitably surprised and congratulated the

couple. Eva said they must come and celebrate at Number 6 another day. Then she and her intended both rose to go.

When the rest had departed, Cobb felt he had not been very successful in probing their pasts. All very innocuous. Indeed, apart from Tony and Lisa, the Heron Closers seemed on the whole a well-adjusted bunch. He went to bed and dreamed of some obscure vengeance that was hanging over the place: the monks perhaps, or revenge for unhappy childhoods, the flotsam of years that drifts always in the unconscious mind – and sometimes in the conscious.

CHAPTER THIRTEEN

The next two days were a little calmer – winter had retreated once again. The tearing north-west wind which they had thought might ruin the sailing club regatta – if it could be dignified by such a name – had dropped a little. Cobb was interested to see the name of the winner of the Saturday race pinned up outside the club-house. Perhaps he was the only one to have finished. He saw the treasurer, Black, fussing round, and beat a retreat, for he did not relish a meeting with Kevin's father.

The evening of the following Monday Susan gave Lisa her usual lift.

'Tony's going away Tuesday till the end of the week,' confided Lisa. Susan thought she sounded relieved, 'He says he's buying some stuff from a Norfolk nursery that's gone bust.'

When she arrived home there was a letter waiting for her in the porch. She picked it up, went into the kitchen and found a note on the table saying her landlady had gone to London and might not be back till late. It was touching, she thought, how Dorothea, who never interfered with her own private life, always let her know very considerately if she were to be out herself.

When she had climbed the stairs up to her room she poured herself a glass of the Chardonnay she kept for an occasional pre-supper aperitif, as a change from a late cup of tea, slipped off her shoes and lay down on the bed for a delicious five minutes of peace before she had to start thinking about making a meal and preparing tomorrow's lessons.

She looked idly at the envelope. The address was printed in block capitals. She opened it as she lay on the bed, feeling in every bone how satisfying it was to have a few moments to herself and nothing urgent to do. She had thought Richard might write to her, but he had not. He obviously considered their chapter closed. She, on the other hand, did miss him, and wondered whether she had been too determined to make herself clear. No, she had not! A few hours in his company and she would be irritated beyond belief by his assumptions that *his* career, *his* freedom were more important than hers.

She slit open the letter and extracted a sheet of cheap notepaper.

WE ALL KNOW WHAT YOU GET UP TO WITH LINDA SWIFT, it said in printed capitals. LEZZIES NEED HORSE-WHIPPING. WHAT DO YOU THINK YOUR HEAD WOULD SAY IF HE KNEW A PERVERT WAS IN CHARGE OF GIRLS?

At first she was incredulous, then she was angry. Linda Swift! Someone who had seen her give Linda a lift and stay talking to her, she supposed. Some twisted mind that equated feminism with perversion. Not that there weren't some lesbians in the feminist movement – why should there not be? But the accusations were so widely off the mark in her case that it was ludicrous. She was not even a very good feminist, whatever the word meant.

Then she remembered the letter that David and Sandy had admitted to receiving and was thoughtful. Who could have a down on her? It *must* be Tony Smith. Was he jealous that she and Lisa got on well and that she encouraged Lisa to stick up for herself? Lisa must have let slip something to him about her ideas.

But how could you prove it? Was it a libel to be called a lesbian if you weren't? To be accused of not being fit to be in charge of girls was something different. She lay fuming and the wine tasted bitter. Then she got up. If it were Tony Smith she'd like to wring his neck.

At Number 3 Lisa was getting a little supper ready for her husband. He liked it ready when he came in, though she was tired after work. He never thought of doing the shopping for them, or even setting the table. He had always been like that. His father had been the same, she remembered. She felt depressed, too tired for it to be just the result of a busy, but not wearing, day in the school office.

At least for the rest of the week she'd have the house to herself. She might start a bit of sewing on the machine. She never seemed to have time for herself when Tony was around. True, he had taken her out to dinner the other night, but it was more in the nature of *I'll do something you'd better be grateful for*, which gave him the moral edge when the next argument erupted.

The next argument was, in fact, not far away. When she heard his key in the door her pulse seemed to race and she ran into the kitchen to check that everything was ready: the chops grilled the way he liked them and a salad tossed with the correct proportions of oil and vinegar.

The meal began badly. Tony was obscurely angry about something, but she could not decide what. To think she had once loved and cherished this man, been as close to him as any human being could be, had followed him, done his bidding, become his slave. She tried to concentrate on eating and was silent. Perhaps if she said nothing he would leave her alone. But he was in a cross mood.

'Mind you come straight home tomorrow,' he said. 'Just because I've to go away doesn't mean you can hang around talking to your women friends. And I've left my washing in the laundry basket. There's some dry-cleaning I had to leave at Taylor's in Eastminster which you must collect.'

'Yes,' she replied. 'Yes, I will.'

'Did the Swann girl tell you what they were all gossiping about on Saturday at Cobb's, then? I saw them all come out. He had *two* groups round. Not us though. We're not good enough for Mr Bloody Cobb.'

'No, she didn't,' replied Lisa. 'I expect he'll be asking us round soon, but we never have anyone back. People don't go on inviting you if you don't.'

'Haven't noticed it,' said Tony. 'Those two pansies always ask us. And the others don't entertain either.'

'But *couples* entertain, don't they?' persisted Lisa bravely, 'I could do a nice little dinner party if you liked.'

'I told you – you don't seem to understand. Dinner parties where people start getting confidential are not what we need. We came down here to be quiet, not to spend our time fraternizing. And money's tight.'

She was silent for a moment, thinking: well then he ought to be pleased we weren't asked to go round to Mr Cobb's.

'I don't know why you didn't buy a house in the middle of a desert,' she said with more spirit than was usual with her. 'You don't want me to be friends with anyone.'

'It's because I love you,' he said with a look that made her feel quite powerless. 'We're enough for each other – always have been. I don't want you getting pally with all and sundry. It's bad enough you have to work and can't stay at home like a proper wife.'

'I don't want to stay at home!' she cried.

He looked at her amazed.

'Eat up your dinner,' he said. She had only picked at her chop. He leaned across the table and gripped her wrist. 'Now, now Lisa. You know we have to be careful. Brenda warned me – she said—'

'Yes – what did she say? You never told me.'

'We must be careful. Silly bitch. It's she who's careless. It would be a different story if I told on her, wouldn't it? She's getting greedy.'

'Brenda hasn't really done anything wrong,' said Lisa, dully.

'Accessory before the fact,' he replied.

She wasn't sure whether to believe him or not.

'Like a spell in prison, dear?' he said.

'You don't love me, Tone – not really *love* me. You just want me in your power,' she said in a quiet voice. She knew they had done wrong, but it had been for her sake. That was what he'd always said. Brenda should never have agreed to it at all. She said timidly:

'It would be you that went to prison, Tone. And anyway, I'm in prison here. It wouldn't make any difference to me.'

He looked at her, his eyes bulging.

'May I remind you that if I am guilty so are you. You have a nice house, a pleasant life, and you've got me.' But he looked also a little frightened. She had never seen him look frightened before. Instinctively she pressed her advantage.

'And what if I don't care any more? What if I tell them what you did with that robe? It was you who put it in Sandy Robson's tool-shed, wasn't it, Tone?'

'What robe?' he said with an attempt at bravado.

'You know what robe. Susan was telling me about it today. She heard Mr Robson found the thing the person was wearing who attacked that girl.'

'Oh – so you had an interesting conversation, did you? You weren't going to tell me about that, were you? And I suppose next thing you'll be saying I attacked the Swift girl. Well, I didn't. Nasty scrawny little thing. None of it's anything to do with me.'

'Why did you do it, Tone? Why did you put that thing in the shed? Aren't you in enough trouble without tempting fate?' She sounded wild, unlike herself, and he gaped at her for a moment.

'Just get it into your head that I had nothing to do with it,' he said again. 'I'm not denying I'd like to get rid of some of our neighbours. Perverts! Though that Robson's not above looking at *you*, too, in a way I object to. And that Cobb with his nasty suspicious mind – I know why he has his little get-togethers. All of 'em are against us—'

'Mr Cobb has nothing on you, I'm sure,' she said.

'And what about that Miss Kant? Another pervert if you ask me! Nosing round and talking to Brenda – what does *she* know about us? And your friend Susan,' he mimicked Susan's rather ringing tones, 'an inquisitive bitch if ever there was one. Well, she'll get her comeuppance. Already Robson and Fairbairn's names are dirt round here – I've seen to that. And so will yours be if you dare to mention your little suspicions to anyone.'

She knew he was bluffing, but she felt sick.

'Do you want your trifle?' she whispered.

'Certainly I do. And I want a promise from you. You do as you've always done. Keep yourself to yourself. Do as I say. Haven't I always looked after you?' He put his hand over her breast.

She could bear it no longer.

'You don't let me have a life of my own! You won't let me be just an ordinary girl – you never have. I earn money too – what if I go to Brenda and tell her I'm fed up? What if I left you, Tony? I'm not a baby now – it's not fair.'

Now he was both angry and frightened.

'You will go to bed,' he said 'And you will do as I say.' He seized her by the arm and slapped her face. 'You're my property, Lisa Smith, and you know it. Come on; say again what you just said. I dare you to.'

She was cowering now and suddenly she began to scream. Roughly he put his hand on her mouth.

'No more of that, my girl. Just remember what you could land yourself in. No more of it.'

He pushed her up the stairs and then threw her on the bed. For a moment she thought he was going to rape her and she gagged.

'You're in it as much as I am. Know when you're lucky,' he said. 'You'll carry on as usual. I shall deal with Brenda, if necessary.'

He stood over her, his face contorted. Would he really hurt her? He had treated her roughly, hurting her when he made love to her, occasionally he had hit her, but he had never yet beaten her up. That would be too dangerous. She knew she had nothing on him that she figured anyone else would care to do anything about and she got out:

'I promise.'

He released her and went out of the room, locking the door.

'I'll unlock it in the morning before I go. Mind you carry on just as usual,' he said in a quiet voice.

She knew she was beaten. Tony would always have the upper hand. She lay there sobbing till she heard him go downstairs and fell into an uneasy sleep, clutching her old teddy bear that had been such a comfort when she was a little girl. But she did not sleep.

In the morning she heard him unlock the door. She was dying to go to the lavatory and crept out of the room. She heard him boiling the kettle in the kitchen. She went back into the bedroom after washing her face.

'I'm off. You've only ten minutes before you go to work,' he shouted upstairs.

She sat on the bed. Then, as was his wont, he softened her by bringing her up a cup of tea, the only domestic thing he ever did. She saw that he truly believed he was in the right, and that he had done her no wrong. She tried to gulp the tea before putting on her face. When she heard the door slam she waited till the car started up. Then she crept to the telephone and dialled Susan. For the first time in her life she knew there was something she could do for herself. Anything was better than going on like this. Tony would be angry, but she wouldn't be there to see.

'I've a headache,' she told Susan. 'I can't come in to school today. Could you call in with some bread, do you think, after school?'

Susan, surprised, agreed, and Lisa heard her car start up and go off without her. She lay for a moment, her face made up, trying to force herself to go back to the bathroom. She would leave Tony the only way she knew how. He would not be back until the end of the week. She would get her revenge.

The weather had once again changed. Now it was still windy but colder, a day when you knew for certain that even if the sun came out, better weather would not pay a return visit to Spickhanger for at least six months. Rain had fallen too in the night. The estuary waters were choppy.

'Windy and wet,' Susan heard on the weather forecast as she steered carefully along the road to Eastminster. She had long ago stopped trying to understand the weather. Recently it had seemed to become even more unpredictable. There didn't seem to be seasons any more, unless you could count a general tendency for the temperature to be slightly higher in September than in February and for snow to arrive in January and February, rather than in June, though even that seemed possible. The autumn term was still the one she enjoyed most; you could look forward to Christmas. January and February could be bitter here. She always seemed to need something to look forward to; at present only the prospect of a different job seemed worth looking ahead for. . . .

Little Lisa had sounded very woebegone on the telephone. She resolved to buy a cake for her when she took her the bread. She remembered that Tony was going to be away.

Miss Kant had been very mysterious last night when, carrying a briefcase, she had come in from her trip to London. She looked as though she had solved an extremely difficult crossword puzzle. Susan had assumed she had been doing some research.

People got involved with that sort of thing when they were elderly. Mr Cobb was the same. Susan loved reading herself and enjoyed discovering the history of buildings and places, but she had no time to spend hours in libraries. She was really interested most of all in people.

Both Jim Cobb and Dorothea seemed to her to be on to something and she wondered if it was the same thing. Dorothea had not referred to Cobb's research after the coffee party he had given at the weekend, and Mr Cobb had not been out into the close or into his garden. He had once been out on his bicycle though; she had heard his garage doors slam late on Sunday night. He kept his bicycle there, along with his lawnmower, and odd pieces of furniture which she supposed he couldn't bear to get rid of. Miss Kant had told her that he had once worked in the North, but had wanted to get away when his wife died. It was true that he looked like her idea of a rather high-ranking policeman, and it seemed now to be generally recognized that that was what Cobb had in fact been.

Her thoughts wandered to their other neighbours. Really, she was getting to be a sort of Cranford character, paying such attention to them. It was years since she had bothered to be so well informed about the 'people next door'. Not since she'd left home, really. But if you were truly interested in people anyone must be worth study.

Nobody was ordinary when you came to know them, and she had had the feeling that at least one drama was being played out under her nose without quite being able to say what. *Twelfth Night* was not in it!

She arrived at school just in time to take her year-group register and hoped the deputy head had not seen her rushing along to her classroom. Then she remembered to tell the office that Lisa was not coming in, so popped in before she went into her first lesson where Linda Swift and others in the sixth form were waiting to take notes on classical civilization. That was her subsidiary subject and one she enjoyed teaching, having learned just enough each week to convey what she had absorbed. Lots of teachers doubled in this way. Thank goodness she had not yet been asked to teach maths. But today, as she outlined the story of Oedipus, she kept thinking first of Lisa, and then of the story of the Cuckoos and of the letter she herself had received.

She made an effort and swept it all out of her mind.

There was a light on in the bedroom that faced the Green when Susan arrived back at Lisa's at five o'clock with the bread and a piece of fruit-cake she had had weighed at the Home Bakery in Eastminster. She rang the bell, but there was no answer. She pushed at the door. Perhaps Lisa was wearing earplugs and trying to sleep, though one would have thought it would be hard to sleep with the lights on. The door opened easily and she saw two envelopes on the table in the little porch. Side by side. One marked SUSAN and the other TONY. With a sense of foreboding, she took up the one addressed to her. Lisa would expect her of course, though she was a little late.

'Lisa!' she shouted. 'Are you there?' No reply.

She opened the envelope, which was not stuck down.

Dear Susan. Please fetch Miss Kant and go up to my bedroom. I can't take any more. This is the best way. Love Lisa.

Susan's heart began to pound. She ran up the stairs, holding both letters, and hardly dared open the door into the bedroom where the light had been shining. But she did and when she turned her eyes on to the bed, forcing herself to look, there was Lisa, lying dressed on top of the coverlet, holding a teddy bear. On the bedside table were placed an empty glass, a not quite empty bottle of painkillers and an empty strip of Temazepam. But there was also the sound of heavy, rasping, breathing. Silly little fool – but she was alive!

Susan rushed downstairs and dialled Dorothea and then 999.

'Dorothea – I'm at Lisa's – she wasn't at school – she's left a
note – she's tried to kill herself. Will you come? I'm about to dial
999 – she's alive.' Then: 'I'm at 3 Heron Close, Spickhanger – yes
– H-E-R-O-N. There's a girl who's overdosed – aspirin, I think –
as well as sleeping-pills. Straightaway! No – I haven't touched her.
Right.'

She put down the phone and went upstairs again, waiting for
Dorothea. Had she done the right thing? She remembered that
Tony was away and then remembered the letter to him, which she
was still clutching. Without thinking she put it in her bag. Maybe
if she came round – *if* – Lisa wouldn't want the world to know her
last message to her husband. She looked at Lisa again, still snoring.
Weren't you supposed to walk them round the room – wake them
up? But how long had she been like this? Had she swallowed the
pills as soon as she'd phoned her in the morning? She looked on
the bedside table. The bottle of aspirins was not quite empty, but
there were no tablets left on the strip of Temazepam.

Below her was the sound of the door opening and Miss Kant's
voice.

'Susan?'

She went out on to the landing.

'She's up here. The ambulance shouldn't be long.'

When Miss Kant got to the bedroom she took a quick look at
Lisa.

'It's not too late is it?' said Susan. 'Thank goodness it wasn't
paracetamol, or she might die from liver failure. I wonder how
many she took? The strip of sleeping-pills is finished but there are
still some aspirins in the bottle.' She was thinking: but I don't
know how many sleeping-pills were there to begin with, nor the
time she took them – it must have been after Tony had gone –
sometime during the day. . . .

'Find her night-dress – they'll keep her in,' said Dorothea.

'There was a note for Tony – I took it. She didn't expect to be
alive when I came back from school. And he's away.'

'It looks to me like a cry for help, not a real suicide. We won't
know till they see how many she took, or when,' said Dorothea,
echoing Susan's thoughts.

Susan handed the note Lisa had written to her and Dorothea
read it with pursed lips.

' "Fetch Miss Kant". Hm. A touching faith – or just to spare you

161

before you went upstairs.'

'Yes, that's why she left the light, to guide me. Poor little thing.'

They waited and Lisa did not stir, but the breathing persisted. After about twenty minutes they heard the unmistakable sound of the ambulance which must have been in the area, for otherwise it would have taken longer to arrive.

Susan had busied herself searching for a nightdress, which she eventually found under the other pillow. Dorothea went down to the men and when they came into the room they took one look and then bundled Lisa on to a stretcher. Susan put the teddy bear on it too. Lisa might like to see it when she woke up.

They both went with the ambulance men. Lisa breathed loudly, and moaned, but did not wake. Susan had never accomplished the first part of the journey so quickly, the same one as to school. They sat on either side of the ambulance with the attendant at the head of the stretcher, and a red blanket draped over Lisa.

'Should we ring Tony?' whispered Susan.

'Where is he? Do we know?'

'She just said he'd gone to a nursery in Norfolk, I think.'

'Maybe she has his mobile number? Let's wait and see how she is. There's more in this than meets the eye, Susan.' Then: 'You said she left a letter to him?'

'Yes – here. Not expecting to wake.'

'Give it to me!' They were speaking in whispers.

Miss Kant opened the envelope, which was also unsealed, and Susan stared at her.

I am leaving you for good Tony. I don't suppose I shall wake but if I do please do not come to see me. I have telephoned Brenda to tell her what I'm doing. She will know what to do. Anyway, you won't have to pay her any more. Forgive me. It is for the best.

No *love from*. It sounded desperate.

'You don't swallow aspirins for fun, Susan, however many,' said Miss Kant. She put the note back in the envelope and sealed it. 'Forget you saw it,' she said. 'If she recovers she can have it. If not – well . . .'

It was still rush hour and seemed to take hours but eventually the ambulance turned into the drive of the new hospital on the Chelmsford road.

162

Susan was still wondering whether Miss Kant's high-handedness had a special reason. The attendant was too busy checking the inert Lisa to show any interest in their conversation. As soon as the vehicle stopped, nurses came rushing from Casualty, and the stretcher disappeared. 'This way to report,' said another nurse, and gestured them into an office. 'Will you wait? Next of kin?'

'No – just neighbours.'

'Sign here. If she doesn't wake up the police will want a statement.'

It was all businesslike, as though it happened every day. Probably did, thought Susan, feeling rather wobbly now that they had accomplished their mission.

'You go home – I'll stay,' said Dorothea. 'You've had a full day's work. Don't worry. Smith won't be coming back tonight. I'll take a taxi home.'

Susan agreed and made her way to the bus-stop. They would probably keep Lisa in overnight. They could see her in the morning, she supposed.

Dorothea sat by Lisa's bed. Lisa had had her stomach pumped and a drip attached to her wrist. She was still half-asleep. It was nine o'clock, dark, and Miss Kant had been given a cup of tea.

'I'll wait till she wakes up properly,' she said to the night sister. 'I can get a taxi back home. You'll keep her in overnight?'

'Next of kin can't be contacted, you say?' asked the sister.

Dorothea explained once again that they did not have Lisa's husband's mobile number and did not know where he was. Lisa might know when she came to full consciousness.

'Well, it looks as though she's going to be all right. We're rather short of beds. She'll have to go tomorrow unless there are complications. But in any case, we like them to come back for a chat with the therapist.'

They both waited for Lisa to wake.

She stirred once, opened her eyes and then seemed to slip into a natural sleep.

'She'll be OK now,' said the nurse.

'Then I'll go,' said Dorothea. 'Here's my card. We'll be back in the morning. Ask her if she wants you to get in touch with her husband. I don't somehow think she will.'

CHAPTER FOURTEEN

Susan was back at the hospital in the morning, having got up early. School would just have to wait.

'Bring her back,' said Dorothea. 'She can't be left alone for a moment.'

'If they let me,' Susan replied. Dorothea still had the note Lisa had written to Tony.

When Susan entered the ward where Lisa had been placed for recovery, she found her lying against the hospital bolster as pale as death. When she saw Susan she stared at her, then:

'Take me away. Take me away,' she pleaded.

'We'll take you home—'

'No! No! Not home. Let me stay with you – he'll be back at the weekend. I wouldn't tell them where he's gone. Why should I? I don't want him to know. I don't want to see him. Take me away. I wanted to die. Why didn't you let me die?'

'I found you unconscious,' replied her friend. 'I couldn't let you die, Lisa. Miss Kant and I will find somewhere for you to go and recover, and you can tell us about it when we take you home.'

A hospital official came up to them with a discharge sheet and a form for arranging to see a counsellor the following week.

'We'd like to keep her in longer, but we've such pressure on beds. She'll be all right. Keep her in bed today, then the sooner she starts her normal life again the better.'

They waited for the ambulance.

'I'm causing such trouble,' whispered Lisa. 'They've made an appointment for me to see a therapist, but I don't want to. I didn't mean to wake up, Susan.'

Susan only squeezed her hand and murmured some platitude. She was amazed that such a timid woman could have plucked up the courage to take an overdose. Fortunately she did not appear to have taken enough to kill herself.

'How many aspirin – and the other stuff – did you take?' she asked in the ambulance.

'I don't know. I took three sleeping pills – they were all I had left, and I stopped counting the aspirin. I remember having stomach ache and I thought I might be sick. Then I must have fallen asleep.'

'A good thing you weren't sick or you could have inhaled the vomit,' said Susan. 'That would not have been a pretty sight for me to find.'

Lisa began to weep silently.

'Sorry. I didn't mean to be unkind. There are plenty of people who are fond of you, Lisa. Just think, you may be sorry now, but one day you'll be glad.'

'No, I shan't. Never. Never. You just don't know,' she wailed.

'Lisa – there is always divorce – if it's about your husband. It's not my business, but surely divorce is better than trying to kill yourself.'

'Oh, I can't explain. I can't explain. I just want to go to sleep and never wake up.'

'You're just depressed,' said Susan. 'Talk about it later when you feel stronger.'

This time Lisa was encouraged to walk from the ambulance. Susan wondered how many of the neighbours would be looking out and how many knew what had happened.

'I don't want to go home,' said Lisa, standing stock-still in the middle of the path to Miss Kant's door. Miss Kant came out.

'You're coming in here for Susan and me to make a fuss of you,' she said and took the woman by the arm. Lisa leaned against her as though she had no strength left at all.

'It's the result of shock,' said the ambulance man. 'Just put her to bed. She'll be as right as rain tomorrow.'

They put her on the long sofa in the sitting-room to begin with and gave her a cup of tea. When she had drunk it she seemed to make up her mind.

'Please take me away – anywhere, so as not to see him again,' she pleaded. 'Anywhere.'

Dorothea and Susan exchanged glances.

'I'll have to go back into school now,' said Susan. 'I shall tell them you're feeling better – no need for anyone to know what happened.'

'I shall lose my job – if I leave here!' moaned Lisa, who seemed to have been thinking.

'We'll see, we'll see. When you've had a rest and feel ready to talk,' said Miss Kant. 'You don't have to stay here, you know. I have friends in London. Don't worry.'

'He'll be back at the end of the week. I can't face him. He'll be back. Why couldn't I do it properly? I'm so ashamed.'

She began to cry and once she'd begun it seemed she could not stop. Miss Kant sat with paper hankies and then went into the kitchen, got out her blender and made some homemade soup.

'I fetched the loaf you'd asked Sue to buy you. And some cake,' she said. 'You must have wanted her to find you, mustn't you? So perhaps you weren't quite sure about what you wanted to do.'

She felt this was at least true, for Lisa looked as though she had wanted anything to happen rather than having to make the decision to go off alone to confront a future without Tony. Miss Kant had something else to say to her, and said it when Susan had gone, as Lisa lay, covered in a fur rug and refreshed from another little sleep and another bowl of soup. Her handbag and make-up had been fetched so she had been able to improve her appearance, though she was still pale with dark-circled eyes.

She unconsciously rubbed her stomach where the pump had been.

'I feel sore all over,' she said.

Miss Kant took a deep breath. 'Why don't you tell me the whole story? I shan't be shocked,' she said. 'In fact, I think I've already guessed. You can trust me.'

'You couldn't guess it – no one could,' Lisa whispered with her hands over her face.

'Let me try,' Miss Kant began. 'Once upon a time there was a girl called Brenda with a brother called Tony.'

Lisa looked up and a mask of terror seemed to fall over her face. She tried to get up, but Miss Kant put a reassuring arm on her shoulder.

'Just let me speak. You can tell me if I'm wrong.'

Susan got back about half past four, having driven as quickly as possible along the winding lanes home from school. She had told the deputy head that Lisa was ill, without elaborating.

'Tell her she'll have to send a doctor's note if she's away more than three days,' was all Miss Probert had said. So far no rumours had been circulated about the incident and Susan had every faith in Dorothea's discretion. That lady greeted her tenant's return with another pot of tea and a piece of the cake that Susan had bought.

Lisa was sitting in the armchair looking as though she had had a shock, but one that had been replaced by a tiny grain of hope, for her cheek had a hint of pink.

'Lisa is going to stay with some friends of mine,' announced Dorothea. 'I'm taking her to London tonight.'

Susan gaped. 'School says you'll have to send a doctor's note if it's more than three days,' she said.

'Miss Kant says I can work for a friend of hers in a bookshop – she needs typing assistance.'

'I've been on the phone all afternoon,' said Miss Kant. 'Lisa has decided to leave her husband. He won't be back till Friday night. She will leave him the letter she has been busy writing all afternoon and I shall personally take her to London. I also have other things to do tomorrow, so I shall stay the night at my club and return tomorrow. I don't think Mr Smith will be making any trouble, Susan, and he won't know anything about Lisa's attempt unless the hospital informs him. So all we have to do now is drink our tea and then I'll get the car out.'

Lisa looked at Susan. 'It's the only way,' she said. 'She's been wonderful, Sue.'

'I know you haven't been happy,' Susan said, turning to Lisa. 'But surely you'd better see Tony first.'

'It's a long story,' said Dorothea, 'and one I expect Lisa wouldn't mind my telling you one day. But we haven't a moment to lose.'

'Look, Miss Kant, why not let me go and have it out with – with Brenda,' said Lisa suddenly, almost perkily. Susan looked from one to the other in puzzlement.

Dorothea joined Susan in the kitchen, where she had gone to add to the teapot, and whispered:

'She's euphoric – she'll come down with a bang. You see, it's the relief at finding herself alive. She didn't really want to die. She just wanted to get out of an awful situation.'

'But surely they could get divorced?' said Susan. 'Even if it isn't a simple story, she needs only to live apart from her husband for a time – is it one year or two? Unless she can prove unreasonable conduct.'

'None of that is necessary, I promise. I'll explain later,' said Dorothea.

'Miss Kant, have you the letter I wrote to Tony?' asked Lisa, standing at the kitchen door.

'Oh, yes. I took it in case he got back. We thought better not leave it at your home. Here it is.' She handed over the letter she had read and Lisa took it.

'I've written him something else, Susan,' she said. 'To tell him I'm going for good. Nothing about how silly I was.'

'Are you sure you want to go away?' asked Susan, trying once more to give Lisa the opportunity to stay and explain things to her husband.

'I asked you to take me away, Sue, yesterday, didn't I – or was it this morning? I still feel the same. You see, I've done something awful and the only thing is to start afresh.'

'I know he wasn't nice to you, but what about your job?' Susan interjected.

'She'll write to the school,' said Miss Kant. 'I'll see she does. Or *I* will. Meanwhile, she needs a place of safety, and that I *can* provide. Go home and fetch the essentials, Lisa. Pack a suitcase. Susan will help you.'

Susan was amused at the way Miss Kant had taken charge, but did as she was bid, and Lisa followed her to Number 3. The house seemed dead when they got inside. There was still the light on in the bedroom, which Susan had forgotten to turn off. Lisa flung clothes in her overnight bag.

'If I want more I shall ask him to send them on,' she said.

'You mean you'll tell him your address?'

'There won't be anything he can do about it. Miss Kant has explained to me. You see I didn't know, Susan – I was too young.' She stopped. 'I don't know how she guessed, but she did. She must be a witch.'

She put her old teddy bear into the case that had accompanied her to hospital, and which Susan had remembered to bring back.

'What will you do about the hospital appointment?' asked Susan. 'And the office? They just won't believe it!'

'I shan't need to go to hospital. I can write and say why I did it and why I'm all right now. I don't want to see Tony or this place ever again. But there are things I can do in London.'

She seemed a different person.

'Ask Miss Kant to explain. We can arrange to meet when I've found my feet. I know I'm not really better yet, but I shall get help. She knows people who'll help me.'

168

Susan went round the house suggesting things to pack. 'Have you got a clock? Your watch? Some winter clothes? Your cheque book – what will you do for money?'

'Tony managed everything. We had a joint account. I can open another as well and then write and ask my next salary to be paid into it.'

Susan forbore to enquire about national insurance numbers, doctors, and savings-bank deposits.

'Miss Kant will lend it me if I'm short,' was all Lisa said. Then: 'I'm going to a place of safety. I could have gone long ago – seven years ago, but I was so frightened of him.'

She took one more look round, then she took off her wedding-ring and put it on the table in the hall on the new letter she had written that afternoon. The key she put under the mat at the front, then she banged the door, walked down the path to Miss Kant's awaiting car and they were off. Susan waved bemusedly and went back in. She hoped to God Tony Smith did not come looking for his wife.

On the drive to London Lisa thought about what she had written to him.

I was in hospital but I'm better now. I have gone away for good. Do not try to find me. I shall tell our Brenda too that I've left you. If you try to report me missing or try to get me back, I shall report you for you know what. L.

She'd really written that! Susan was full of curiosity and eagerly awaited Miss Kant's return, for she was still in the dark. How could a woman change from a reeling shadow, a suicidal wreck, in the space of one afternoon? She must have confessed something – or Miss Kant had wormed it out of her – or guessed it already. Lisa looked as though she had had a burden lifted from her shoulders that had been there for almost a lifetime.

Tony Smith did not, in fact, return till the Saturday and by that time Miss Kant was back, having deposited Lisa with the family of a woman doctor in Hampstead whose grown-up daughter owned a small bookshop and needed a typist. Susan found Dorothea sitting drinking coffee at home on Friday on her return from school. She had not quite known what to say at the school office, but apparently Dorothea had persuaded Lisa to write immediately to say she had not been well, enclosing a doctor's note and giving in her notice.

'Doctor Appleby will write to your head,' Miss Kant went on. 'It's a long story,' she said, though Susan had not, in fact, asked. 'Lisa just has to wait till things blow over. The lady I chanced upon in East Ham – you remember – Brenda? – has been telephoned by me and is going to write to Mr Tony Smith.'

'He'll have to be told about the suicide attempt though, won't he?' asked Susan.

'Lisa hinted enough in her letter. He'll see it when he returns. Maybe he's already telephoned home and found no one there.'

'I don't envy him. Aren't we being a bit hard on him?' asked Susan. 'After all, people do quarrel and still stay married.'

'It was Lisa's own decision. She only wanted someone to tell her she was right, then she could leave him.'

'But she might still be frightened of him once he knows where she is. Are we to tell him? Not that *I* know where she is,' she added.

'He won't follow her, you can rest assured,' said Dorothea. 'Divorce papers will not need to be served on him.'

'But he was cruel – he frightened her!'

'You might say that. He's a criminal.'

That was all she would say for the present and so Susan tried not to worry.

She saw his car parked in front of Number 3 early on Saturday morning, but no sign of him. She was half-expecting he would knock on their door with an axe. Her imagination always got the better of her. She had almost forgotten the letter about Linda Swift and herself and wondered whether to show it to her landlady now. She was pretty certain Tony had penned it. In that case, why didn't she accuse him? She felt torpid, uneasy, and slightly sick. For the time being, she said nothing.

Miss Kant was on the phone on the Saturday evening when there had still been no sign of Tony in the close. She came out of the sitting-room and called up:

'Susan!' When Susan looked over the stairs she said: 'You needn't worry any more. That was Lisa. She's already seen my doctor friend's agency in London, which helps with her sort of problem, and she's got the temporary job I told you about.' Later she said: 'I expect he'll be selling up soon.'

Susan cleared her throat. Surely this was all rather sudden.

170

'Lisa thought the garden centre was not doing well – so she thinks he went to Norfolk to see about a sale,' added her landlady.

Sure enough, on the Monday morning there was still no Tony around and the car had gone. Then an estate agent appeared and a FOR SALE notice appeared in the garden.

'What will she do about her things? I mean, practically everything she possessed was in the house. She only took a small suitcase.'

'She'll be along to collect it, I expect,' replied Dorothea calmly. 'Or I'll get a van for her.'

The next news arrived in a letter addressed to Susan which awaited her return from school on the following Monday. It was from Lisa and began by asking Susan to collect various items of clothing that belonged to her. She didn't want to go into the house herself, but would be back the next weekend if Susan would kindly fetch them. She enclosed a duplicate key wrapped in tissue paper. The letter was typed and bore an address in north London of a working girls' hostel. After describing the job she was doing in the bookshop, Lisa ended with the following:

You see I was not really married to Tony. Ask Miss Kant to explain, but don't ask me about it, Sue, it's too awful. Love from Lisa.

Cobb called in just afterwards and Susan heard him talking in the kitchen to Miss Kant. He did not stay long; so when Susan came down to ask her landlady if she'd like to share an omelette, she brought Lisa's letter down with her.

'Can you tell me what it's all about? I'm completely at sea,' she said. 'I didn't like to ask before as I knew you wouldn't tell me till Lisa said you could.'

'Let's have the omelette. That was Mr Cobb. He says the garden centre is up for sale too! Smith's done a bunk.'

'But why? Surely they both earned a decent income? Lisa told me they were paying off the mortgage of the house and that he owned the garden centre.'

'He may have owned it, but he was in debt. The house was in his name alone so he can sell it.'

Susan threw down Lisa's letter.

'She's coming to collect her stuff. And she says she was never married to him!' she cried.

'Yes, the law would have quite a lot to say about that – as well as about the letters he wrote and the way he tried to incriminate Sandy Robson.'

'Miss Kant, will you tell me simply, in words of one syllable, what this is all about? I'm going mad. What do I say to Lisa when she comes? She says *you* will explain it all to me.'

'Well, if she says that,' said Dorothea scanning the letter, 'it's all right, and I can tell you. This must go no further than you and me. It would reflect very badly on the poor girl, you see, though it was not her fault. That is quite clear. Smith, of course, was being black-mailed. That's why he never had enough money.'

'If Lisa was not married to him, who was?'

'Lisa Smith was.'

Miss Kant smiled and then looked angry.

'Our little Lisa was not Lisa. Her real name is Brenda. The woman I saw in London who looked like her, the one who said she was called Brenda, is Lisa and *she* was married to Tony Smith.'

'But why all the mystification? It's not illegal to live with some-one you're not married to.'

'Indeed not, but there's much more to it than a simple question of leaving your wife and living with someone else. Lisa you see, the girl you knew as Lisa, was born Brenda Smith and she was Tony Smith's sister.'

'My God! No! You mean . . . ?'

'Tony Smith could be accused of the sin of incest, now called abuse, I believe, which is also a crime, make no mistake. He and "Lisa", whom we ought to start calling Brenda, I suppose, were the children of a couple who were killed in an air disaster over ten years ago. But long before that he had approached his sister sexu-ally and she was at first completely in thrall to him. He was, she says, crazy about her.

'She was a timid child and one suddenly bereft of her mother and father. She was fifteen when the accident happened, but he had already made her a sort of slave. Whether the parents ever knew, I don't know. He was completely unscrupulous. And, of course, as she told me – he did 'love' her.

'What happened was that he persuaded a cousin of theirs, a certain Lisa Landon, to marry him – all above board. He couldn't "marry" his sister because that would have been a crime he could-n't get away with. So he persuaded the cousin, who was really

called Lisa, to swap identities after the marriage – for a little financial consideration, I should imagine. His real sister, the real
Brenda, took the name of Lisa and lived with him as his wife. So
as to turn away suspicion he made the real Lisa falsify her age on
the marriage certificate, also an indictable offence. They came
away from the East End to a place where no one knew them and
the cousin continued to live in Wanstead. She and Tony were
married at a registry office there. Then he went back to his sister
Brenda, with whom he now began to live with as husband and
wife, calling her Lisa. Bob's your uncle.

'None of this would have mattered, I suppose, to freethinking
progressives – apart from the illegality, if "Lisa" – our friend, I
mean – had been happy. But she began to realize what she had
done, or rather what had been done to her. She had never known
any other man and she'd been fond of her brother. He *was* besotted with her – which didn't stop him treating her in a very brutal
fashion. The marriage with the real Lisa was, of course, never
consummated and the brother and sister went on living here.

'I think Lisa thought she could never escape him. She thought
that if she confessed, it might land them both in jail. Then Brenda
started – or I should say the real Lisa started – to ask for money to
expand her business. He'd never thought of that, I suppose –
thought all women were there to do his bidding. "Brenda" – the
real Lisa – is a rather unpleasant character, I would think. They all
had the same grandfather, a market-gardener with stalls in the East
End.'

Susan sat there trying to take all this in.

'You're making this up – it's not possible!' she exclaimed.

'It's all true. She was distraught, terrified of him, and decided,
when he went away to Norfolk on a matter concerned with his
business, to kill herself. But the poor child was caught. She really
only wanted to get away – anywhere – away from him. She'd
begun to want a normal life but, as I say, she thought she'd be put
in prison if it were discovered that she was living incestuously with
her brother. That's what *he'd* told her. She was staggered when I
told her that as she was a minor when she was seduced she was
perfectly free to escape. She wasn't even married!

'Of course, if she *had* managed to kill herself, other matters
would have come to light and then he would have lost everything,
so he's escaped rather luckily, I think.

'Quite by chance I'd seen the false Brenda in East Ham at the market and thought at first it was our Mrs Smith. She did look like her; that was why they did it – there was a remarkable resemblance between the cousins. The similarity between Lisa and Brenda had always been noted with surprise, even though our little "Lisa" was the same age. That was how he was able to prevail upon her to go through with it. Don't you think that Lisa and Tony looked alike too, apart from their eyes? It struck me straight away. I thought at first *they* could be cousins!'

'But how did you find it all out? Lisa – Brenda I mean – I suppose I'll have to start calling her that – never confessed to you, did she?'

'Only after I'd asked her. I said I thought I knew what the problem was. She couldn't believe I could have guessed. Her life, she said, was too frightful to put into words. So I told her what I thought had happened. I was right. You see, I have this little hobby of family history and I looked up the marriage between Tony and Lisa and also looked up a *Brenda* Smith. There was no Lisa Landon of the right age in the birth registers. There was this woman calling herself Brenda who looked like our Lisa. So I looked at the births to a Smith of East Ham and there they were: Father, Mother, Anthony and Brenda, the same age as our Lisa. So, Brenda of the market place, I thought at first, must be his sister. The idea occurred to me that they might have switched names. One day I said "Brenda" to *our* Lisa in a shop in Eastminster.

' "Oh, Brenda!" I called and she looked up and was just going to say "Yes?" when she remembered! I'd had my suspicions before that. I didn't like Tony Smith. I was sure he'd had something to do with the planting of the robe and with the letters to the men and with spreading those rumours around at the marina about David and Sandy and Kevin. Cobb had come to the same conclusion. It was absolutely none of my business, though, and I would have said nothing. If people want to live with their brothers, that's nothing to do with me. But, you see, she *didn't* want to. She was terribly unhappy. I expect she was not really a party to the "marriage" at first, but she agreed to call herself Lisa. It was all a complicated and unnecessary ploy. He had to drag the other woman in to satisfy his sense of power.

'He thereby cooked his goose, for the real Lisa is still married to him and can now sue for divorce and get a nice little settlement, if she's so minded. And *our* "Lisa" whom we'll just have to get used to calling Brenda now, is as free as air. He'll be frightened that if he tries to do anything to get her back she'll press charges. She told me she wanted to start a new life.'

'So the overdose was the beginning of her freedom?'

'Exactly. I've found her work with my friend Dr Madge Appleby's daughter, who owns a bookshop. In her spare time Madge helps man an abuse support line.'

'It's an unusual story,' said Susan. 'I still can't see really why he bothered to *marry* the other girl.'

'To show his marriage lines if it were ever necessary. To pretend to Lisa that he was now "married" to her. After all, *she* was now Lisa, wasn't she?'

'But how could a man get away with it? She wasn't *so* stupid? There can't be many girls who would allow it to happen.'

'Oh, I wouldn't be so sure. She's probably a masochist. She was grieving for her parents. Her brother obviously loved her. She was confused about love and sex and she both loved and feared him.'

'It's pretty horrible, isn't it. I bet it was going on for ages before he decided to "marry" her.'

'Yes – that's why I wanted you to promise you would never tell anyone else. It would do no good to the new Brenda if anyone ever knew what she'd been – a victim of her own brother. Mind you, I think he must be a peculiarly horrible sort of man.'

'She said he stood over her with the contraceptive pill.'

'Yes, she's a maternal young woman and wants children. Of course, that was the one thing he wanted to be sure she'd never have. Having a child was not in his plans at all. Apart from the danger of some genetic tragedy, he wanted her to stay with him and never grow old, never talk to another man, never see a man except when he was around, never put anyone else first. She *was* his slave. But she had to work, as he needed money for his black-mailer and his business. He quite enjoyed flirting with women to make the little thing feel jealous and thus secure her undying devotion. Then he overreached himself. He has a fanatical hatred of gays and couldn't resist a little mischief.'

'Do you think he could have had anything to do with that man Thrush?'

'No, I don't think so. Not in his line. Though he probably got Thrush to spread the rumours at the marina.'

'And he couldn't have attacked Linda?'

'No. He was at the party all the time, I'm sure of that.'

'Does anyone else know? I mean they must have had some relatives around, some witnesses to the real wedding.'

'No. They took two people off the street and parted once the deed was done. The false Mrs Smith was only twenty and completely under his thumb.'

Susan shivered. '*I* had a letter too,' she confessed, 'accusing me of lesbian tendencies with Linda Swift. Tony's doing also, I expect.'

'He didn't like you because you were friendly with his "wife". She told me that he doesn't really like anyone. She's worried about him still – that he might kill himself. I don't think that at all likely. I think he'll find some other girl to victimize.'

'At least it won't be his sister. To think of what she must have suffered.'

'These cases are very complicated. She's not out of the wood yet. It's only a beginning. She's now admitted to someone else, you see, what really happened, so she can begin to face it. She told me that sometimes she even thought she *was* married to him, that he was not her brother. She couldn't bear the truth. But she was so relieved when I told her – you saw her face.'

'Yes, she was transformed. I wonder whether she'll find anyone else. It'd have to be a strong sort of man to know all she'd gone through, wouldn't it?'

'Perhaps there are such men,' said Miss Kant. 'If she comes back at the weekend, just be friendly. I don't think she'll want to talk about it.'

'Well, you have done a good deed, I must say. I don't know how you dared – and you never moralized to her about it or anything. She must be grateful.'

'I wouldn't want her to feel grateful. Gratitude is very enervating. She needed a kind of parent figure, I suppose, who wouldn't blame her. But I'd like to have seen Smith's face when he read her letter – and even more when he confronted his legal wife. She'll put the screws on him, I expect. Perhaps she'll suggest they share their guilty secret and set up business together! I wouldn't put it past her.'

Susan took the anonymous letter she had received and tore it into little pieces.

'Is there no one nice and normal? It's so horrid – you can't even like a pupil without someone suggesting you're a pervert.'

'Well, let's hope we can all settle down now in peace,' said Miss Kant.

CHAPTER FIFTEEN

Cobb, who had not been told anything specific about the Smiths, guessed that Miss Kant had come to the aid of the young woman. All the Heron Closers knew that Lisa Smith had tried to kill herself, that she had now left her husband, that Tony Smith had disappeared and that both his house and his business were on the market. Cobb carefully refrained from discussing it with his neighbours.

He was still following the tracks of Percy Thrush and trying to disentangle the truth about that deceased handyman. He asked himself why he was so determinedly curious: what did it matter? What was there to discover? Tony Smith had undoubtedly been behind the anonymous letters to Sandy and David who would be able to prove that they were neither drug smugglers nor corrupters of the young, spreading disease. Smith must also have been behind the letter Susan had mentioned to him, though the poor girl had torn it up. But had Smith been behind the piece of doggerel that Cobb still carried round in his pocket?

PERCY THRUSH
DID NOT FALL
HE WAS PUSHED
'TIS A PITY YEARS AGO
HE WAS NOT DUCKED

Doggerel did not seem to Cobb to be in Tony Smith's line, but he wasn't going to mention any of this to Graham. This was *his* puzzle. He had his own ideas but he needed a bit of help from an old friend up North who might be willing to please his old boss and look something up for him on the police computer. They had begun to rationalize and improve their computer records.

Cobb kept looking at the letter. It was typed. But so many

people had typewriters, or word processors. He could hardly go round his neighbours asking if they had written it. He was sure the letter was a 'teaser'. The envelope, of course, had been written in block capitals to make it look like an anonymous letter. He tried to remember the writing in the letter David and Sandy had received.

Someone wanted him to go on asking questions. Why him? Why not ask him directly? Someone knew more about Thrush than he did yet. He had had a profitable day at the Family Record Centre the afternoon he had seen Dorothea Kant there, and awaited developments on that score. He felt certain in his own mind when he sat down and thought about the whole thing calmly, that there had been *an intention* to push Thrush over the sea-wall.

Whether there had also been the intention to kill him was another matter. You could not count on semi-drunkards banging their heads in the right places. Yet someone might have *meant* to kill him off, even if the police no longer believed this.

It still might all be supposition on his part, yet he felt in his bones he was right, doggerel or no. That Thrush had banged his head on the concrete might have saved the 'murderer' from carrying out the crime.

Would it be murder or manslaughter to push an old man off a wall and thereby kill him? It depended on the intention. If the intention had been to kill, then wasn't it, philosophically, murder? Did it matter whether the final blow was delivered by fate or by a human hand? Manslaughter would arise out of an accident, though he was sure many murderers pleaded manslaughter, knowing that judges and juries were not thought-readers. His wife Edna had ended up dead, even if that had not been intended.

Who would want to be rid of Thrush? He returned to his former questions whilst waiting for the result of his enquiries elsewhere. Computers might be efficient, but their managers took a damned long time to cough up. His old mate might not have easy access to all he needed.

Why should anyone want to get rid of Percy Thrush? He tried once again to disentangle all the other aspects of the events of the late summer and autumn; the trouble at the marina, the letter to David and Sandy, the robe in the tool-shed, Kevin and his two mates, Mrs Simmons, and the Smiths. What counted was *intention*. Who might have had that intention and why? How could Thrush be so dangerous to someone that a firm intention was translated into action?

Cobb made a cup of coffee and sat at his table in his open-plan sitting-room with a clean notebook, trying to begin again and sort out his thoughts for the last time. If Denis Pearson in Bruddersford didn't find anything out, he would give up. Today he would think round the whole case. He hadn't heard a squeak from George Graham for days and wondered if Graham knew anything about little Lisa's suicide attempt.

He ruled a title at the top of a double page, then divided the page into three columns, the old faithfuls: Motive, Method and Opportunity. Then he squeezed in another column: Type of Personality.

It looked very amateurish and he laughed at himself. The boss had become an amateur, pipe-smoking sleuth. Police work wasn't much like detective stories; it never had been. But now he was released from the profession he could be as amateurish as he liked. It was his wits against someone else's.

Under motive, he wrote: Was Thrush blackmailing someone? Leading to motive to remove him by:

(1) Pat Dawson? Had he a conviction for drunken driving? Did Thrush know he had killed a person (say) and had so far escaped undetected?

(2) Sandy and David, esp. David. Thrush may have done a bit of rumour-spreading for Tony Smith down at the marina but decided he might act for himself and blackmail David Fairbairn on account of something he knew about his past?

(3) Could Mr Whitwham be blackmailed if someone knew and had told Thrush about, say, some irregularity in a customer's bank account? Could *Mrs* Whitwham have resolved to get rid of him for this reason?

(4) General query against Tony Smith's name.

There were doubtless many shady matters in that man's past, but here he was connected with the replaced robe and the letter to the men.

It was thundery and dark and Cobb put his reading-lamp on. He looked again at the possible victims of possible blackmail and added a sixth: Eva Maitland, who might have acted for her lover, Dawson. If Thrush was blackmailing any of these couples he could only have come upon information to their disadvantage, either in prison, where perhaps one of them might have been – Dave Fairbairn, for example, years ago, for 'seducing' an under-age boy?

Or *someone else* knew a person's secrets and had perhaps mentioned the facts to Thrush? Or someone who knew Thrush had wanted to settle a private score?

It was getting too complicated. Any of these couples might have been victims of blackmail, and Thrush could have come upon information about any of them anywhere, perhaps from Tony Smith. He could have been in prison with one of them and been surprised to meet him later, back in ordinary life?

It would need a thorough investigation of the pasts of his neighbours, for which he felt disinclined. What if Pat Dawson *had* been a drunk driver? What if Dave Fairbairn *had* been in jug for what was no longer a crime? What if Whitwham *had* served a sentence for fraud?

None of it seemed likely and if they had – or one of them had – paid the penalty, there was nothing more to lose, surely?

If blackmail were not the nub of the question, what else could be? He was still on 'motive' and had many question marks and a lot of confused ramblings.

He pulled himself together and lit another pipe. He would exhaust his ideas about Motive before he got to Method and Opportunity and Character. He looked vaguely out of the window, feeling rather like a writer trying to disentangle his characters and plot. Perhaps he himself was making up the plot and it was all a waste of time? But before he left 'blackmail', he must check that he had covered all possibilities.

Blackmailing Miss Kant seemed excessively unlikely; likewise, Susan Swann. Tony Smith might have been eminently a subject for blackmail, but Lisa had sworn he was asleep all night the night of the death of Thrush, as she said, she had been with him. Of course, as his wife – though he had his doubts about that – she could have confected an alibi for him. But what could Tony Smith really fear from Thrush? Thrush had not appeared very intelligent, though he had probably enjoyed spreading rumours. Probably got paid for it too. If Lisa had not gone away he would have asked the Smiths again.

He put another question mark against Smith and against Mrs Maitland. What about *her* past? She was awake late that night and had rung up Pat Dawson for company. But she might wish to shield Dawson, or vice versa.

David Fairbairn, then? Could he have gone out after Sandy had got back and gone to sleep? Possible again. No one knew Percy

Thrush had been asleep on the beach.

They could all be possible murderers! That was the trouble. Well, not quite all, but he could imagine enough motives to sink a ship. Only one of them could be the correct one. *If* this theory was tenable at all, *if* Thrush had been dispatched a little prematurely out of this world . . . but he himself seemed to be the only person who thought Thrush had been murdered, with the exception of the writer of the doggerel, he, Cobb, was the only person to believe that there had at least been an *intention* to murder.

He would like to chat with someone about it, but there was no one he could omit from his suspects, except perhaps Susan and Dorothea. He wanted to think this through by himself.

He couldn't help feeling that more than one person in Spickhanger wanted Thrush disposed of. Now why was that? Had he himself thought the man such a nasty character when he had worked for them? He tried to think dispassionately of Thrush. A nondescript little man, foxy-looking, slightly shifty, but a good worker.

He decided to make a cup of tea, and tried to think, as he filled the kettle and waited for it to boil, of any other reason apart from blackmail that might have motivated the disposal of Percy Thrush. The only other motive that seemed plausible was revenge. He had shied away from it, since revenge was never far from his own thoughts when he thought of Edna, which he did every day. If he knew, say, that Thrush had killed Edna, even by inadvertence, he would have got his hands round Thrush's throat with pleasure, ex-policeman or not.

But would he have killed him? He shuddered. He was a human being, and most human beings wanted revenge or retribution for a man who had killed, didn't they? Whatever progressive opinion said; whatever people said when they used the top half of their brains; whatever was said about rehabilitation, the influence of a bad home, or unemployment.

Whenever a person read of an old lady of ninety being raped or a teenaged mother having her cheap little earrings torn off by a thug, the immediate feeling was surely: *What wouldn't I do to such a person if I could?* That was why we had prisons and punishments, and a police force. So, *think*. Could Thrush have committed some crime for which he could not be forgiven? It argued a personal affront, a personal revenge. For when brought up against it, people would only kill in revenge for a crime perpetrated against someone they knew and loved. Impersonally they would like violent criminals to be hanged, but when it came to the crunch, only if a man knew that a crime had been committed in which he was personally involved – say a parent of a murdered child – would he take action and carry out the revenge himself. This was no lynch-law case but a personal vendetta, and he became more and more convinced of this as he drank his tea.

He had a gut feeling that Thrush *had* done *something*! Had he attacked Linda Swift? He was stymied here, as he had no access to records. He would have to be patient. Anyway, once a sentence had been served, unless someone was regarded as a possible danger to society, his prison record was wiped out to all but a few in the know. Even the computer could deal only with certain crimes. Or was he ignorant and was there now – where? – a record of every crime, every criminal in the book, going back for years and years? It seemed unlikely.

He felt in his bones that it was Thrush who had attacked Linda. Apparently he had not raped Patricia Simmons. Were there two rapists in one little place over a few days! Had Darren got the idea from hearing or seeing something? But Darren had not worn a monk's robe. Mrs Simmons had been quite simply raped by a man hiding in a hedge on a rather remote country road; a man had seen her and marked her down, a man known to take drugs. Had he seen Thrush attack Linda two nights before?

Who else might there be who wished to avenge themselves upon Thrush? He tried to think of the most unlikely person.

Susan Swann. Was she a closet lesbian? Was she in love with Linda Swift and therefore so incensed at the attack upon her that she wished to remove a male animal from the world to avoid future attacks. No, Susan was not a likely lesbian, and she had been asleep in bed that night, having to get up early for school the next day.

He must learn to discipline his thoughts. What offences might the unfortunate Thrush have committed which might have led someone to avenge themselves upon him? Well, the most obvious was an attack upon a woman, although Thrush looked more like an indecent exposure type. Of course, he had not actually raped Linda, had he, just wanted to frighten her? Here the Cuckoo idea came in and that was a real clue, something that Cobb felt might explain the whole thing. He thought about what Susan had said.

All these thoughts stirred him up and were perhaps not good for him, since they brought back the atmosphere of crime, the impotent anger he had felt when Edna was killed. But Thrush was not a drunken driver. Cobb had never seen him drive at all. With a start he realized he had not yet even got to Method and Opportunity and was already half asleep.

Under Opportunity he wrote: All suspects had, at a pinch, opportunity, except Tony Smith if Lisa were to be believed, and Susan if Dorothea were to be believed, and the Whitwhams if they were each telling the truth and had been asleep. Lisa had had other problems on her mind and she was not the type to go round pushing old men over walls, not being able to say boo to a goose. Really, if all were lying, if anyone was lying, *anyone* could have done the deed! It was becoming just another academic exercise to keep his brains from addling.

He tackled Character. This looked more promising. Given a motive and given an opportunity he thought first of Bill Whitwham who was pre-eminently the representative of the law and order brigade on the close. If Whitwham had wanted to avenge himself on one who'd committed a crime against him he could easily have done so and Thrush would not have suspected that the treasurer of the Spickhanger residents' association was going to push him over a wall. But why choose such a place at such a time? That was a good point. Tony Smith was also the type to use violence for his own ends and *perhaps* David Fairbairn, though not Sandy. Mrs Maitland was an enigma. Miss Kant wasl strong-minded. Pat Dawson and Mrs Whitwham were less strong-minded – *on the surface.*

Means and opportunity seemed to depend upon motive. That was another good point. And when the robe turned up at Sandy's, was there not an implication that somehow it had had something to do with it? Had someone other than Tony stolen it from Susan's car? Most of them shopped in Eastminster and could have done so. Cobb put *Temporary Conclusions* under his columns and then wrote: *Motive*: Revenge most likely. *Method*: chosen in such a way as to frighten Thrush, (or put him at his ease?). *Opportunity*: Fairbairn, Dawson, (in cahoots with Maitland), Whitwham (shielded by his wife). Tony Smith. *Personality type* for *this* crime: Anyone strong enough to push a man off a wall. Someone very determined: T Smith? D Fairbairn? D Kant?

He added J Cobb? and went to fill his teacup.

*

Dorothea was washing up when Cobb called round the next morning. She had refused to buy a dishwasher as she did not think it worthwhile and Susan always did her own washing-up. There was, however, a washing-machine chuntering away and a coffee-pot on the stove and she was reading *The Independent*, which was open on the table.

'Do come in. Have you come for those bulbs?' she asked. 'I've heaps of tulips I don't need.'

He sat down and she poured him a cup of coffee.

'I suppose I mustn't ask what's happened to the Smiths?' he said, sipping his coffee appreciatively. 'I gather *you* must have had something to do with it. I saw you and Susan go with her in the ambulance – and then you were walking up and down in the garden with Lisa the next afternoon.'

'She's lucky to be alive,' replied Dorothea. 'Poor little girl – and that brute of a man.'

'I gather she's gone, and I presume *he* won't be back either?' he hazarded.

'I expect one day you might hear the whole story, but it's better kept under wraps. Most unsavoury.'

'Is that what you were doing at the Family Record Centre in Islington?' he asked. 'I thought it might be something to do with a marriage.'

'You're too sharp for your own good,' she replied.

'I came to ask your advice really,' said Cobb. 'I'm still exercised by the Thrush death. Can't get it out of my mind.'

'Once a policeman!' she said. She, at least, was certain.

'Well, so many untoward events have happened in the last few weeks, I thought at first they must all be connected. Seemed too many coincidences – robes and an anonymous letter – and attacks.'

'Susan has had a letter too,' said Dorothea. 'Accused her of being a lesbian. It was just before Smith went away.'

'Sue a lesbian – nonsense,' said Cobb. 'I'll take one of those biscuits, if I may.'

'She was supposed to be having a love affair with a pupil,' said Dorothea.

'Linda Swift, I expect,' he suggested.

'The very same. Another of Smith's little japes I think. What an odious man.'

'Well, there's nothing shameful about being a lesbian. Of course it's different if a pupil is *seduced*, but Smith had sex on the brain.'

184

He paused, then went on: 'I'm sure it was Thrush who attacked Linda.'

She looked at him for a moment then put down her cup. 'Why are you sure?'

'What Sue told me about him looking strangely at Linda last year after an innocuous remark about a cuckoo.'

'Yes, I agree. Though why that should upset him I don't know. He wasn't called Cuckoo. Susan told me about the anonymous verse you received.'

'But he might have had that as a nickname as a child, meaning 'barmy' – or a family who takes over other people's nests.'

'That must be it. It seems an odd reason to attack a girl though. He must have been crazy.'

'He looked such a harmless old thing, but we're taught to beware of harmless old things in the force. I came really to ask you about a philosophical point.'

'Ask away.'

'There are two points in fact. *One*: if, say, Thrush was the product of a broken home – had been abused as a child – been cruelly treated and yet survived damaged, 'Nature' might have easily got rid of him; I was reading Darwin last night. But 'Nature' did not. He wasn't aborted and he didn't die of neglect, but survived, say, to be a man full of hatred. Perhaps he had a father who attacked girls, or beat him? Well, would you say he was then responsible for his actions? Entirely?'

'Which of us is entirely responsible for our actions? If you were a Christian – or even a philosopher of the Kantian sort,' she smiled, 'you would put forward the free will argument. We can all choose.'

'Do we all partake of original sin?' asked Cobb. 'Are some people, as apart from actions, evil?'

'There are perhaps degrees of wickedness, though I don't think orthodox theologians would agree. Sin is, of course, a Christian concept. Nowadays, people would think there might have been mitigating factors that made it harder for someone like Thrush – if his background was what you suggest – to behave well. But his will is supposed to be as free as yours or mine or Lisa Smith's.'

'I take it you're not a Christian believer yourself?'

'Alas, no. I do, however, believe in original virtue! When you teach a lot of students and you see some with appalling backgrounds who survive them – and others with every mortal advantage who throw away their lives or act selfishly, you begin to wonder. The mystery is that anyone with a deprived childhood survives to be a pleasant person and not actively wicked.'

'You may be coming round to divine grace, then?' he said.

'No – I think it's just the luck of the draw. Some people are just nicer than others, aren't they? Thrush was probably not very nice. Yet he might have had a brother who was perfectly OK and didn't go round attacking girls.'

'I was thinking through the old "Motive, Opportunity, Method" thing – and pondering over what sort of person would attack a girl or attack Thrush himself. And there was another conundrum I'd be glad to hear your opinion about.'

'Have another cup of coffee. I'm not Socrates, or Immanuel Kant!'

'In my opinion, probably because of my old legal training, it is the intention which makes the crime a crimee. Say someone pushed Thrush over that wall but did not intend to kill him – just wanted to frighten him. Would that be a crime, in your opinion, if the man died as a result?'

'Well, it would be unfortunate for them both, but if the intention was not there – no, I don't think it would be a serious crime. Not a good thing to do though.'

'It would be manslaughter, I'm sure, nowadays,' remarked Cobb.

'But if the intention were to kill it would be murder. Not that the sentence might be all that different nowadays, might it?' said Miss Kant.

'There are no sentences that judges are allowed to impose for murder other than life. And life does not mean life, as Whitwham keeps saying. If it were an accident, the man might get off with a suspended sentence.'

'And if it were *planned*, and the man died – that *would* be murder. Thrush hit his head, didn't he. But he could have just fallen.'

'I'm still worried about intention,' said Cobb.

He put his cup down and looked her full in the face. 'The fact is I have suffered myself as a result of what would probably have been a manslaughter verdict. A drunken driver killed my wife. They never found him. That's why I retired. I couldn't bear to go on helping the "law" any longer, when all I wanted to do was to have my revenge on whoever it was. If he'd ever have been found,

I know I would have wanted to kill him – even if he hadn't intended to kill. Purely in revenge and to feel that there had been retribution for stupidity.'

She was silent for a long time, then:

'I am very sorry,' she said. 'I didn't know. Is that why you don't drink?'

'Yes.'

'But James, you *wouldn't* have killed that man if you'd found him. You knew he didn't *intend* to kill your wife. If he *had* intended, then you might have wanted revenge. But you're just not that sort of man.'

'I often wonder. I think I *would* have killed him, and then killed myself. Young policemen often used to ask me: why don't we give murderers the benefit of a choice of suicide or prison? I had no answer. This is a civilized country, I would parrot; we are not supposed to encourage suicide. Even of a man who actually wants to die. You see, like you I am not religious either. Yet I'm frightened of what we all might do if we were given our head in self-defence or as victims. There'd be no end to vendettas. I'm always surprised by how the relations of victims react. Say, if it had been a child who was killed – on purpose – what other punishment but death would be right?'

'Yet we are not asked to forgive on other people's behalf, are we? We are not gods who may magnanimously "forgive". There is such a rush now for an injured party to be seen to "forgive"! A remnant of Christianity, perhaps? We learned *Forgive them that trespass against us*, and *Turn the other cheek*, but I feel it's more a knee-jerk "progressive" reaction now that is expected of victims, and that very few people do "forgive".'

'Perhaps truly religious people do, but they can surely never *forget*?' said Cobb, 'It ruins people's lives to feel they have no redress and are powerless. I suppose we could all be murderers, but we would murder for justice, from motives of self-defence or the defence of others, not from "evil" motives.'

'*You* wouldn't go round attacking old ladies. *You* wouldn't rape a girl,' said Dorothea, 'Where does *your* conscience come from?'

'I came from a loving home,' he said, and rose to go.

'I take the Kantian view about intention,' said Dorothea. 'It must be *my* background,' she added.

Back home Cobb felt curiously relieved. He had never told anyone down here in Essex the details about Edna and perhaps it was a good thing that at last he had found he could unburden himself. Miss Kant had cleared his head for him. Now all he could do, as far as Thrush the Cuckoo was concerned, was wait reports from Denis Pearson. He was not optimistic; he looked at his old notes again and lamented any idea of a conclusion.

He had had more abstract matters on his mind than any further discussion of the 'duck' doggerel, so he had not mentioned it to anyone but Susan, who he knew would tell Dorothea. Perhaps it was Tony Smith who had written it after all, as a last *billet doux* before his departure for Norfolk.

He remembered he'd never taken those bulbs and seeds from Number 2. He'd ask her tomorrow. He had large Michaelmas daisies growing too riotously in his front garden, but the prolonged last flowering of his hybrid perpetual roses was a delight. He needed some rock plants for his half-finished rockery, must buy more spring bulbs to put in the side garden, and perhaps some herbs, like rosemary, for the back. Miss Kant's garden was lovely with forget-me-nots and scilla and aconite in spring, and roses in summer. She tended it as carefully as Edna had once tended theirs.

His eyes pricked. Poor Edna. How he missed her, would always miss her. He saw her in their old garden in summer, gathering campanula and marguerites and in winter watering her winter pansies. A life of peace that would never return. If people had all been like Edna, there would have been no wars, no murders and no unloved children. Life was so bloody unfair. But at least some-one else agreed with him. He would never marry again, but it would be pleasant to go on knowing Miss Dorothea Kant. When he had solved the Thrush puzzle he might perhaps ask her to accompany him to the 'chess pub' in Chelmsford – might even cadge a lift. He was smiling now. Occasionally, life could be pleas-ant.

CHAPTER SIXTEEN

Susan was giving out pencils and pieces of paper to Form 'One Q' the very next morning. '1Q' had been so named to draw attention away from the fact that they were the top stream. Unfortunately nobody had noticed the juxtaposition of the two characters that gave the opposite impression to the one intended. The bottom stream was called 1A.

Susan wished the children could be given desks with lids in which to put their books. An older teacher had explained to her that they did not have many books to go round, and that the younger children always lost them in any case. Work-sheets were still the rule, and pencils were collected at the end of the lesson, which made it into a gigantic endurance course-cum-logistical exercise on the part of the teacher. The national curriculum had, on the other hand, squeezed out many of the more pleasant parts of teaching, and Susan's lessons on the myths of Greece and Rome could only just be squeezed in now under an optional 'History' rubric.

She had decided this morning that the children should learn how to take notes, and had prepared an introduction to the Greek gods. She was guiltily armed with a piece of chalk to spell difficult names on the blackboard, intending to give them information slowly to see if they could note down salient facts. 'Chalk and talk', it was called, but at least she would be able to take the papers in at the end and see what the children had made of it.

The most frustrating part of her job was the lack of follow-up. As the children had no books, they could not do any homework except with the wretched work-sheets and these were often conveniently lost, too. She had prepared a simple work-sheet for the next lesson in a week's time, when each child could compare his or her efforts to remember what had been said with the actual facts on this paper.

Unfortunately, however, in her experience, the 'next lesson' was often a chimera. Form 1Q attended approximately one out of three of her prepared lessons, often having better things to do – a medical inspection, a trip to London, or special individual meetings with the heads of years and departments.

The school was far from being a sink school but it was a monument to bureaucracy and it amazed Susan that anyone ever learned anything at all. What happened was that the children whose parents were keen, or belonged to public libraries, went and borrowed books and did the work themselves, or helped with it; you could not really expect the average eleven-year-old to trot off to the public library every teatime. The school library was unfortunately often closed on account of various incidents that had taken place with the third year pupils, always the most difficult.

As she gave out paper and pencils a small boy in the front row spoke up.

'Miss, I saw you the other week,' he said.

'Oh, yes? Adrian, is it? Where was that?' she answered injudiciously. One was not supposed to carry on a private conversation with any one child but to attend to the mass. The mass at the moment was relatively quiet since they were first years and had not learned the bad behaviour of some of the older, so-called children. This being the top stream, one might catch their attention before the perils and boredoms of adolescence caught up with them. They might then emerge five years later with decent GCSEs.

English and Art and PE and social studies were taught in different groups of the first years all mixed together but mathematics and French were taught in ability groups. She had therefore, for administrative reasons, the same group here as the top maths group, which was, strangely enough – surprise surprise – almost the same as the top French group, a set of serious children.

Adrian continued to regard her earnestly.

'I saw you at Duck's Cabin,' he said.

'Where?' she asked, absent-mindedly, looking for a list of names to check whether any child had disappeared between his or her group register and the trek to this distant classroom.

Then again, more sharply, she asked: '*Where* did you say?'

'Outside Duck's Cabin, miss, on the Tidewell Road. You was in your car looking at the builders.'

'Why do you call it that?' she asked. 'Do you mean the old corrugated shack opposite?'

'Yes, miss. My great-gran – she always calls it that.'

'Duck's Cabin you say?'

'Yes, miss.'

The rest of the class was now listening to the exchange. Why was it that whenever you did not want their attention you got it?

'Yes, I was having a little run in the car,' she replied. 'Now, I'm going to tell you a story about the gods whom the Greeks thought lived up in the sky on Mount Olympus.'

She wrote the word on the blackboard. 'You'll see the word later on your work-sheet,' she said. She suddenly decided against the taking of notes during this lesson.

'Today I'm going to tell you a story for a few minutes and then you can ask questions. Then I shall go through what I have said and with the help of the words on the blackboard I shall want you to write down what you remember.'

The children would ask irrelevant questions but they must learn to concentrate. They seemed to enjoy listening to her and did ask questions that were not to do with quite extraneous matters.

She walked round afterwards as they attempted to write down what they had learned, and thought about what Adrian had said. So, *Duck*'s Cabin, was it? Not Thrushes or Cuckoos?

'The 'olden days' in Greece were over two thousand years ago, not two million,' she remarked, looking at what one child was writing. 'Anyone who is interested can get a book out of the school library – and don't forget your public library as well.'

As they all trooped out at the end of the lesson, she stopped Adrian.

'Did your great-grandma know the family who lived in that cabin?' she asked.

'Yes, miss,' he answered. 'My great-gran's ninety-two – did she live in the olden days like you were talking about?' He was obviously under the impression that the Edwardian period, when his great-gran was born, was not that far away from the time of the Greek gods. She could not blame him. Until she read more she had mixed up dates of the Celts and the Romans and the Anglo-Saxons.

When she got home, Susan could not keep the information to herself.

'Do you know, a child who saw me the afternoon I took the car out to where Thrush used to live – remember, I told you? – said today that his great-grandmother, who's over ninety, calls it Duck's

Cabin! What do you think about that? Another bird! Was Thrush a Duck? Or did another family live there before? It doesn't look all that old – perhaps built seventy-five years ago?'

'Duck?' said Dorothea, frowning. 'That's odd. You'd think they'd call it Thrush's Cabin – or Cuckoo's Cabin, if that was their nickname. You ought to tell Mr Cobb about it. He's still on the track of the attacker of Percy Thrush – thinks someone intended the man to die.'

'He's got a bee in his bonnet about it,' said Susan. 'You'd think we'd had enough excitement, now that the attack on Mrs Simmons has been more or less cleared up and our incestuous neighbours have departed.'

'I didn't go into details with him about Lisa. He'd guessed something was not quite right over at Number 3. He told me his own wife was killed in a hit-and-run accident, probably a drunk driver. They never found him.'

'How ghastly.' Susan's eyes filled with tears. Life seemed to be a more terrible business than she had ever imagined. She felt low. School exhausted her. She returned to that topic with her usual grumbles.

'I wouldn't mind if I felt I was doing any good. The older children enjoy the acting, but I know the head of faculty thinks the present project ought to be the last Shakespeare I do.'

Susan laboured for a certain Ronald Baker, the head of the Faculty of Arts, to which English and drama, along with the theatre arts and painting and craft belonged.

'I'm so glad I've retired,' said Dorothea. 'Poor Sue. Wouldn't you rather be doing something else?'

'You bet,' groaned Susan. Her dream was to enrol as a mature student at RADA and try once more to see if she could work in the theatre. She had earlier chosen to teach because her parents saw it as a nice, safe job. Which it certainly wasn't. Neither nice nor safe. But what job was, nowadays? She tried to cheer up that evening and read *Middlemarch*, feeling that Eastminster High had had enough of her energies for the day.

The other inhabitants of Heron Close were settling into their seasonal routine. There was a good deal of tidying of the garden and last-minute putting in of bulbs. Apparently someone had already leased the Smith garden centre. Shrubs had disappeared and the forecourt was full of tubs of autumn-flowering bulbs to catch the eye of motorists.

'They've no idea where Mr Smith has gone,' said Vera Whitwham to Mrs Maitland on returning from a shopping expedition in that direction with her husband. 'Isn't it odd? But Miss Kant says that Lisa has gone to London and is all right.'

'She's well out of that marriage,' agreed Eva Maitland.

'Got wed too young, I expect.'

'Bill and I were married young. I suppose I was just lucky,' replied Vera. She went in to her husband, who was once again boiling over at the antics of the adolescents in the town.

'Schools have no discipline any more,' he said. 'Loud-mouthed, dirty, and, I suspect, drunk. They couldn't have been more than eleven.' He was referring to two boys in the supermarket who had been swearing and shouting to the evident terror of the manager and the other shoppers.

'It can't just be the fault of the schools,' said Vera peaceably. 'It's the families. They think they're rearing wild animals, not human beings.' Vera had a pretty turn of phrase when she wanted, he thought.

'Well, let's hope there are no more attacks round here,' he said.

'The police caught the man. After the trial he'll be put inside,' she said soothingly.

'I don't suppose women will want to come and camp round here any more, though.'

'Wonder who our new neighbours will be?' said Vera, to change the subject. 'Quite a few people have been round to look at Number 3 and I expect if Mr Dawson and Mrs Maitland get wed there'll be another house on the market. I do hope it's someone young, with children.' Then she remembered that children grew up rather quickly into wild animals and hoped he would not descant upon the fact.

Still, he had seemed recently to want to patch up his quarrel with his son-in-law. Poor Val. She'd had to come without her husband when she visited them. It was silly – not that she minded having her daughter to herself, and cooing over the new baby, but Bill had been so angry about Val's husband Tom's left wing views that they had almost come to blows. Tom was a good man, even if his opinions were rather extreme, and he adored their daughter and the baby. It would all come right in the end if she were patient.

At Number 6 Eva Maitland was cooking a quiche for Pat Dawson, who now took almost every meal with her. They were both old enough to know their own minds, were well suited, but she knew that people of their age liked time by themselves, even if they lived together. She hoped Pat would take up golf after a bit. There was a course a few miles away. If only he'd drive again. He wanted her to visit his own grown-up family in the near future and she was rather dreading it.

She might persuade him to move with her somewhere less remote; she wanted to put the money she'd had left by her husband to good use. She'd helped him make it for several years and had a right to it. He had known she would look after it well. He'd been a lot older than she, for she'd been not much older than Linda Swift when she'd eloped with him. And it had worked out well, once he'd got his divorce. She smiled reminiscently and then thought: well, I deserved a break!

It hadn't quite worked out as she'd hoped down here. The place was a bit too isolated now that she felt better about going out alone, and it was so cold in winter.

She was feeling much less depressed, but she sensed that Pat was a townie really. She imagined a little second-hand bookshop they might buy if they sold up here.

Pat Dawson was looking forward to a nice supper. Eve had brought him out of his shell. He'd always wanted to marry a 'daughter of the people', as he thought of her.

Not like his first wife, Yvonne, who had had pretensions to culture and couldn't cook. He too was thinking that perhaps they might move away. All that business with the attacks on the women and the trouble with Kevin and Thrush had slightly unsettled him. Not that he'd had much time to brood over it. He'd been too busy sampling Eva's charms.

She seemed better now, though; she'd been so nervy earlier on in the year. It was because she was so frightened that they'd got talking, and one thing had led to another. . . . They might buy a little dog and he'd get her driving lessons. He never wanted to drive again.

Occasionally, even the proximity of Eva was not enough to make him stop wanting a drink, but he told himself it was now or never and he must learn to stick to mineral water: Evian and Eva! Sex was better than drink, on the whole. It had been life in London that had led to his problems; away from it he'd weaned himself off alcohol and it was thanks to Eva above all. She was an unexpected bonus in his life and he was eternally grateful. He'd do anything

for her. She was a plucky woman and they'd be good for each
other.

Sandy and David had also resumed the even tenor of their ways.
Neither wished just yet to set foot in the marina again, but they
were not going to be persecuted by false rumours. They would
stick it out and ignore any further letters if there were any.

'I don't think there will be any more,' Cobb had said, and they
believed him. But the thought that the planted robe had had something to do with the attack on Thrush gnawed at Sandy. They
speculated about Tony Smith. Why had he had such a down on
them? Not that they would ever be able to prove anything, of
course.

'Thank God he's gone,' said David. To think they'd entertained
him in their own home!

'The rest of the neighbours are OK though,' Sandy said.

'We could do worse. Even Whitwham.'

'He's too busy worrying about violence in society,' said Sandy.
'Chaps like him were brought up to think homosexuals were all
pansies and couldn't say boo to a goose, so he's not afraid of us,
even if he despises us.'

'Neither was Smith.'

'Oh, I think he felt in some way his maleness was threatened.
There's more than meets the eye in his departure. Susan Swann
knows something, I'm sure.'

'It's not our business,' replied David, and Sandy had to agree.

Cobb was still waiting on the Saturday for the report from his pal
when Mrs Swift, Linda's mother, came to 'do' for him. She flicked
a negligent duster round his ornaments, but was good at ironing,
which he hated. She was busy cleaning his bathroom when Susan
knocked at the door, having decided to pass on to Cobb the bit of
information about Thrush's shack. It was Dorothea who had
reminded her.

Cobb could hardly contain his excitement when he heard. He
had still not mentioned the doggerel to any of them but Susan, and
when she had finished her story he took it again from his locked
desk and showed it to her.

'What do you think of it now in conjunction with what you've
just told me?'

'You think Thrush was living under an assumed name? It seems too far-fetched. Why should he?'

'Who else would know he might be?' asked Cobb, his eyes on her.

'I didn't hear of Duck till this week,' said Susan hastily.

'No, I'm not suspecting you,' he laughed. 'But don't you see? If the police were checking up on him it would be under the name Thrush – and if he was called Duck – if that family of his were Ducks not Thrushes, or Cuckoos – they wouldn't look for him under that name.'

'But he's always been called Thrush here, hasn't he?'

'Let's ask Mrs Swift.'

He called her down and made a cup of tea for her, as was his wont. He didn't mention the name Duck but asked her what she knew of Thrush. Had he ever been called anything else?

'He was always known as Thrush,' she said. 'He's only been around Spire for two or three years – came to the close looking for work when the Whitwhams moved in. The old lady who used to live in his place died a few years ago. I assumed she was called Thrush. They say she was in hospital for ages. My dad might have known. They do say East End criminals often used to come to live round here.'

'I wonder where Percy was before the last two or three years,' mused Cobb. 'It probably wasn't here. I believe someone told me he'd worked in Birmingham,' he suggested at random.

'I wouldn't know anything about that. People round here often work away. One even went to New Zealand,' said Linda's mother. 'Can I finish the bathroom now?'

'Don't let's mention any of this to anyone else,' said Cobb to Susan. 'I had a hunch there was a Duck around. I might hear something new next week.'

There matters were left for the moment.

'He's making enquiries elsewhere,' said Susan when she returned. 'Thinks Thrush used to work in Birmingham.'

'Well, if he was a policeman he'll know how to go about it,' was all Dorothea said.

Cobb wondered as he sat in his clean house, eating his solitary supper, whether Thrush – Duck – had ever been inside, ever been convicted of attacking a child, for example. He felt sure he'd had a record, had changed his name because of it. Perhaps the old shack had been left to him after his mother was dead and nobody had claimed it at first. But he could not have claimed it, surely, unless he'd used his real name? Yet it was no crime to take an assumed name. People did it all the time. No law against it.

He'd have to go to the Land Registry to find out the name of the previous owner of the shack and see what name Thrush had used when he took over. He might just have squatted in it when he came back to the area. Or it might have been waiting for him. Old Mother Duck or Thrush must have left it to him, and she might have known his alias. Mothers often did.

Cobb was impatient now, was sure that something would turn up soon from the computer records. There were other places he could look if this came to nothing.

'Here I am,' he thought, 'chasing moonbeams, when as far as the police are concerned there was no crime.' He felt like a crab proceeding sideways with nothing but instinct to help him. *Someone* knew, though. That was the puzzle. Someone wanted Percy Thrush's attacker brought to justice. He would wait to see what Denis had turned up before alerting him to a new possibility.

The postman was late on Monday morning and Cobb had given up trying to listen for the advent of the red van which bumped up and down on the ruts of the lane before coming to a standstill at the entrance to the close. In the old days one postman would have traipsed along the village lanes with a much smaller bag of letters and he would certainly not have had to stagger along with all the junk mail that filled Cobb's hall.

Cobb bent down swiftly, hoping that this morning there might be a letter from his old friend. He had given up when he found it stuck by mistake to a large envelope offering him £100,000 for buying certain items of underwear or, as runner-up, a tour round the world. The letter was in a small brown envelope with Denis's unmistakable loopy handwriting. Cobb had not wanted to telephone. He disliked the instrument now he was free of the office.

He looked at the envelope with an absurd sensation of 'now or never', and a little sick feeling stirred in the pit of his stomach. He calmed himself, and took it, unopened, into his sitting-room. His own professional reputation was safe: nothing to do with him depended on the message he held, so why did he feel as though he would be responsible for more than the possible unmasking of Percy Thrush, and the reason for his perhaps being pushed off a not very high sea-wall?

197

Denis Pearson didn't write at length, but it was enough.

I searched your Percy Thrush on some old computer records that ought to have been destroyed. Eventually, I turned up a man of that name but in the following form: 'Duck aka Raven aka Thrush. Born 1939. National Service 1957–9. No record in army. Sentenced under name Percy Duck 8.8.1975 to life imprisonment for rape and murder Sutton Coldfield. Other offences taken into account.'

I found a later entry elsewhere showing release 8.8.90 to hostel. He should have reported quarterly but I can find no further info. Any use? Good hunting!

Denis.

Cobb sat down feeling rather dizzy. He had expected it some-how, the confirmation of all his hunches and the incontrovertible proof that there was more than met the eye in the whole Thrush saga. And he had *guessed* Birmingham! Now he must go to London to Colindale to check the story of that rape and murder.

He looked at his watch. He'd go straight away, sleep overnight, if necessary at a B and B near Liverpool Street, and stay till he had all he wanted. He rang a mini-cab firm in Eastminster and packed a bag, not forgetting his notebooks and sharp pencils. He felt absurdly excited.

CHAPTER SEVENTEEN

Cobb was away two days and returned on the Wednesday afternoon looking preoccupied. He had a lot of thinking to do. Not only had he been to the National Newspaper Library in North London, but he had also spent some time on the telephone to various institutions. Now he had to check with the local newspaper office where he would more easily find a further confirmation of his suspicions. That could wait until the next day.

He looked out of his window. The sun was glinting on the peaceful gardens and the old pond, and the sound of the wind was faint amongst the trees, most of which were now brown and yellow or bare instead of their summer green.

He would go for a walk to the beach to get a breath of fresh air. All this gadding about in London and the stuffy archives had made him long to be back in the country air. He was becoming quite a cabbage. Still, he had found almost all he wanted. The problem was only what to do with the information.

He had no intention of handing anyone over to the law. Besides, there was no proof of intent to kill. The only proven 'unnatural' death, if it could be called that, had been of the victim in 1968, who had, apparently, been raped then strangled and left naked except for her tights on a piece of waste ground near a park. Duck, or Thrush if you preferred, had been arrested, convicted and sentenced. Cobb's pertinacity had been rewarded; the newspaper reports had been detailed.

Tomorrow it only remained for him to check the records of purchases of land more than seventy years earlier by Thrush's father. He hoped he might find that in Eastminster by visiting the estate agent acting for the new purchasers.

As he walked along the beach, the sea grey now and more turbulent, he thought of the long-dead girl. If it had been a few years earlier Thrush might still have been given a capital sentence, but in fact not many murderers did receive that sentence even before the change in the law. But Thrush – or Duck – had *not* raped Pat Simmons, even if he had previously been guilty of a rape that had led to murder. Cobb's problem was now to link the story of the long-dead victim to someone local. He reviewed his tentative conclusions on the subject once more as he walked by the steel-grey waters.

Next afternoon he was coming out of the estate offices with the information he needed when he saw Susan Swann on the other side of the road with a shopping basket. She waved to him. He crossed over to her.

'Do you need a lift home?' she asked him. 'I've got the car in the town carpark.' She looked curiously at him. 'Have you found out about the Duck thing?' she asked. 'I mean, I nearly went in there myself and then I thought it was none of my business.' She gestured to the estate agents. When they were both stowed in the car, he replied:

'No. It's not my business either, is it. But I did find that our friend Thrush used to be called Percy Duck, if it's of any interest.'

'My God!' she said. 'So he *did* change his name! Why?'

'It's a long story,' said Cobb and said no more until they were out on the minor road, which led round the back of the estuary, heading for Spickhanger.

Then: 'I feel sure now he took your monk's robe and attacked Linda Swift,' he said.

'Oh, that bloody robe,' she said. 'Why did it turn up at Sandy's, then?'

'That would be Mr Smith putting his spoke in,' said Cobb. 'Anything to incriminate a man he didn't like – Dave or Sandy – it didn't matter which.'

'Then did Tony Smith attack Thrush? Push him over? Why?'

'I don't think it was Smith,' replied Cobb.

'But if Pat Dawson saw a man in a robe, that person must have been the one who stole it from my car at school and next day put it in Sandy's tool-shed! Who was it?'

'I'm not sure. But I think I might have an idea,' Cobb replied carefully.

'Well, Thrush – I mean Duck – is dead now; there's nothing we can do about it. Are you going to the police?'

'I have no proof. I've worked out why he might have been

hated. As to pushing him, I don't know.'

'Perhaps he just got frightened. Couldn't someone have dressed up to frighten *him* the way he frightened Linda? That must be it. And perhaps Tony Smith saw. Could it be Dave or Sandy, then?'

'They'd have every reason,' said Cobb.

'No one really liked Thrush – I mean Duck,' said Susan.

'I can tell you this, Susan,' said Cobb carefully. 'Thrush – or Duck – was a convicted criminal. Though I shouldn't say it, maybe he wasn't much loss.'

'Mr Whitwham is always saying capital punishment should be brought back. What was Duck's crime? Murder?'

She put the car into low gear as they began the slight rise up to the village of Spire.

'Someone did die. A girl,' he replied.

'A girl? You mean a little girl – someone's daughter?'

'Well, she would be someone's daughter, but no, not a *little* girl – a bit older than your friend Linda.'

'They said – my letter said – I was having a lesbian relationship with Linda, you know,' she said after a pause, 'I think it was from Smith.'

'I hope you didn't let it upset you,' said Cobb.

'No, I knew it was nonsense. I tore it up.'

'I've just been checking who built the old shack Thrush lived in,' continued Cobb, changing the subject. 'It was his father. They all came from the East End. There was a large family. Our Perce was the eldest of his father's second wife's. All dead now, I believe. Our friend came back here after his release, changed his name, and hey presto! He may have intended to go straight. Why he should suddenly attack young Linda we can only guess. I imagine he thought she knew about his miserable childhood and was taunting him about the Cuckoos. It must have been a sudden impulse. Would he have carried it through? I think he would. I believe someone coming up from the sailing-post past the barn – Darren Bogworthy in fact, interrupted him. It gave the fellow an idea of a rape he might then pin on Thrush.'

'The one who they say raped Mrs Simmons? So seeing Thrush – I mean Duck – struggling with her gave him the idea.'

'Yes.'

'They're absolutely sure Thrush didn't rape Pat Simmons?'

'Quite sure. My police friend tells me that it's pretty certain that Darren Bogworthy will be convicted after a confession. He'll say he was under the influence of drugs.'

'But Linda – if she weren't such a level-headed girl. I mean, I know she panicked at first, but anyone would've. She might have been scarred for life – or even gone round the bend? Why should he get away with it? Of course,' she went on, 'we weren't to know he'd done worse before.'

'No,' said Cobb. 'We weren't to know.'

The car came down the lane now and Heron Close lay before them in the afternoon sun.

'I like late autumn,' said Cobb.

Susan sighed. 'If only it didn't lead to winter.'

'I think I'll drop in on Dave and Sandy,' said Cobb.

Susan stopped the car and leaned back for her basket. He thought what a pretty girl she was – or rather woman. He had to keep reminding himself that it was not politically correct, was sexist nowadays, to call a young woman a girl.

Susan smiled at him. By God, if she'd been his daughter, his and Edna's, and someone had raped *her*, strangled *her*, he'd have wanted him dead, might have done more than give him a gentle push. It was perhaps a good thing he *had* retired.

'You look angry,' she said.

'No – just sad,' he replied.

'I've got a rehearsal this evening for my play,' she confided. 'It'll take my mind off Percy, I hope.'

Susan returned exhausted the evening after the first meeting for those interested in *Twelfth Night*. She was already late for school on Friday morning, but managed to give Dorothea an abbreviated version of Mr Cobb's deductions. Miss Kant was suitably impressed.

'So Jim thinks it was certainly Thrush – Duck who attacked Linda? If that's the case, thank goodness he's not here to attack anyone else. To think people come to the country for peace and quiet.'

'I expect he returned to his childhood haunts,' said Susan.

'I've decided to go to town today, to see Lisa,' said Dorothea. 'I promised I'd keep in touch and she still hasn't collected those things of hers. I'll take them along.'

'I don't expect she will ever come back here. I wouldn't,' said Susan.

*

Cobb could only wait. He had done all he thought he should. Now it was up to someone else to tie up the loose ends for him. He occupied himself planning his garden – he rather liked the colour of those large, straggly Michaelmas daisies. Edna had liked mauve. Really, it would be easier just to grow roses and not bother with planting herbaceous borders. Not large pink and orange floribundas like those in the gardens of several 'Spirants', which he thought were rather awful, but *old* roses. He doubted, though, whether the pebbly, salty soil would provide the right nourishment for them. He decided to get a load of topsoil and some bone-meal, and plant some next March. They had still not had a frost – might he even put them in now? He was pondering this problem and raking sycamore leaves from the tree that overhung his garden when Miss Kant came out of her garden next door, carrying a briefcase and a small suitcase.

'Take anything you like from my garden,' she said. 'There are heaps of seeds you could still garner from the back.'

'I haven't got green fingers like you,' grumbled Cobb. 'Are you off on a jaunt, then?'

'I'm going to see Lisa, and then staying at my club for the weekend,' she replied, as she climbed into her old car. 'I've a college reunion,' she added, poking her head out of the car window.

'I hear that was a good turn you did for little Mrs Smith,' said Cobb, 'I hope she'll be happy now.'

'If I'm not back by seven on Monday, I've left a note for Susan on the dresser about taking some plants to you and the men at Number 4 – she had to go off in a hurry. Would you remind her? They said they were going to have a few days away this weekend themselves, so she needn't bother till Monday.'

'Certainly. Have a nice time.'

' 'Bye then. Good gardening!'

Cobb returned to his contemplation of an ideal garden and saw both Whitwhams come out of their house.

'Going to Eastminster,' they shouted. 'Anything we can get you?'

'A loaf of bread would be nice,' Cobb shouted back and Vera gave him a friendly wave.

Really, there were compensations for retirement, he thought. Time to stand and stare. Time to chat to neighbours.

Sandy and David were dressed very formally for them and he wondered where they were going. They were said to patronize various expensive restaurants in Suffolk when funds were good.

'We can't slave all day every day over the kitchen sink,' Sandy had once said. They must be making a weekend of it.

The Smiths' house was still empty and already looked neglected. Lisa had always kept the windows bright and shining and now in three weeks they had become dusty and smeary. He looked up, as Pat Dawson and Eva Maitland came out of the latter's house, wheeling two bicycles and looking rather self-conscious.

'Good for the middle-aged flab,' said Dawson, as they wobbled past him in his garden and started down the lane to Spire.

Cobb was all alone now on the close and for a moment he felt a little depersonalized. But he conquered this in his usual way through a burst of activity, cleaning his own outside windows with great energy. When that was finished he went in to read a new book on the Dark Ages which Dorothea had lent him and which his criminal researches had left him no time for.

That weekend it was chilly but the sun managed to break through. England had so many varieties of weather, thought Cobb. On the Monday it rained and he fell asleep in the afternoon, it was so dark. He woke to hear Susan's car arrive. He thought about preparing his supper. When Edna died he determined not to let himself go, not to eat snacks or raid the fridge, but to eat the way he knew she would want him to. As they had had no children, his wife had often treated him rather maternally, and now that he was alone he was determined to err on the side of coddling rather than neglecting himself. But it was seven o'clock by the time he had made his omelette, nicely flavoured with chives from his garden, eaten it and then finished off some home-grown apples flavoured with a clove or two and washed it all up.

He sat down to see if there was anything worthwhile on television. He didn't like to miss anything good, but was usually rather relieved when he could read a book and take notes without feeling anything of great importance had passed him by on the screen. There had been nothing of interest on the news, just the usual recital of international misadventures. The time was past when he had thought that by voting in a certain way he could do anything about them.

He was just settling down to the Dark Ages once more, with a map, and making plans for a visit to St Peter-juxta-Mare, when there was a tap at his back door. He opened it to find Susan.

'Has Miss Kant telephoned you?' she asked him. 'You told me she said that if she wasn't back by seven today – she's at her club and was going to see Lisa – that she'd left an envelope on the dresser about some plants. I'd almost forgotten about it but as she isn't back I remembered. On the envelope inside all it said was: "Open this and go to see Mr Cobb". It wasn't stuck down, and inside there was this envelope with your name on it. Nothing about bulbs or plants.' She sounded puzzled, worried.

'She did say she'd left a note for you about some plants for Number 4.' He scratched his head. 'You'd better come in.'

Susan came into the kitchen and gave him a brown envelope.

'Have a cup of coffee,' he said. 'There's some left in the pot.' He busied himself pouring one out and then sat down with her at the table. He slit open the envelope. Susan watched him as he read it.

'Well?'

'It says to go up to her bedroom together,' he said. 'There is something for me there.'

'Her *bedroom*? What on earth is all this about?' Susan was remembering Lisa's similar note.

Cobb did not reply, but said: 'I'll come with you – if I may.'

Together they left the house, Cobb locking the door behind him. He was always careful in that respect, even in Spickhanger. They both went into Number 2.

'I've never been in her bedroom,' said Susan. 'We only meet downstairs, though I've been a few times into her study for books.'

They walked up the open staircase and Susan held back when she had indicated the door to Cobb. He gestured her in. She did not quite know what she expected to find. He followed her in. The curtains were drawn, but in the half-light they saw a dark cover on the bed. Cobb drew the curtains.

'It's . . . no it isn't! I thought it was the monk's robe,' said Susan. They looked down at the bed upon which was spread a dark shape. 'It's her MA gown,' said Susan. 'I know she has one because we joked once about the teachers at Eastminster who used to wear them in the old days.'

'Her MA gown,' said Cobb thoughtfully. Then he saw a note on the bedside table, propped against a vase.

Dear Susan and Dear Bill.
Expect a letter in the post on Tuesday, unless there has been another postal strike! This is just to tell you not to worry but

to listen to the late Anglian TV news bulletin on Monday. DK.

The vase was full of dying, feathery leaves, and next to it there was a small painting of tall, spiky-looking flowers with dark red blooms.

'Did she say she'd left a note for me about some plants?' enquired Susan. 'Well, there's no note here. What does it all mean? Is it something about Lisa, do you think?'

Cobb looked again at the dark MA gown with its scarlet hood lying on the bed like some sacrifice. It was all clear to him now.

'I think, Susan, all we can do is wait for the news on television,' he said.

'And for the promised letter,' Susan said. 'I've never been in here before. Why has she put her gown on the bed? And why are you looking at those flowers so intently?'

'Let's go downstairs,' he said. 'Come to my house for a drink. I've still got the bottle of Scotch my policeman friend brought me – unless you want to wait by yourself.'

She had tried to prepare Susan for the worst, he thought. His mind would have worked in the same way.

They went back into Number 1, Cobb reminding the girl to lock up.

When he had poured her a drink and added soda, and poured himself a Perrier with lemon, he said:

'Those flowers – the ones in the picture – and the leaves in the vase – she grows them in her garden at the back. You can keep them in pots. Do you know what they're called?'

'Haven't a clue,' said Susan. 'I've never taken much interest in gardening. Dorothea always says that no one under thirty-five ever did.'

'The flowers are *amaranth*,' said Cobb. 'I do know, because she once pointed them out to me amongst others.'

'Amaranths – amaranth? There's a poem about fields of amaranth,' said Susan.

'They have another more colloquial name – two in fact: the prince's feathers – and love-lies-bleeding,' he murmured.

'The dead ones in the vase do look like droopy feathers. Fancy having some in a pot by her bed. "Love-lies-bleeding"? Oh, Mr Cobb, I'm frightened. Is she foreseeing someone murdering her or something – Tony Smith!'

'I don't think you need worry about *him*,' Cobb answered.

'What did that poem say?'

Susan knitted her brows. 'No, it wasn't a poem,' she said at last. 'It was something I once had to recite at school. I'm trying to remember the author – wait! I've got it: Walter Savage Landor. Something like: *"Helen died; Leda the beloved of Jupiter went before."* We had it for a competition for spoken English.'

But Cobb was busy rummaging through his bookshelf.

'Landor . . . Lawrence – yes, Landor. Knew I had it!' He looked rather shamefaced. 'I read quite a lot of poetry,' he said, 'but this was something I read when Edna – my wife – died.' He looked in the index. As he came back to the table she saw it was an anthology.

'Here we are. You read the passage, will you?'

She took the book from him.

'Read it all. I'm sure you read very well.'

Susan cleared her throat glanced first at the passage:

'Laodemeia died: Helen died: Leda, the beloved of Jupiter went before.

'Oh, now I remember!

'It is better to repose in the earth betimes than to sit up late: better than to cling pertinaciously to what we feel crumbling under us, and to protract an inevitable fall. We may enjoy the present while we are insensible of infirmity and decay: but the present, like a note in music, is nothing but as it appertains to what is past and what is to come. There are no fields of amaranth on this side of the grave: there are no voices, O Rhodope, that are not soon mute, however tuneful: there is no name, with whatever emphasis of passionate love repeated, of which the echo is not faint at last . . .'

'Ah,' said Cobb. 'I should have known – I think I did – it was the " 'Twas" in the poem about Thrush being pushed. It sounded like pastiche of some old story or folk-song.'

Susan looked blank.

'I wasn't sure,' said Cobb, heavily. 'But she wanted me to know. We'd better watch the news.'

'What did she want?' Susan asked. But he only repeated:

'Yes, she wanted it.'

She stared at him.

'I'll tell you later. Will you watch the local news with me? It's after the main news.'

'What are we expecting to hear?' cried Susan.

He took the book from her.

'I don't think I'm wrong this time,' he said.

He switched on the television and turned the sound down until the end of the main bulletin.

'Amaranth,' said Susan. 'Love-lies-bleeding.'

'Yes, love-lies-bleeding. A very poetic conceit for a horrible end.'

'Well, Thrush – I mean Duck – didn't lie bleeding – at least, not much,' said Susan.

'Nobody loved Thrush,' said Cobb.

'I thought all that was over. Why did you rake it up? You did, didn't you?' she accused him, stony-eyed.

'Only because it didn't make sense. I hate things not to make sense. Miss Kant wanted things to make sense too.'

'Look, it's coming on.'

He turned up the sound and they waited. Reports of arson in Southend, a lost child in Basildon. Susan lit a forbidden cigarette, nerves stretched to breaking point. Then, suddenly:

'. . . The body of an Essex woman, was found this afternoon in her room at the Hero Club, an exclusive club for graduates, in Marylebone. Foul play is not suspected. . . .'

That was all.

Susan was white-lipped.

'The police will be ringing your phone at Number 2,' said Cobb. 'I'm surprised they haven't before. She probably left a note.'

'Then it wasn't murder – Foul play? How do they know?' Susan swayed and sat down suddenly.

'Have you the number of her club?' asked Cobb.

'Yes, I think it'll be in the telephone book we kept near the phone.'

'I'll take you back to your house again, if I may, and ring from there.'

Susan felt limp. She still could not take all this in. 'Are you sure?'

'She told us to listen, didn't she?' He shook his head, weary and sad.

*

He was soon on the line to London.

'Chief Inspector Cobb, Retired. South Riding Police, ringing from Essex. May I speak to the officer if he's still there?' Then: 'I was told to telephone you,' he semi-lied. 'About the accident today at the Hero Club. Would you mind telling me if the body is that of a Miss Dorothea Kant? You can't? Then will you please ring George Graham, Chelmsford police, and ask him to ring me?' He put down the phone. 'I'd forgotten I have no authority any more.'

'I'll wait up, if you don't mind.'

'I think you'd better get to bed.'

'I shan't sleep. Would you ring me when you hear from Chelmsford?' she asked.

Cobb promised and left, patting her arm as he said goodbye.

'Try not to think about it, Susan. It isn't murder – of that I'm sure.'

He sat alone with his glass of Perrier reviewing all the facts he knew. He was not going to tell more than was necessary. The police weren't the only people to keep secrets.

Later, when he had almost despaired of Graham's ring, the telephone bell sounded. Before the phone had even finished ringing its first burst, the receiver was in his hand.

'George. I asked them to let you know I'd rung – they wouldn't tell me anything. Was it my neighbour? Yes? She left a note telling us to watch the news. Yes. Oh, I see. No, she may have been depressed. A note for the coroner? "This is the best way". I see. You'll ring me in the morning. Yes. OK.'

He put the phone down. Distalgesic, brandy and a plastic bag over the head. What a way to go.

He went heavily up to bed, and then remembered to phone Susan.

'Susan – it *was* Dorothea.' He heard her catch her breath. 'Yes. Suicide. Will you be all right? I can make you up a bed here. All right, if you're sure. Wait till morning. The post comes at about half past eight. She may have written to you. Try to put it out of your mind till then. No, I know. Take a sleeping-pill, my dear – she wouldn't have wanted you to lie fretting.'

In the night he reviewed his old friends: Motive, Opportunity, Means and Character. The motive had been the problem all along. But as for means, a man like Duck, knowing he'd frightened a girl by dressing in a monk's robe on a dusky evening, would be scared

out of his wits. No wonder he'd fallen. A bloodless crime. But –
what, if just to be sure, she'd . . . no, there was only the bang on
the head against the concrete. That couldn't have been foreseen.
Had he died straight away? He thought it likely. Then he remembered again the intention he had so earnestly discussed with her,
perhaps unconsciously knowing even then, but wanting to be
certain. What had he said, and she'd agreed? The crime was in the
intention.

Now he knew who and how. She'd *wanted* him to guess – that
doggerel! A give-away. Who else but Dorothea would have used a
fake antiquarian ' 'tis', and a pun, so exactly? Not even Susan or
Dawson. The letter would explain it all, but he almost knew
already, had guessed, once he'd seen the Colindale reports. And
the flowers. Not just a poetic touch, but also a cry of the heart. Yes,
she was capable of killing for that. And capable of exactly this sort
of crime – which would not be a crime if he said nothing.

And he was going to say nothing.

She'd left it to him, he knew.

CHAPTER EIGHTEEN

Next morning Cobb was sitting waiting once more for the sound of the post van coming down the lane. Last night seemed dreamlike, or like a story he had once read. But it was not fiction. It was a fact, and facts were what he'd lived by until Edna had died. He could eat no breakfast yet, but sat on. Had Dorothea managed to see Lisa in London? The death would be a blow to her. He had admired Dorothea Kant. He still admired her.

He heard the sound of the van faintly in the distance so he got up and went to the window. He saw the young postman walk perkily to Number 2 then turn into Number 4 and put something through the box. Susan would be up. Poor girl, she had to go off to school in the middle of all this. The postman came up his own path next and pushed through a handful of mail. Cobb waited a moment, and then retrieved it. He took the bundle into the kitchen and made another cup of tea. He sipped it as he looked through his post. Another circular, a letter from Yorkshire – he recognized his sister-in-law's writing – and a long buff envelope, with the address typed. He looked at the post-mark: London NW1. This would be it. Before he could open it he saw Susan at the window.

'I've got a note from her,' she burst out. 'It says will I give you the keys to her desk. You can explain everything to me this evening.' She thrust a ring of keys at him. 'This one's the desk one. She told me once where her will would be if she had an accident, or anything . . . happened to her.'

She paused a moment. 'I'll go now, Mr Cobb, I must go to school.'

She had been crying but had decided not to miss her day's teaching. It would be better than sitting full of unanswered questions, in a dead person's house amongst her possessions, thinking about her, agonizing over the past and the future. Cobb would take care of everything. Cobb was good and kind and practical and Dorothea had trusted him.

Susan felt rather wobbly and wished someone could give her a lift. Cobb showed no surprise that she was off to work.

'Drive carefully. Try to forget it till tonight,' he said. She shook her head, went out and got into her car.

Cobb weighed the key in his hand and then went back to his tea.

He opened the buff envelope and took out a long letter.

It began with a scribbled P.S:

Before I forget, will you please extract from my bureau two large scrapbooks and several green-backed files and burn them. I'd rather no one but you and Susan knew of their existence.

Then the letter proper began.

Dear Mr Cobb

Perhaps I might say this time, Dear Jim?

For years I have pored over the daily reports, increasing exponentially as the years have gone by, and ever increasing still, of the victims of vandalism, destruction, violence, sadism, wanton, gratuitous acts of cruelty; they have almost been a relief from my own obsession. Am I, unlike these patient victims, a monster? Or have I been just more rational in my planning? I don't know. I hate violence except when I am defending myself against it. Then I take my sword – as a mother might whose child has been slaughtered, and 'civilization' goes out of the window just as surely as it did when we had to defend ourselves against Hitler, the murderer of innocent Jews.

You will by now, I expect, have guessed that I was responsible for the death of Percy Duck, an event which I must confess gave me at first a sensation of pure gratification. I planned to kill him long, long ago and even now cannot quite believe that he is dead. You know that I think it is intention that counts and I had the firm intention to remove him from this world. I wanted him to have a taste of his own medicine. Alas, I can no longer believe in hell, where he would undoubtedly have gone – or is the theology I was once taught now too old-fashioned?

212

He was found guilty of murder in 1975, almost half a century ago. The evidence was decisive and he was sentenced to life with a recommendation of 20 years. He was therefore eligible for release in 1995 but years taken off for good conduct, and the fact that he had admitted his guilt allowed him out earlier on parole.

If we had still been hanging murderers in 1975, if Duck had been offered the option of suicide, an option I believe all murderers should be offered, I do not think he would have taken it. He 'could not help himself' he said.

There is not one of us perfect and I suppose nobody is utterly worthless, but the girl I loved, whom Percy Duck murdered, was beautiful and brilliant as well as good, and when he was on trial for her murder I swore I would avenge her. I do not believe in lynch law but in my terrible grief it helped me first of all to imagine putting him to death with a sort of wild justice.

When Rachel died, I wanted to die too, but I have not had the courage before, and I wished to avenge her. It has taken a long time. Duck was stupid as well as cruel. I'm sure you will have by now read the details of the case.

I have been regularly and secretly to Rachel's grave since her death. Her parents keep it up. They knew nothing about us. That was almost the hardest thing to bear, for I loved her too. Twenty-one may still be young, I know, to make up your mind you are homosexual. But Rachel knew, and she loved me. I adored her, but we were discreet. I was seventeen years older, and was her tutor at college at the time. Duck was the care-taker of a school in the area where Rachel did her teaching-practice.

I felt certain he would eventually go back to his native county when he was released. When I was driving round this area, planning to move here myself, I saw a report in an Eastminster paper that a certain Mrs Joan Duck had died. I ascertained later that a man, who went by the name of Thrush, had taken up residence in her old shack. Nobody remembered him as Duck, though some solicitor must have acknowledged his right to the dwelling. (You could have checked that in your investigations!)

He had lived near Spire as a child. All his brothers and sisters – it was a large family – seem now to be scattered. Not one of them did he contact, or I should have known. Many of the present inhabitants of Spire came in the last twenty years; the old were all carted away to homes elsewhere. When I moved here – I was one of the first – the Whitwhams were advertising for a handyman-gardener. I helped them with the notice and added 'perhaps a retired caretaker'. This brought him here, as I knew it would.

Duck was not a psychopath but I knew he could not suppress his urge to rape. Nobody here would ever be able to prove it was he who had frightened Linda, so if I had not done what I did he would have gone on to worse acts. The police did not take the crime of 'frightening' Linda seriously enough.

I knew I would be playing God, but if you do not believe in a deity, that is only a matter of semantics.

After the first euphoria, my feelings of relief were succeeded by a tremendous guilt, even though I felt that he deserved to die. I had waited a very long time for this opportunity to come up and had begun to believe it never would. The attack on Linda Swift played into my hands and firmed my resolution. I knew his habits and I also knew he was a coward. Who knows what he might have done next? Who knows what other crimes of his still lie undiscovered? Linda was lucky. There may have been other Lindas who were not. Even after over thirty years the man had not changed, whatever 'expert' psychiatrists might have said.

You will by now have discovered my MA gown. Poor Sandy! Tony Smith did his best to suggest the men at Number 4 had something to do with the death of Duck, by the clumsy manoeuvre of stealing Susan's robe from her unlocked car in the school carpark. This confused everyone. He knew nothing, was an arrogant fool. More than a fool: a really vile man. Like Duck, who perhaps had more excuse, I don't know.

I intended first of all to give Duck a fright in his half-intox-icated half-sleepy state. Then I'd push him off the wall. I hoped he might die of fright, but that would be too much to expect. Yes, I, an intelligent educated woman, planned to kill him with a brick. It was fortunately not necessary. He had made himself an easy target for anyone to use his own ploy against him, and then I pushed him over the sea-wall, uttering her name as I pushed him. He'd surely remember that name even in a fuddled state.

Revenge is sweet only if the victim knows the motive. As I hovered over him with a brick I saw that the lump of concrete 'rock' had done my work for me. I left him dead, as he left my Rachel dead after raping and strangling her. Even now I can hardly bear to write these words. You will have found the details in your newspaper research, or from your colleagues in law enforcement.

According to the law, I would probably be responsible for his death by manslaughter, but as it was my intention to kill him I believe I was guilty of murder. I know that what I did was immoral but I believe it was just, a symbol for others in my position whose stories you will find when you open my desk, others whose loved ones will never return, who died at the hands of rapists and murderers. Think of the parents of little children, whose lives, already ruined, go on being ruined, unable ever to repair their loss, unless they believe, as I cannot, in eternal punishment or in a just God.

You will say, not only reparation, but also the satisfaction of the ancient eye for an eye and tooth for a tooth; in this case, a body for a body. . . . Barbarous? Perhaps. But I have always thought it odd to take upon us as human beings to 'forgive' those who have not sinned against us, but against the lovers and husbands and wives and parents and brothers and sisters of the murdered. I could even now escape punishment for what I did by pretending I intended only a little shock to the system. Yet I am led to an inescapable conclusion – in accord with all my philosophy of life. The reason for my anger is the betrayal of so many innocents in our society when the punishment does not fit the crime. It is not remorse or guilt or masochism that lead me to my suicide, but my sense of justice. I may faintly hope too that I might see my beloved Rachel once more, for if there were an after life, she would come from Heaven to take me away from Hell. My only regret is that I could not die in the body long ago when she did – when my soul died. . . . I tried once, but at the last moment I could not bear him *to live on if I were dead.*

The letter went on, in a beautiful script that Cobb appreciated even as he was saddened and dismayed.

I knew someone would find Percy Duck in the morning and am sorry only that it was Mr Robson, who is a sensitive soul under his camp jauntiness.

You may find it ironic that I began my intellectual life as a pacifist. I am not sorry for what I have done but I must judge myself if there is no god to judge me. This is probably the only world we have. Strange that in the ages of faith men thought nothing of dispatching the souls of murderers to death, to await God's vengeance, but we take it upon ourselves to keep alive those who have taken away a life, because we believe only in this world. My own life is nothing. I do not fear to die, for it has been a living death. I have evened up the score, if nothing else. And now, to be true to my own convictions, I must perish too.

I have always loved and desired my own sex, but I did not 'seduce' Rachel. Who could I blame for that 'perversion' visited upon me? God? Rachel was like me, and we loved each other. We had arranged to share a house after she had finished her training, although we were not yet lovers. I have never taken advantage of my position as teacher or tutor.

At least the bad has now perished, along with the good. Percy Duck has already been turned to dust in the crematorium, and my body will rot or be consumed, like Rachel's.

I do what I do now not from hatred of life but as an affirmation of its value and a protest that life lingered in one who took away the only life a young woman had, a man who had very likely raped and murdered before 1975 and a man who could easily murder again. Only the advent of that oaf from the marina stopped him raping Linda, I'm sure of that. Remember, Jim, how many violent crimes are never discovered, how many innocent victims are women and children, just as in warfare.

There remain only practical matters. I have left Susan my house. She will be able to leave teaching if she wants. She is a gifted young woman and – to make things clear to you and her – I have never had any designs upon her virtue. You will find my will in the bureau.

You too have suffered, I now know, from a crime perhaps almost as grave as that which killed Rachel Wolstenholme. But you are a moderate, temperate man, and in the end you would not have taken action, even though you think you would.

Unlike Mr Whitwham, you do not believe in the state taking vengeance on behalf of its citizens. Perhaps I don't either, or I'd have been denied the satisfaction of a personal revenge. I hope one day you will be happy again and I hope that Susan and 'Lisa' will both find someone to love them. David and Sandy would have a fellow-feeling for me if they knew, wouldn't they?

I have written quite enough. I ask you now only to scatter my ashes in the same cemetery as Rachel Wolstenholme. I enclose all the details for you to do this. As my last wish, I ask you, as long as you are alive, every year on the anniversary of my death, to place on her grave a pot of love-lies-bleeding: Amaranthus is more evocative than 'rosemary for remembrance' or 'myosotis for forget-me-not'. Will you do this for me? If I need forgiveness it is only from the god in whom I cannot believe, that I should receive it. Otherwise forget me; I do not ask for forgiveness from any human being.

You will find all my affairs in good order. I have written to my brother in Ontario. Tell Susan the details of my case – as far as you think fit. I leave it to you whether you inform anyone else in authority.

Farewell,

Dorothea Kant.

Cobb remembered the reports he had read at Colindale. Duck had gone to a pub nearby after the murder and people had noticed he was wearing a lady's woollen scarf he had taken away from his victim. He said later he had been carried away, did not intend to kill her – just lost his temper when she would not say good-evening to him. A likely story. A beautiful young woman represented a 'lucky' person to Percy and he needed to feel powerful after being powerless all his life, thought Cobb, as he sat a long time at his table reading and rereading Dorothea's last testament.

Then he took his spade, went to her garden and dug up one of the now re-grown amaranth plants. He replanted it in his own.

His dictionary gave the meaning of amaranth as 'not withering'. It would not flower again this year now, but would remind him to buy a new plant next year, and maybe also sow some seeds in spring.

Susan and Cobb opened Dorothea's desk together that evening.

217

Messages from the Metropolitan Police and from the secretary of the Hero Club were being dealt with. There would be an inquest, although the short note she had left appeared to have said all that was necessary:

> *This is the best way. I am taking my life because there is no longer anything to live for. Please advise J Cobb, 1 Heron's Close, Spickhanger, near Spire, Essex, who will undertake funeral arrangements. DK.*

'Lisa' had telephoned in great distress and Susan had attempted to calm her down. Now Cobb and Susan were sitting in Dorothea's study before the oak bureau and taking out two enormous scrapbooks and file upon file of newspaper cuttings from the cupboards and drawers. Her last will and testament was in an open envelope, with the solicitor's name and address clearly marked on the cover in the immaculate handwriting. When they had taken it all downstairs, Susan said:

'I still don't understand. Will you explain to me? I can make us something to eat and you can tell me about it. The others will be coming round, I know. It's spread all round the close.'

Cobb told her over their meal the essence of Miss Kant's letter and Susan kept shaking her head.

'I don't know how an actress on stage would receive all this,' she said. 'I just feel stunned – I can't take it in. Silence seems at first the only response.' There were hot tears in her eyes. 'She was noble,' she said. 'I never dreamed she was a lesbian, but then, of course, I am not, and she wouldn't have . . .' her voice trailed away miserably.

'I am not going to tell on her,' said Cobb. 'What good would it do? It's all over and done with. She's paid for her crime.'

'No one but you ever really thought Thrush – I mean Duck, *had* been murdered – or even attacked,' said Susan. 'She needn't have died – it seems such a waste. That horrible man. What if it had gone wrong with Linda? He could have killed her, never mind rape her. Why do men do these things?'

Cobb was silent, crumbling his bread. Then:

'Perhaps men are weaker vessels – some of them anyway. Forgive me for trying to unearth the truth.'

'In which case, was it even Thrush's fault the way he was?' asked Susan, following her own thoughts about human iniquity.

'That's what she was asking herself, when I made enquiries about Duck Cabin. Perhaps it should have been called Throstles' Nest. Anyway, I gather the father was a very unpleasant character. In those days people didn't report such things as child abuse, but I'd guessed that was what he did.'

'So Percy Duck was victim too?'

'It might seem so, but Dorothea thought we all possess free will. I'm beginning to wonder. That's what keeps me from joining the Bring Back the Birch or Chop off their Heads brigade.'

'My ex-boyfriend, Richard, used to talk a lot about free will and determinism,' said Susan. 'I never understood the half of it. Seems to me we're all born with both good and bad and some are just better than others. We don't all start with the same brains, or physique, so why should we start with the same capacity for virtue?'

'I agree with you, I suppose,' said Cobb.

'There but for the grace of God,' said Susan.

'You can't have punishment without the idea of responsibility for your actions,' he said after a pause.

'Richard used to say that God was dead and therefore everything was permitted.'

'Dostoievsky or Nietzsche said it first – and it's only *if* he's dead. I don't believe that Dorothea felt quite like that. '

This Richard seemed to have been a young man full of sententiousness. She was well out of his clutches, he thought.

'Will you leave teaching and go to drama school?' he asked. 'She's left you the house, you could get about two hundred and thirty thousand or more for it, I should think – prices round here are getting as bad as London since the diesels were introduced.'

'I hate to feel I'm profiting from misery,' she said.

'Dorothea would have wanted you to make the most of your chance. Life is very strange. You know that I lost my wife through a crime – a driver out of control. Probably drunk. Should I have tried to track him down? Was I at fault in leaving it alone? I was a policeman and the police are trained to believe in justice, not vengeance.'

'Violence breeds violence; there's a never-ending chain, isn't there?' she said.

'I did want revenge. Now I don't feel I do any more. But I cannot honestly say that I feel sorry for what Dorothea did. I suppose I shouldn't,' he said quietly.

'A girl she loved – raped and strangled – it's all so horrible. You don't want to feel the world is like that. Think of the girl's parents too. How could Dorothea behave normally after she had disposed of Thrush?'

'She probably felt at peace, and then with all the fuss about monks' robes and the rape of Pat Simmons and the problems of Kevin and his friends and "Lisa" Smith, it must almost have seemed even to her as if his death *was* an accident. But she knew she would have to pay in the end, if only by punishing herself, for she realized I was on the right track. She *wanted* me to find out!'

Susan found there was nothing she could say to this.

'Do you think we might burn those scrapbooks?' said Cobb. 'I don't want to keep all the evidence of man's inhumanity.'

Dorothea Kant was cremated in the same crematorium as Percy Duck. None of the other Heron Closers but Cobb and Susan knew the truth, but the Whitwhams and Sandy and David attended the cremation, along with many other friends of Dorothea's, including Mrs Swift and George Graham, neither of whom had been told the whole story. An official from the Humanist Association conducted the service according to the deceased's wishes.

The Whitwhams looked bewildered, but the flowers were beautiful, and Susan read the passage from Landor. Afterwards, Patrick Dawson and Eva Maitland joined the rest of the mourners at Cobb's.

When it was all over, Cobb extracted the notes Dorothea had written on the local history of the Hundred and began his own researches. It took his mind off more emotional matters.

Later, he took her ashes to be scattered on Rachel Wolstenholme's grave.

AFTERWORD

When the new century began, the growth in ownership of mobile phones, along with the refinement of DNA analysis, was transforming the work of the forces of law and order, although police computers were not yet centralized. Susan thought of the death of Percy Duck, alias Thrush, as *The Tragedy of Dorothea Kant*. It was, in Susan's opinion, partly an accident. It might have been a murder, would have been if the man had not hit his head as he fell and thus completed Dorothea's work for her.

In spite of technology, such crime as violent unprovoked stabbings, shootings and gratuitous aggression – actions usually with far less motivation than Dorothea Kant's – was growing. It was ironic that Dorothea had considered that her crime was worse because she had wanted the man dead. A crime of passion if ever there was one.

Cobb took a long time to stop feeling guilty for his part in Dorothea's suicide. She was guilty, yes, but had he not wanted revenge on his wife's killer? Did not the many hundreds of people whose loved ones were killed by drunken drivers feel just as vengeful as those who had loved the victims of psychopaths or murdering paedophiles? That way, however led to lynch law: he knew all the arguments against revenge The Old Testament preached one thing and the New Testament another. What about war, when killing was in sell-defence, or when the innocent were slaughtered? What had the church to say about that? Who was then 'guilty'? Or had we now dispensed with guilt? Yet he often wondered if he had been nothing but a busybody, ex-policeman or no. He said nothing to George Graham about Miss Kant's letter, and eventually burned it. He knew most of it by heart.

221

Susan Swann was to leave teaching altogether and to become a mature student at RADA, having sold Number 2, left to her in Dorothea's will, to a young couple who had a baby, with another on the way.

Sandy and David promised to keep in touch with her. They had both enjoyed her production of *Twelfth Night* and admired her for carrying on with it after the traumatic events of that year. It was to be Susan's last school production, and Linda Swift as Olivia was much praised.

David and Sandy remained at the close, always preparing work for new exhibitions. Sandy now had plans for investing in a little restaurant between Spire and Eastminster, an area woefully lacking in anything but pub lunches. With the influx of more and more incomers who liked good food and wine and did not want a long drive to a decent meal, he thought he'd be on to a good thing.

'It could be a nice little earner – promise you'll come and eat *chez nous* and bring all your actor friends,' he said to Susan on one of his trips to London. David had rolled his eyes up to heaven, but Susan had laughed, and promised.

Another young family came to live at Number 3, the Smiths' old house, and Cobb got used to the sound of children playing on the green. When 'Lisa' went back to the school to see Susan's play, the teacher of physical education, Bob McAlister, who had always fancied her, chatted her up. She had told her old colleagues in the office that she was getting a divorce. To Bob a little later she confessed the whole story. They were married the following year and left the district.

A marriage at the local register office had already taken place. Pat Dawson and Eva Maitland lost no time in moving away. They went up to Norfolk where Dawson was soon to find work at a newly set up radio station.

Mrs Whitwham had been much upset over Miss Kant's end, although she never knew the whole story. She started to attend church again, and urged her husband to expend his energies on a political party, not that she thought it would make much difference. Their grandchildren come every weekend on a visit to the close, and Bill Whitwham and his son-in-law have agreed to differ about most things.

The marina flourishes with a new name, a new committee of management and a new handyman, a gentle youth who for a time accompanied Linda Swift on some of her bird-watching expeditions, until she went away to university.

Kevin Black, having been given a suspended sentence, found a job in Eastminster and made things up with his father. He limited his drugs to pot and went up to London for his love-life.

The place did exert a certain pull, thought Cobb. He hoped that Dorothea was now at rest; he often thought of her. He knew he would never marry again, although there were several nice women with whom he played chess and who doted on him.

Tony Smith never resurfaced. Rumour said that he had gone to Australia.

Duck's Cabin was pulled down, and when the new development on the land was finished it looked similar to Heron's Close, but with smaller houses and gardens, and without the splendid view.

Patricia Simmons took some time to recover. Darren Bogworthy remained in prison for some time. Wayne Spitt got married.

There was one other person who still rejoiced secretly over the death of Percy Duck, alias Thrush.

Eva Dawson, ex-Maitland, née Evie Duck, had thought her brother was behind bars for good when she had left Spickhanger for Norfolk. It had been the greatest shock of her life when, in search of her childhood roots after the death of Mick Maitland, with whom she had lived for thirty years, and having bought a house at the close, she had come upon her brother working as general handyman and gardener there. Her 'agoraphobia' had developed rapidly after this, though she did not think he had ever recognized her. When 'Thrush' died she had once more been able to leave the house.

A pity she could not have got rid of him herself, she always thought. After the attack on Linda, which she felt sure was her brother's work, something inside her had boiled up. She knew Percy's past, and his present habits, and knew too that he often fell asleep after drinking on the beach. She had mustered up all her courage and crept out to look for him, having made up her mind to punish him herself for his latest crime, a quarter of an hour after Patrick had eventually returned to his own house.

She had found Percy 'asleep' only a short time after the gowned figure of Dorothea Kant had left him for dead.

Holding a cushion ready to smother him, Eva had bent over her brother. The sight of him brought back all the memories of their drunken and violent father, who had abused all his children.

It was fortunate that her work had been done for her, and that the cushion was unnecessary.